THE COTTON RUN

Also by Daniel Wyatt

Two Wings and a Prayer
Maximum Effort
The Last Flight of the Arrow
The Mary Jane Mission
The Cotton Run
Pennant Man
Route 66

"The Falcon File" series:
The Fuehrermaster
The Filberg Consortium
Foo Fighters

THE COTTON RUN

Daniel Wyatt

Published by
Bladud Books

Foreword

The American Civil War was not only a conflict that pitted brother against brother, state against state, American against American, Union against Confederate, Johnny Reb against Billy Yank. It wasn't only a struggle in support of preserving slavery, liberty, or the Union, although these motives were significant and honorable. The American Civil War was, for the most part, a fight for business interests and new markets. History unfailingly shows that there's money to be made in war, and the American Civil War was no exception.

The North had the advantage, the means to wage war. They had more people, more railroad tracks, more factories, more steel, and a much stronger economy. For example, the Gross National Product of the entire Confederacy was equal to less than one-quarter of New York State. The Confederacy, however, did have cotton, the commodity that had blessed the Southern states with rich bountiful crops for several decades. With King Cotton, the South thought it could rule the world. Before the hostilities of 1861-1865, the South's top customers were the Northern states, France, and England, the latter having one in four of its population employed in the textile industry. Lacking the means and power to produce enough manufactured products itself, the Confederacy depended on imports to anchor its economy. Shipping was crucial. The exchange of cotton for outside goods was the lifeblood of the South.

Within two days of the Confederates' firing on Fort Sumter to initiate the war, President Abraham Lincoln announced a naval blockade on the Confederate coastline with the intention of starving the fledgling nation into submission. The Southerners reacted the only way they

1

could. With no industrial base and no merchant fleet of its own to speak of, the Confederacy relied heavily on British manpower and shipping interests. Immediately, the art of blockade-running sprang up, ushering in an infamous era of adventure, danger, greed, and deceit. From a handful of Southern ports, courageous sea skippers and their crews (a sprinkling of British and Rebel officers and sailors) ran the blockade, their ships stacked high with bales of cotton. They set sail for neutral ports to transfer their cargoes and return with military and domestic goods, reaping a hefty profit along the way.

The spring of 1863 saw four of the original Confederate ports still open: Galveston, Texas; Mobile, Alabama; Charleston, South Carolina; and Wilmington, North Carolina. The most strategic of these ports was Wilmington, for it was the closest by rail to the Confederate capital of Richmond and the crucial fighting in Virginia. The chief depot for Robert E. Lee's Army of Northern Virginia, the Wilmington docks carried the hopes of the Confederacy. From there, the neutral cargo-transfer destinations of the Bahamas and Bermuda were only three days away. These ports were the main sources of the South's communication with the outside world.

> *"Without firing a shot, without unsheathing a blade, we can bring the whole world to its knees before us. With equanimity, if needs be, the South could refrain for a year, or two years or more, from cultivating a basketful of cotton. But what would be the result? There can be no doubt. Old England would tumble from her proud industrial perch, the whole of civilization toppling with her, joining in her ruin. No sir, you dare not make war on cotton. No power on earth dare make war on it. Cotton is King."*

> Senator James H. Hammond of South Carolina, March 4, 1858

One

The captain slid his hand through his reddish-blonde hair and sniffed, his tall, hard-muscled body absorbing the breeze. Rain was on the way. No doubt about that. He could smell it in the damp, heavy air. He turned west, where his weathered clean-shaven skin caught the last of the setting Carolina sun.

Time to move out.

Inside his cabin, Captain Joshua Denning switched from his white frilled shirt, black tie and black slacks into his functional, all-gray ensemble. Outside, the *Silver Sally* crew slipped the ship's cables on schedule at nine o'clock, and pulled away. In order to dodge the numerous sandbars at the mouth of Cape Fear, Denning preferred to depart Wilmington an hour or so early and make his escape just as the tide reached the high-water mark, which tonight would be shortly after midnight.

The southerly eight-knot cruise in the inky darkness gave the meticulous Denning time to check his last minute details and plot his strategy. Night had brought a gloomy hush to Cape Fear. Pressed in around him were seven-hundred pound cotton bales piled firmly on the ship's deck, so high that his tanned, well-built Southern sailors in similar gray garb to his had to stand on the bundles to perform their tasks. This was a lucrative cargo at their feet; a Confederate fortune of five hundred and sixty-four bales of American Sea Island, the finest-fibered cotton grown in the South, two hundred and seventy-five bales of the general purpose Georgia Bowed, and thirty cases of turpentine.

Skimming down the Cape Fear River, Denning now had one of two choices: New Inlet, off the port bow, with Fort Fisher and Fort Buchanan as covers, or Old Inlet, guarded by Fort Caswell and Fort Holmes, farther down river. The mouth of the river was divided into these two openings, only six miles apart and separated by the triangle-shaped Smith Island and numerous underwater sandbars, the worst of which were the Frying Pan Shoals.

The *Silver Sally* drew even with New Inlet.

Denning brought his telescope to his eye. . . and shook his head. Too many enemy gunboats for his liking. And they were too close. First mate Matthew Balsinger had a saying for it: *as thick as fleas on a dog's ass*. Denning didn't wish to take on the cross wind either. The escape route now had to be Old Inlet and the Frying Pan Shoals, no matter what was waiting for him.

As the *Silver Sally* slid on, the only sound aboard was the soft drone of the ship's powerful engines. Clouds from the southeast had blotted out the quarter moon. The mild breeze up the river before nightfall had peaked at twenty knots. From the port rail near the bridge, Denning watched the silhouettes of the pine and palm trees along the bank give way to the towering oaks and the weighty smell of the swampland along Smith Island. The moon poked through the clouds for a brief moment.

He checked his pocket watch, angling it to catch what little natural light there was. It was 11:25. Forty minutes till high tide.

Perfect.

They neared the southern mouth of Cape Fear River.

Through a thin path between two rows of bales, Denning observed Balsinger's solid figure in the night. Denning raised his hand—the signal. Balsinger slipped away and commanded the engineer below deck to stop the engines. They were getting too close to the opening of the river now to use the voice tube. Denning heard the defiant growl of the engines drop. The ship drifted, then slowed to a moderate crawl. He threw his partially smoked cigar in the water, then tapped the barrel of his revolver strapped to his thigh. It was loaded and ready. No Union captain was going to take him, not if he could help it. After several more minutes, the ship stopped altogether. Slowly, quietly, the anchor was lowered overboard. Denning eyed his watch again.

It was 12:05. Maximum high tide down to the last minute.

The ship rolled on the incoming waves. Still, Denning waited. He peered through the darkness for the vital sign from Fort Caswell, at the tip of Oak Island off starboard, a few hundred yards over the water. By now all lights aboard were snuffed out. The engine room hatches were covered with tarps. Smoking was forbidden. The hinged masts and telescope smokestacks were lowered. The *Sally*'s signal officer, holding the coding apparatus, stood facing the fort. Denning and the officer could see the same danger that those in the fort saw. Two blockaders were combing the waters off the channel. Beyond the ships, a lantern-lit vessel, which Denning took to be the senior officer's ship, was at anchor. The Federals had always kept their distance from the Rebel shore batteries during the day. But now, under night's blanket, they were roaming closer toward the Cape Fear mouth.

At 12:11, Denning caught the all-clear lantern blink from the batteries. His signal officer identified the Morse Code and replied promptly. Through his powerful brass telescope, Denning studied the inside position of the Union gunboats just out of range of the Rebel guns. He would soon depend upon another arsenal of friends: *stealth, speed*, and *tide*. They were friends he knew well, and so far they were as faithful as his crew.

"Up anchor—and I don't want to hear it," he whispered his new order.

"Aye, sir." The nearest sailor telegraphed the order to the next man, who in turn whispered to the man next to him. And on it went, quickly.

No one made a sound as the sailors waited for the next cue from their captain who they knew would not hesitate to fire a pistol shot through the head of anyone who showed an open light aboard the vessel. Once Denning saw the anchor on ship, he quietly climbed the steps of the bridge and darted for the pilot house, midships under the smokestacks. Inside the house, a husky man was bent over the ship's helm, opposite a long, rectangular piece of glass facing the bow. He was intent on the cone-shaped cover placed over the compass, allowing him to plot his moves without light escaping. Across from him in the darkness sat the navigator, ready to plot a course to Nassau once they broke the line of gunboats. Silently, Balsinger brushed past a row of cotton bales and eased alongside the pilot house.

"All ahead two-thirds," Denning said calmly and quietly to his helmsman, Homer Cogswell. Balsinger nodded at Denning, then left to relay the order to the engineer and his stokers.

"Mind your helm. Hug the shoreline until I say so."

"Aye, aye, skipper."

"Keep your weather-eye open. Get us through, Homer."

"Aye, skipper."

Under the pressure of the engines, Cogswell was heading the ship into the teeth of the enemy. He steered around the underwater sandbar, Burch Shoal, off the tip of Smith Island. Despite her extreme length and burdensome load, the *Sally* handled smartly for him, as she always did. The tall lighthouse and the walls of Fort Holmes formed through the glass. . . and slid past to port. The jagged features of oak and pine tops drifted by. He guided the ship burdened with cotton into the region of the dreaded Frying Pan Shoals. The waves became choppy now, and no wonder. They were reaching the point where Cape Fear met the Atlantic Ocean, where the river ran to join the tide. Cogswell—the only Catholic officer aboard—made the sign of the cross with fervor.

Denning continued to study the warships.

Most remained at anchor. The others were cruising offshore near the horizon, eight to ten miles removed from the inner line. Cutting through the more heavily defended first line was always the most hazardous. From what he could determine, there was a gap to starboard, between both sets of Union positions. He watched it closely, his eye pressed to the long lens. After several minutes, he nodded, satisfied. The gap was widening out to sea.

"There's an opening, Homer," Denning said. "Two points off the starboard bow. Steady as she goes." With that, Denning bolted off to stand on a low stack of bales outside the cabin.

The *Silver Sally* veered away at half-speed from the safety of Smith Island, slicing through the dark waters, her engines no longer hidden by the sound of the pounding surf, her hull no longer camouflaged against the sand dunes. The only protection now was the low mist. On deck, the men hid behind the bulwarks. All orders now would be relayed in an organized set of whispers.

And *God help* anyone who messed up.

Less than a nautical mile from shore, Denning brought his telescope to eye level. He focused on the blackness, looking for any man-made objects that seemed out of place. The unmistakable outlines of three massive warships loomed ahead in the night, spread out in a semi-circle. No one aboard had to tell Denning that they were within gun range of all three blacked-out cruisers and the senior officer's anchored ship off port side. Earlier in the year, the runner skippers had been able to use the well-lit gunboats as guides. Then the Union officers realized their ships stood out like beacons and they switched to a method where only the senior officer's ship in the middle of the fleet was lit by just a single lantern. The runner skippers adjusted. They used the ships to get their bearings on the position of the rest of the squadron. Denning swore by the same strategy now, careful to observe that the senior vessel would often try to lure the runners into a shoal. But Cogswell was no idiot. He knew where the shoals were. He wouldn't be fooled.

Denning stood over the engine room, where he met Balsinger. "Stop engines," he whispered hoarsely to the engineer, trying to control his voice. "Now!"

"What's the matter, skipper?" Balsinger asked.

"Look! There!"

Balsinger focused his eyes to where Denning pointed, toward the dark image of a Union gunboat now turning toward them, a hundred yards off the bow. Denning feared that the Union captain had caught sight of something. If Denning could see them, it was possible the Yanks could see him. "Just hope he doesn't spot us."

Balsinger could only nod.

Denning hid behind the rail with Balsinger and other deck hands. The paddle wheels cracked to a stop. The runner took some time to slide silently to a creep. Denning strained his eyes in the cloudy night. Then he saw it, through the thinning mist. His pulse quickened. The sound of the gunboat's engines swelled in the night, as they steered closer to starboard. Denning primed himself for a possible collision. They had never been this close to the enemy before. He felt so helpless. The gunboats were armed with potent deck guns that could blow any ship to bits in seconds. The *Sally* only had small arms. Hand guns.

Denning leaned toward his first mate. "Steady, Matt." Denning was already calculating where he'd be in the next crucial minutes, providing the gunboats, especially the nearest one, remained on their present courses. "Get to the pilot house. Inform Homer that as soon as he hears our engines start up, he's to steer to port, away from the nearest gunboat. Go." His voice was a mere caution. "And stay down, damn it."

"Aye, aye, sir."

Denning squatted over the engine hatchway, looking down at the sweaty, bare-chested engineer. "Stay sharp."

"Aye, sir."

Denning returned to the rail, barely making a sound. The enemy ship chugged closer. He could hear voices aboard. Northern accents! They couldn't be any more than forty yards apart now. He expected any second to see the captain fire a warning flare into the sky to alert the other ships. In minutes, a half-dozen warships could be hunting down the *Silver Sally*.

But to Denning's shock nothing happened. No collision. No shouts. No orders to pass the shell. The warship merely steamed on by, at one point only twenty yards away. *They don't see us,* Denning thought to himself, amazed.

"They missed us. How could they miss us?" Balsinger said, in a low voice.

"I don't know," Denning answered. "But they did." He watched as the gunboat slid off in the opposite direction.

"Start 'em up," he whispered down the hatch.

The engineer and stokers flew into action.

In a few minutes, the *Sally* was a safe distance behind the first line of gunboats. Denning worked his way forward on the ship and extended his telescope again. He saw the large gap in the second line that had presented itself earlier. It was still ready for the taking.

At the pilot house, he pointed ahead for Cogswell. "See it?"

The pilot nodded. "Yes, sir."

"Full speed!" Denning said to a sailor beside him. The order was quickly relayed by the other sailors to the engine room. The crew immediately positioned themselves in the proper places. Despite the darkness, they shot the masts and smokestacks up. The *Silver Sally* cut the water at an incredible speed, assisted by her streamlined body, a draft of only eight and a half feet, and a hull only five feet above the water line. At eighteen knots it didn't take long to leave the second line of enemy boats in her wake. There was no catching them now. Denning had poked a hole through the center of the Cape Fear blockade and got away with it for the eighth straight time.

Denning strolled toward the ship's stern, Balsinger by his side. The breeze filled the sails and stiffened the Bars and Stars Rebel flag. The feint smell of burning coal drifted down from the smokestacks. Beneath them, the engines rumbled a mechanical beat of a smooth sixteen knots.

A hard-working seaman with a rich bass voice, Balsinger was as tall as his captain, but thicker around the waist. Earlier in the evening, Balsinger's glassy dark eyes and exhausted expression had given him away again. He had been out on another drunk the night before, but that never bothered Denning as long as Balsinger made sure his in-port flair for the opposite sex and stiff liquor didn't get in the way of his obligation as the *Sally*'s first mate.

"You play much chess, Matt?"

Balsinger shrugged. He thought he caught the captain smiling. "A few times, skipper. Why?"

Denning clenched his cigar between his teeth, the red fire lighting his face on an inhale. "I think I'd call that a checkmate. Wouldn't you?"

"If you say so, sir."

"I'm going to sack out for a spell. Fetch me if you have to."

"Aye, sir. We'll look after things."

Denning lay on his bunk inside the plush cabin in the rear quarter-deck of the *Silver Sally*.

Joshua Denning's naval career had been a chain of ups and downs, much like his disposition of late. He had never been that interested in the Navy, per se. When he grew up, he had just wanted to get away from the farm and those damn chickens. He wanted to see the rest of his country, sail the oceans, and set foot on other countries. His father had the good sense to see that his son had no aspirations to be a Virginia chicken farmer and packed him off to the Navy academy at Annapolis where Joshua could fulfill his dreams of adventure on the high seas. At school, Denning had risen from an intelligent country boy to a bright young officer fascinated by politics and business.

After graduation in 1852, Denning had spent nine years on active service with the United States Navy. By February 1861, a frustrated Denning asked for a leave of absence. He felt he had spent a long enough time commanding an antiquated frigate. Three years as her skipper seemed like eternity. He was tired of navy life. He saw no future in it, except for a moderate officer's pension once he retired. He was irked by pompous, overbearing superiors who couldn't envision the changing nature of naval defense, with modern guns and metal hulls.

Where was the adventure he sought?

With his savings, he had sailed to Europe. It was an extended vacation to observe the world, to ponder his future as an unmarried modern man, closing in on forty years, with no definite plans in sight. He left behind him a splintered nation, states seceding and a harsh line drawn between North and South. He had been in Paris not even two months when the stunning news broke of the firing on Fort Sumter. Hostilities had begun. The news in the same week of a Union blockade on Southern ports and of Virginia seceding caught his attention.

Virginia separating! How could they?

Thousands of miles away, he had pondered the situation over. Coming out of Annapolis, he was one youngster in a throng of eager newly-commissioned officers. He had high hopes. The future was his. He had sworn allegiance to the United States of America, to defend her at all costs. Not anymore. Now his loyalties were to his native state of Virginia. Although his father had owned slaves for a time, slavery was never an issue with Denning. The blacks should be freed eventually, he had always felt. He was no abolitionist, either. The matter needed time, that's all. But for Virginia to leave the Union in support of slavery was absurd. *If* slavery was the reason.

Virginia seceding? Virginia had been the home state of seven presidents, such founders as George Washington and Andrew Jackson. The other states—North Carolina, South Carolina, Texas, Florida and the rest of them—what did they need independence for?

Independence from what? What was the matter with people?

Denning had remained in Europe until the spring of 1862, then sailed across the English Channel for Great Britain, where the shipbuilding yards of Clydeside in Scotland, and Liverpool in England, had finally opened Denning's eyes to an opportunity he couldn't ignore. The industrial dry docks were swarming with Confederate government agents supervising the construction of a fleet of new and radical ships called blockade runners. Denning pictured himself commanding a runner. Not only could he help his fledgling country by running cotton through the blockade, but he could also make a profit, far more than his navy pay could provide. It was the law of supply and demand in wartime. His country was threatened by an enemy, regardless of the fact they were fellow Americans from the North. There was a civil war across the ocean, and it was his duty as a Virginian to fight in it in the way he could. Of course, he sided with the South. He could not comprehend raising his hand against his relatives, his friends, his home. Never mind his Navy oath.

By this time, Denning was out of money. Fired by a combination of patriotism, profit, and adventure, he convinced a large British bank that had invested heavily in the cotton industry to finance the purchase of one of these light, slender, pencil-shaped paddle-steamers. And he would be the ship's commander. He demanded one of the longest and fastest runners ever built, with a beefed-up keel, and a new, revolutionary steel hull which was lighter and stronger than all the other hulls. He knew that any strong magnetic compass aboard the ship would give inaccurate readings over long distances and would have to be compensated for. A good navigator worth his salt would take care of that and make the adjustments. Denning's ship had to have the most powerful of engines. Eighteen knots under a full load was an absolute necessity.

The finished product was a seven-hundred ton rakish runner measuring two hundred and seventy-seven feet by thirty-six feet by fifteen feet with three telescope smokestacks, one more stack than considered normal. The *Sally* was one of the newest ships—a super runner. Under the cloud of war, Denning had entered the newfangled world of paddle-wheeled, steam and steel ships.

Denning's investors were impressed with his leadership experience on frigates and his five-year expedition surveying and mapping the Atlantic coast for the United States Navy, including the first detailed excursion to Cape Cod. As part of the agreement, the English bank had its own demand for collateral. Half the crew had to be English until the ship was paid for. Denning wasn't certain whether British sailors would accept orders from a Southerner. The bankers insisted. After some hesitation, Denning agreed. He knew they had him by the short hairs.

It took only three successful return trips through the Union blockade for Denning to open his own foreign bank accounts in both Hamilton, Bermuda, and Nassau in the Bahamas. From his profits, he reimbursed the forty-five thousand pounds he owed the banking firm for the ship.

He immediately replaced the English crew members with Southerners, mostly locals from Cape Fear who knew every channel, beach, swamp, and submarine sandbar in the area. The crew was thirty-three in all, from seventeen to fifty in age, all well-paid, splitting over twenty thousand dollars in gold per trip.

With his full Southern complement, he also demanded that the officers and enlisted men all be armed and ready to fire their weapons with accuracy when ordered, something the English sailors couldn't do. It had annoyed Denning that the British had faced the fewest risks. The Union policy of the war at sea assured them of that. When blockade-runners were captured, the foreigners were set free. The Southerners aboard became prisoners of war and were banished to a Northern prison where the chances of living beyond a year were slim to none. Denning simply wanted to provide his fellow Southerners with the incentive to succeed, as well as being able to defend themselves. He was glad to see the British off his ship. They were risks he couldn't afford. Once they were gone, Denning was in total control.

The only way he wanted it.

Captain Joshua Denning blew the oil lamp out and looked up to the ceiling. He was going to play this game through for what it was worth. What was to become of him? He didn't know. His mind drifted. The academy came to mind.

Then he thought of him. Again. Damn. Why? How many times was it that week? Carlisle. *That son-of-a-bitch Bobby Carlisle.* Where was he? Still in the navy? And did it matter? To hell with him.

Denning closed his eyes and listened to the beat of the engines.

And he fell asleep in minutes.

Two

Hatteras Inlet, North Carolina

Less than two hundred miles up the coast from Wilmington rests Hatteras, a long, low sandbar of an island forty miles in length, split in half by an inlet on one end and a bulging cape in the middle. The region is home to sharp reefs and thousands of shipwrecks dating back to the middle 1500s. Early in the nineteenth century, Hatteras had been claimed by a gang of ship wreckers who would snuff out the Cape's lighthouse flame to lure ships to the reefs and the nearby Diamond Shoals in order to commit acts of plunder, murder, and illegal salvaging. By 1851, an east coast naval captain had summed up Hatteras by saying that "she was cursed by both God and Satan by mutual consent."

When the war began, the ship wreckers vanished without a trace.

As he sat impatiently outside the office of his superior, Captain Robert Carlisle agreed silently with those good men who sailed the "Graveyard of the Atlantic" before him. He was familiar with the Cape's reputation as an inhospitable land. The place was indeed cursed, a miserable place for a Union port.

Carlisle snapped his officer's cap under his arm and made a weak attempt to fix his wiry, untamed hair this muggy evening after being summoned to the headquarters of the 514th Blockading Squadron of the United States Navy. For twenty minutes, now, he had been contemplating the reason for the meeting. It had better be good because he was in a foul mood, suffering from another migraine headache, the third one of the week.

Carlisle heard muffled conversation beyond the closed door to the private office. Hearing his name mentioned, he leaned forward as much as he dared, but he couldn't distinguish the rest. Out of the corner of his eye, to his right, he saw the waterway through the window. USS *Connecticut*, his ship, named after his home state, was in dock. It had been undergoing an engine overhaul for the last eight days, allowing Carlisle and his crew some time off. There wasn't a lot to do on leave except drink. They were slated to head out to sea in two days on another patrol. Since joining the competitive squadron in January 1862, their patrols had not netted them a single blockade runner. This irritated Carlisle, as it did his stiff and starchy navy-man father, according to his once-a-week letters from Washington. The two other ships that Captain Carlisle could see in the inlet had each caught two blockade runners in the same space of time. Perhaps the squadron leader was going to relieve him of command or demote him. Or both. The *Connecticut* was his first sea command. He didn't want to lose her. It would look bad on the family. He licked his dry lips. He thought longingly of the flask under his coat. What he wouldn't give for a drink right now.

Five minutes later the door slowly slid open and a tight-mouthed adjutant appeared, flowing with an air of contrived importance. He faced Carlisle, taking in his flat nose, droopy moustache, and unruly hair. "Captain Carlisle. Squadron Leader Baines is free now."

Carlisle snapped to attention. Conscious of his bothersome limp, he stumped bow-legged to the wide office opening and stopped near the adjutant. Carlisle reminded himself to speak clearly. Don't mumble. Be confident. *Be a Carlisle.*

"Captain Carlisle to see you, sir," the adjutant announced.

"Fine. Send him in."

Carlisle entered the room and cracked off an excessive, perfectly performed salute. The adjutant clicked the door closed.

"At ease, Carlisle." Squadron Leader Baines sprang up from his chair behind his plain wooden desk and folded his arms. "Sit down."

"Thank you, sir." Carlisle found a chair in the small office. He did not feel intimidated by the imposing presence of his superior. From past encounters, he knew the methodical Baines to be a strict but fair man. "You wished to see me, sir."

Baines stood by his desk, stroking his bushy white sideburns. He wore his uniform as if he had been born into it. "Yes. You have new orders. A special assignment. You'll be kind of a roamer on the high seas, for lack of a better word. You'll be on different patrol routes, for example, not stuck to one assignment. You're to be somewhat of an experiment. If this works out, then who knows what?" He smiled. "Sorry. I realize you're probably confused."

"Yes, sir, I am," Carlisle admitted.

"Carlisle, we're discovering by experience that the two squadrons patrolling Cape Fear can't support each other. It's almost as though they're. . . well. . . they're working against each other. Some ships, like yours, might have to be more. . . mobile. And cover more of the sea. Become a little more free to hunt. Are you understanding me now?"

"Yes, sir. I do believe I am."

"First off, I have asked for and received permission from the Department of the Secretary of the Navy for your ship to sail into neutral waters in search of ships carrying contraband goods bound for the Confederacy. Unofficially, you understand. I know this is usually the area deployed by our naval base at Key West. However. . . there are no printed orders sent through the chain of authority. This is word of mouth only."

Carlisle relaxed. He was not going to be relieved. It also smelled of his father's influence. "I understand, sir."

"Of course, we have to be careful in how you deploy your new assignment. The cargoes have to be ultimately destined for the Confederacy, which means no runner can be overtaken sailing into the close proximity of Bermuda or the Bahamas. Do you understand?"

"Aye, aye, sir."

"Outbound is another case entirely."

"Can we anchor inside their harbors, sir?"

"Yes and no."

"I don't follow, sir."

"If you wish to get that close, then yes. You need not, however. You cannot conduct search and seizure inside neutral waters, only on the open sea. Therefore, you might as well stay out of their harbors."

"Of course, sir," Carlisle said. "I understand."

"Remember, under international law, belligerent warships entering neutral ports must leave within twenty-four hours or be interned."

"By whom?"

"The British. So, don't provoke them."

"I see. But I heard tell that they don't have the forces in the Bahamas and Bermuda to enforce the international policies."

"Never you mind," Baines warned. "Even then, there will be a legal fine line here. The international law of the sea will certainly be bent to the limits. The war will be our excuse if the British decide to file any complaint. We can conduct our business in the name of urgent national interest at a time of crisis. Great Britain does not wish to wage war with us. And we certainly don't want a war with them."

"Carlisle," Baines went on after a long pause. "I know that you've been plagued with some mighty bad luck lately. That's why I wanted to speak to you personally." He paused again. "Some new ships will be in service this year. We've come a long way from two years ago when we had only ninety ships in the entire national blockading fleet. Now we have hundreds, with more coming. Would you like one when we've got one ready and shipshape?"

"Yes, sir. I'd be much obliged, sir." Carlisle's reply was enthusiastic.

"I'll see what I can do. Our Navy is growing stronger and more proficient all the time. In the meantime, keep your head up."

"Aye, aye, sir. I will," Carlisle said, noticing that his migraine had lightened up. This was good news, better than he had anticipated. He liked Baines, one of the good navy desk men. *Good old Baines.*

"One other thing."

"Sir?"

"Load up with as much coal as you can. You'll need it."

"Aye, aye, sir."

"Dismiss."

They saluted each other.

Baines turned and sat down behind his desk. He waited until Carlisle thumped to the door frame. "And good hunting, Carlisle."

Carlisle smiled, glancing at his superior, who had returned to his paperwork. He wanted to ask if his father was behind this, but didn't dare. That wasn't done in the Navy. "Thank you, sir. Thank you very much."

* * * *

16

Carlisle trudged his way to the gray two-story house commandeered for military use as Union officers' quarters. The long walk bothered his knee and he swore to himself. From higher ground, Carlisle caught a glimpse of the docks, Fort Hatteras, and the waterways winding back to the Atlantic Ocean on his left, and Pamlico Sound on his right. It was very quiet. A slight breeze. Set before him was a broad view of the United States Navy operation at Hatteras Inlet. Thirty miles beyond the mist and the horizon lay the mainland of North Carolina.

Carlisle was born into a decorated US Navy family, who had set high goals for themselves, a tradition the youngest Carlisle—Robert—found difficult to live up to. Most of his life his standard identification was that he was the son and grandson of the famous seafaring Carlisle clan. His paternal grandfather, Lindsay Carlisle, was a hero of the War of 1812, during the Battle of Lake Erie, in which he and his gunboat of men had held off three British ships until help arrived. He later retired as Chief of Staff to the Secretary of the Navy. Carlisle's father, Wilbur, a current advisor in the revamped Navy Department in Washington, had organized and led the American troop landings on the California coast during the Mexican War. Once that had been accomplished, he oversaw the blockade of the Gulf of Mexico until the war ended. Both father and grandfather had climbed the naval ranks faster than the third generation Carlisle—now in his late thirties—had.

So what was the problem with Robert, the family wanted to know.

Carlisle thought of his nine-year-old son, Jonathan, back home in Connecticut, at boarding school. He had already decided that his only offspring wouldn't have anything to do with a navy career if he didn't want to. *No damned academy for him.* He'd be better off forgetting about the navy altogether. Maybe he could be a banker, or a doctor, or a newspaperman, or a lawyer. All honorable professions.

Carlisle reached the steps of the house and lowered himself into a veranda chair. At least his headache had finally dispersed. He rubbed his knee and withdrew the flask from inside his uniform jacket. Uncapping the container, he tilted it, and held it long to his lips. The brandy stung his throat, but he savored the taste with aggressive delight. He had been relying on his brandy more often now since his wife had died a painful, untimely death in February. He had loved her deeply, but always doubted if she had ever loved him back. He fixed her in his mind in an instant, then erased her just as quickly. He took a second swallow. His friend Bottled Brandy was helping.

Blockading was hell, he reminded himself. He wiped his mouth. For what? Thirty dollars a month pay. Freeze his ass off in the winter, and bake his skin brown swatting mosquitoes in the summer heat. Carlisle considered his crew. It was even worse for those of lower rank in his command. Sixteen dollars a month to be part of an excursion that sometimes lasted weeks, in which they had to stand watch for hours. Tempers flared frequently. A sailor's day at sea consisted of long bouts of boredom interspersed with short periods of excitement, if any. So far, the moments of excitement had been few and far between for Carlisle and his crew.

Why couldn't the higher powers increase the pay? But, then again, the mere thought of having to fight and die in some vicious land battle in some horrid place no one had ever heard of before was enough to make Carlisle appreciate his calling. If one could call the Navy a calling. In addition to being safer, the Navy had more to offer than the Army. There was still the chance of catching a blockade runner. There was still the hope of sharing with the crew a piece of the valuable booty at a Northern auction. Besides, a promotion coupled with the possibility of a new ship was attractive. He might have better luck now outside neutral ports. He knew the international naval laws concerning neutrals would be observed only when it suited the warring nations. Neutral rights on the open seas were often ignored.

Then, suddenly, the anger toward his Rebel adversaries grew within him, and he swore under his breath. He had loathed Southerners since his academy days.

"Filthy bastards!" he muttered to himself. "They're the cause of all this."

He guzzled twice more, and wiped his chin. Then he popped the cap on the flask before thumping into the house for dinner.

Three

By the third year of the war the United States of America was caught in the thick web of a martial law dictatorship. Trouble was, most citizens didn't know it. It was a time when thousands of Northerners had been jailed on suspicion without cause, unable to seek legal advice. Only a favored few had rights, depending on who they were and who they supported politically. Military courts had replaced civil courts. All transportation had been nationalized, and it was rumored that all telegraph communication might be forced into the same fate. The two men behind this terrifying consolidation of power were about to meet for one of their regular gab sessions in a corner of a Washington hotel dining room.

Edwin Stanton finished his afternoon meal and ordered the wine once he saw Colonel Lafayette Baker arrive in the lobby. Stanton peered over his small, wire-rimmed spectacles at his younger associate moving towards the table.

"You're late," he frowned, as Baker neared the table.

"I was busy at the office."

"Is that so," Stanton remarked.

The two bearded men waited for a servant to clear the table. Stanton poured the newly-arrived wine for both him and Baker. Stanton was an ill-tempered, chubby, fidgety man, a lawyer by trade. A former director of the Atlantic and Ohio Telegraph Company, he entered federal politics in 1860 as attorney general to then-president James Buchanan.

19

Although a Democrat and a fierce rival of the current President Lincoln, Stanton was appointed by Lincoln as secretary of war two years later in a move that stunned political circles. Washington quickly saw Stanton as an opportunist, preoccupied with his own growing power, someone who took advantage of every situation dumped in his lap. In one short year, Stanton had taken the backroom reins of the country with the help of Baker, a man of questionable reputation, and never let go.

And Stanton still wasn't finished.

Colonel Baker had risen to his position almost as rapidly, but by other routes. A roughneck from a low-to-middle-class background, he had been a founding member of the infamous 1856 Vigilante Committee of San Francisco that had policed the city during the wild California Gold Rush. The talk was that the group had cleaned up the town. But insiders said they had crossed the line. The Committee ran the city their way, making up the rules as they went along, looting and confiscating where and when they saw fit, all in the name of the law.

Later, Baker moved east and established connections in Washington. When the war started, Baker was made a special agent in the War Department and was sent to the Rebel capital of Richmond to gather information about the enemy. The Rebels sent him back, believing he was spying for them. At the Second Bull Run battle he rode a hundred miles through enemy lines to deliver a dispatch from Stanton to Union General Nathaniel Banks. When the Internal Revenue Act of 1862 was passed as a war measure, Stanton hired Baker, who in turn hired detectives to collect from defaulting taxpayers and imprison them if they failed to pay. The jails were soon filled to capacity. Baker's position was merely a front for his own federal secret service, the National Detective Police. Baker now had a force of two thousand NDP detectives and spies under his iron-fisted control. Next to Stanton, Baker was the most feared man in Washington.

"Anything new from your agent at the front?" Stanton inquired, glaring at Baker.

"Haven't heard from him in days. But I do know that both Hooker and Lee have moved out from their winter headquarters."

"So what?" Stanton said. His eyes held Baker's without blinking, as he measured the detective's words. "The newspapers have already reported that! Your man is supposed to be there for the inside information, Baker."

"I know it, sir. But the spring campaign has just started. He won't let me down."

"I should hope not."

Baker said nothing. He knew Stanton hated spies. He considered them sneaks and bloodsuckers. But Lincoln insisted on them. Spies were good for the North only as long as they were of use. Spies could also turn against their masters and become double agents, like he did to the Rebs.

"Lee has to be defeated," Stanton continued. "The sooner, the better. For all of us, the South included. Put them out of their misery. Lincoln wants to let the Reb states back in the Union after the war. He told me that under his plan as long as only ten percent of a state's population agrees to an oath to the United States, then they're in."

"What kind of oath?"

"They must promise to support the Constitution of the United States and obey all federal laws concerning slavery. He's even thinking of pardoning all Reb military and political leaders. Can you imagine, Baker?" His eyes grew larger. "Let Lee, Jackson, Longstreet, Davis off dirt free?"

"What can we do about it?"

"Plenty." Stanton's face twisted. "A few choice Republicans are concocting postwar reconstruction plans to divide the South into five conquered military districts controlled by a military governor for each district. These are our kind of people, Baker. They won't allow any Southerner to vote unless he takes the oath to the Union. We'll make the Rebs pay."

Baker knew that Stanton stood to gain the most. The governors would answer to a Washington controlled by Stanton. It would make the secretary more powerful than ever. "Who are these so-called choice Republicans?" Baker asked.

"Senators Chandler in Michigan, Wade of Ohio, Conness from California, and Representative Davis of Maryland, to name three."

Baker wondered what lay beneath the surface of the Republicans' proposals. The NDP chief saw the proposals as a plan for the Republicans to stay in power and create a Southern branch of their party by relying on Negro votes. They wanted to keep their Congress gains of 1860—free homesteads, high tariffs, subsidies to railroads, a banking

21

system favorable to the big business empires in New York. If the Southern-based Democrats returned to power, they would oppose the Republican reconstruction plans.

"Does Lincoln know what these men are up to?"

"Yes, unfortunately," Stanton said. "And he'll veto any such bill. That I know. He *can't* win the next election. He'll destroy everything we're putting together. Right now, he doesn't have much support anywhere. And he had to bring the emancipation thing into the picture. The troops are now fighting to free the slaves. And they don't like it. Neither does our Republican round table in Washington. However," Stanton grunted, "if we win the war by next year, or at least manage some great victories on the battlefield, it's likely that Mr. Lincoln could win again."

"So, we're stuck."

Stanton nodded. "Yes, Baker. Stuck."

Forty minutes later, deep in the basement of the Treasury Department, not far from the White House, Colonel Baker was preparing a coded dispatch for his agent in Wilmington, North Carolina. This machine was not for military purposes, but for Baker's personal business. By using it, Baker had an excellent control of the clandestine flow of shipments—cotton, meat, guns, and medical supplies—between Washington and Richmond. His connections on both sides in the conflict were of great advantage to him. He was also becoming very wealthy, very quickly.

Baker walked up to a subordinate in the busy office, a young man unfamiliar with the message's true contents. "Barkley?"

The man turned around. "Yes, sir."

"Drop what you're doing and send this through our channel in Richmond."

The man looked at the sheet for a moment. "It's in code?"

"Of course it's in code. Get to it."

"Yes, sir."

Wilmington, North Carolina

Eli Jacoby slowly opened his hotel room door.

"Yes, what is it, boy?"

"Mr. Jacoby," said the young telegraph messenger. "Message for you, sir. From Richmond."

Jacoby gave the young man a gold sovereign and took the sealed envelope. He locked the door, then spent the next few minutes deciphering the message by using his cipher-code book and his own notes. He soon discovered that all secret shipments expected to cross the Potomac bound for Wilmington were still to be grounded. Jacoby frowned, wondering when it would pick up again. He was losing money.

Born a Southerner, Jacoby was no respecter of Southern ways and customs. He had high-level contacts in New York, Washington, Boston, and Philadelphia, a network of Northern commodity speculators in the Union war effort. This group had been making a killing selling to Rebel interests on the side, and at the same time they were all making money on the transfer of cotton north. It was made to look perfectly legal by the sinister misuse of cotton and border passes issued by both the Lincoln and Davis governments.

Jacoby appraised his image in the mirror, which reflected an influential citizen of the South. He was not the most handsome of men, with his slight paunch, square face, and cold gray eyes. Balding on top, he had long hair on the sides and back, and a patchy beard speckled with gray around a thin mouth. But he was the best-dressed man in town. He liked that distinction.

Today, he needed a hair trim and was impatient to be doing something. The barber shop was just around the corner, a good place to pick up useful war gossip.

Four

Chancellorsville, Virginia—May 1863

The sun climbed over the wilderness clearing where Major Luke Keating shaved closely around his thick moustache and chin whiskers. Finished, he put his mirror away and threw his dirty cavalry coat on. Then he began to make his rounds, his spurs clinking as he went.

The major heard the familiar early morning noises amid the piercing reveille. Tents were sparser this year. Most of the men had slept on the ground, wrapped in bug-ridden blankets. The sounds of yawns, stretches and curses began, as they did every morning. The coughs were heard over everything else. Deep, raspy coughs, the result of braving the outdoors for nearly two years. It never failed to fascinate Keating how the camp could rise, snort, and cough almost in unison. Some soldiers were smashing their rifle butts into their coffee beans as they continued to cough and clear their throats. They were the lucky ones. Most soldiers didn't have the luxury of coffee, only substitutes such as potato or peanut brews. Within a few minutes, breakfast was on and the smells drifted over the camp. Over the last two years, rebel camp life had become an alarming struggle for proper food, shelter, and clothing.

And it was getting worse.

Keating had received his orders before sunup. Today his unit in the North Carolina cavalry would move out and engage. They would do battle and good men would fall. He tried to picture how many fewer campfires there would be tomorrow morning. He wondered how many more men would die in the coming campaigns until their political allies in Europe would step in and assist the Confederacy. The situation was desperate. No longer was the cavalry hailed as dashing cavaliers on horseback who rode light-heartedly through the countryside. That was a popular story in 1861. *Only a story.* This was no pleasant little romp in 1863. The cavalry were as starving and as ill-equipped as the other soldiers in Lee's army. However lean they were, Keating's Confederate unit were still part of a proud, formidable force, feared by the Yankees as excellent fighters. With good reason. The cavalry had been instrumental in most of the Rebel victories so far.

They were the eyes of Robert E. Lee.

Keating was stiff after the walk. The steady pounding on his frame was getting too much for him. For months, he had felt much older than his thirty years. For months, his bones had been whispering in voices of exhaustion that his brain was trying to ignore. Although he usually made a habit of keeping to himself, this morning he took up a tin of hot, strong coffee and stood with other officers, all junior in rank to him. In appearance, they weren't much different than Keating. Their uniforms were the same homespun butternut or gray, with black facing, broad-brimmed dark hats, long riding boots, along with gray or filched Yankee blue short jackets and trousers. The difference was the more youthful faces.

The second son of a well-to-do former North Carolina senator who had made his fortune in cotton, Keating had been in the Union peace-time army only a year before dropping out and joining his father in business. He had officer experience, a scarce commodity in the Rebel army when war erupted. He quickly joined up again. So far, Keating had taken part in all the great campaigns of Stonewall Jackson, his general commanding. In two years he had been a witness to some terrible bloody battles and some awe-inspiring victories such as their last major skirmish at Fredericksburg in December past, where the Union forces lost three times as many men as Robert E. Lee.

Keating watched as a piece of hardtack floated on the surface of his coffee. Two little boll weevils, which had worked their way into the biscuit overnight, bobbed about. He skimmed them off, then coughed, and guzzled. One look around the camp left Keating with nagging doubts. How could Lee's army continue under such appalling conditions? Where were the proper supplies in this ragged army? Pay was low and erratic if not nonexistent. Scurvy, typhoid, measles, mumps, dysentery, and pneumonia ran rampant. More soldiers were dying from diseases than bullets. Keating knew that the blockade runners couldn't supply them with all the military necessities. According to letters from home in Wilmington, the blockade was tougher to break with each passing month.

Lieutenant Franklin Taylor's nerves were strung taut as a deer. He had been up for more than an hour since daybreak, circling behind his own Rebel lines on a narrow path through the forest. Even the birds weren't making noises this morning. Was that a good sign or a bad sign? Taylor's youthful face showed his worry. He had lost track of his critical lifeline—the telegraph wires—coming out of Fredericksburg, and he wondered how he would get word to his base if he had to. At the same time he kept his eyes open for those Union snipers, the best damn shots in the army.

Taylor barely resembled the man he had been when he joined the Army of Northern Virginia the previous summer. His tattered and patched butternut-colored Signal Corps uniform hung loosely on him. Before the war, he had been round and full in the body, living in relative comfort near Charleston, Virginia, a part of the state that contained people with a strong Union sentiment. In less than one year, Taylor, ill-fed on depleting Southern rations, had lost almost forty pounds. Sores covered his face, his scruffy beard matched the rest of his unkempt hair. The lice on his body no longer upset him.

His unsightly appearance was typical of the majority of soldiers in the still-haughty Army of Northern Virginia. What separated him from most of the others was one outstanding possession. He still owned a pair of boots, and Yankee boots at that. The right big toe was beginning to wear through, it was true, but he was fortunate. Half the remaining soldiers in the Signal Corps, not to mention most of the entire Army of Northern Virginia, were barefoot.

As a Signal Corps telegrapher, his duty was to keep a close watch on the Reb and Union troop movements. He knew that since the end of April, Union commander Joe Hooker had marched east from his winter headquarters at Fredericksburg, leading four corps of his 130,000-strong

Army of Potomac. Hooker then ordered seventy thousand of these men behind Robert E. Lee, while the rest were left to face the Rebs across the Rappahannock River. It was a dangerous spot for Lee and his much smaller total force of only sixty thousand men. However, Franklin knew Bobby Lee had yet to back down to any Union commander. Hooker would be no exception. Lee had split his forces to shore up his flank. Portions of the two great armies had already clashed yesterday, sending Hooker into a defensive position in the Wilderness clearing around a two-story white brick building called Chancellorsville House. Taylor believed that this particular piece of ground only six miles from his Signal Corps tent at the edge of Lee's army would be where Hooker wanted to face Lee to defeat him.

A fierce battle was coming. He knew it. He could smell it.

Taylor also differed from his comrades in another way. When ordered to send coded messages along the telegraph wires and flag signals between units, he did so. But when he had the chance, he also sent what he felt were essential messages to a Union telegraph office based in northern Virginia. The latter was his all-absorbing job. Thousands of Union lives were depending on his dispatches. Taylor's employer was not the Army of Northern Virginia, but the National Detective Police headquartered in Washington. His code name was *Yankee*. Once a month one thousand dollars in gold would be deposited by a high-ranking detective into a secret account opened under Taylor's assumed name. The account had been growing for many months. Taylor would be filthy rich by war's end.

While his southern friends were fighting their hearts out for the Confederacy, Lieutenant Franklin Taylor was a Union informant inside Robert E. Lee's Army of Northern Virginia. And he had been getting away with it for a year.

Five

Hatteras Inlet, North Carolina

The *Connecticut* should have put out to sea that morning, but it didn't look anywhere near ready to go. Now, Robert Carlisle was concerned about morale—his crew's as well as his own. He wanted the ship out and hunting pirates.

One of the engine mechanics, smothered in grease from his face down to the rolled cuffs of his blue coveralls, stepped from the ship to the pier. Carlisle approached him.

"How much longer?"

The mechanic shook his head. "Not today, sir. Not for a few days. We need some parts from the mainland."

Carlisle turned in the direction of the officers' quarters on the rise and pounded away on his stump. "What a piss-poor way to run a navy," he said to himself.

The Bahamas

Navigator Ben Woodson rested his leg on the frame below the window glass. Pointing ahead, he confirmed for pilot Homer Cogswell a small palm-tree-dotted island one nautical mile off port and reconfirmed it on Homer's chart. Cogswell nodded. They were on course. Cogswell and Woodson were a polished partnership, crucial for any successful cotton run. They were the heart of the *Silver Sally*.

Woodson scratched his free hand through his receding short gray hair and his white beard. In the summer of middle age, he looked at least ten years older than his fifty-one years. His jowly face was brown, lined, and haggard. A native Georgian from the seaport of Savannah, he was a man of great marine skill who took a fierce pride in his work. Another officer who met Denning's high standards, Woodson was a seasoned elder of east-coast mapping expeditions, two battle cruisers, and overseas duty before jumping ship and country to run the blockade for the Confederacy. Where the money was.

Smoldering pipe in mouth, Cogswell enjoyed the taste of his favorite tobacco, Georgia Navy Gold, the most expensive money could buy. The sweet sting lingered in the cabin as he stared down at the charts on the table. He was directing the ship southward through the Northwest Providence Channel toward the capital of Nassau, steering south by east. His mind drifted back to his earliest days at sea, on sailboats. He recalled how by gripping the two helm spokes, he could actually feel the breeze in the sails. Now, years later, he was feeling the engine rumble on the spokes, vibrant and humming. The modern steamships were certainly faster, but not as challenging and romantic as sail. He thought it would be great to own a sailboat, just for fun. Maybe when the war was over, when things calmed down and life returned to normal.

Cogswell knew these waters nearly as well as he knew the beaches and sandbars of Cape Fear. He noticed that the water was changing from a dark green-blue to a richer, softer green. It was a sign they were drawing near to the shore. Ahead, the sun caught the white, cylinder-shaped lighthouse outside Nassau. Only ten miles divided the crew from another good time before they had to make the return run to Wilmington.

Joshua Denning stood on the bridge across from the pilot house, in white shirt sleeves rolled to the elbows. He lit a fresh Virginia cigar and made his customary check of the channel, propping himself against a stack of cotton bales. His ship was surrounded by small fragments of land. He drank in the pleasant, hot weather. The steamy sun hung in the sky. Wispy clouds floated by and a slight breeze helped to keep the heat at least bearable. About four hours of daylight remained.

At that very moment, caught in the violent world of war, he felt at peace. He glanced over the rail at the calm, sparkling water rushing past the steel hull. The sea had a pulse of its own and for a few moments he allowed himself the luxury of relaxing. The subtropical waters off the coast of Florida were never more attractive than they were in these late daylight hours. And they were never more dangerous, due to the long underwater shadows cast on them. These were unforgiving waters with canyons and coral reefs that would rise and fall in fathom lengths in the space of a few feet. The stark underwater changes in depth had been responsible for the destruction of many a ship, along with the careers of a few inexperienced and overconfident pilots who had contested the Bahamas channels.

The sun's deep yellow rays brought out the glittering colors of plant life below the water line, the red, brown, blue, green growth. Looking aft, Denning saw a barracuda and a three-foot-long turtle bobbing to the surface. Bright-colored fish darted everywhere. The deep canyons drifted by.

High tide had passed. As a precaution, Denning posted extra look-outs to guide the approach to port. He blew out a cone of cigar smoke and marveled at Cogswell's wizardry. Cogswell was the highest-paid man on the crew, and he was worth every sovereign he received for his nautical skills, all twenty thousand dollars in gold per trip.

The captain leaped onto a row of bales as if he were years younger and saw the Nassau dock coming into view. A flight of squawking pelicans flew over, circled, and teased the crew before heading back for shore. Concluding a survey of the horizon, Denning glanced up. "Keep a sharp lookout," he called to the sailor high on the foremast before returning to his cabin. Matthew Balsinger was waiting for him.

It was payday for the crew. Denning dug out two heavy metal-and-wood cash boxes from the safe and opened them. Balsinger, who doubled as the ship's paymaster, hungrily eyed the contents—hundreds of gold sovereigns in Nassau currency. He was looking forward to docking and spending his own generous share.

Denning remained on his feet, gazing through the open cabin port-hole at an island in the distance. He turned and said, "Matt, let me ask you a personal question."

Balsinger looked up in response from his chair, folding his arms across his strong chest. "Sure, skipper."

"What do you aim to do after the war?"

"Don't rightly know. Never really gave it any honest attention. Why do you ask?"

Denning puffed on his cigar, turning back to the porthole. "I heard some gossip back in Wilmington."

"What kind of gossip?"

"They're saying the Davis government is going to commandeer the blockade-running business, either partially or totally. Maybe even the ships."

"Will it finally come to that?"

"To be sure. It hinges on whether Davis can enforce it over states' rights," Denning said. "But it's inevitable." He moved around the cabin slowly. "The president wants his share. His whole plan would shift the profits from our pockets to his. What I'm trying to say is that everything is stacked against us. If it ever does come down to commandeering the runners, we have to be prepared to retire the *Sally* on short notice, and look at that retirement some of us are considering. With less profit, the ship's wage scale would surely drop. It wouldn't be worth it anymore." He paused. "I feel I should tell you that Morehardt Steamship Company has approached me with an offer."

Startled, Balsinger said, "They have?"

"One hundred thousand dollars. In gold."

"Good price. Damn good price!"

"I'll say. About what I paid for it once you convert the gold to English currency. I'll trouble you to not let any of this go beyond this room just yet. Let's keep a lid on it."

"I gathered that. My lips are sealed, skipper."

Balsinger was surprised by the information but had no reason to doubt the captain. Balsinger had barely saved anything for the future, preferring to always spend what Denning paid him—two thousand dollars in gold on every return trip. He was in no position to consider retirement. "At any rate, I guess you can't blame Davis," Denning continued. "He has to cash in. And to think the price of cotton was ten cents a pound before the war." He shook his head. "By the middle of next year, it'll more than likely reach a dollar."

"That works out to about seven hundred dollars a bale!"

Denning nodded. "Look what cotton has done for us. For everybody."

"It's made us damn rich. That's what. We've never seen such money."

A shrill whistle came down the voice tube. Denning reached for the extension, and stuck it to his ear.

"Captain, we're coming into port."

"Thanks, Willy. Ring the bell."

"Aye, aye, sir."

Denning returned the tube to the wall bracket and smiled at Balsinger. "Take it easy this time, Matt," he said. "Don't blow your whole pay again."

Six

Nassau, Bahamas

A tall, muscular, black man waited for the skipper at the end of the gangplank. "Captain Denning, suh?"

"Yes. I'm Captain Denning."

"I have a message for yuh, suh."

Denning snatched the envelope, read the contents, and frowned.

As instructed in the note, he found his way to the White Light Tavern, an all-green, gabled establishment hastily built during the war. On entering through the elbow-to-elbow crowd near the door, Denning caught the strong whiff of fresh liquor. They were starting early. Some of his crew were mixing with the bar women. A group of British speculators at the counter were engaged in some chatter. Another cluster, this one British and Southern naval officers, were proposing toasts in the corner.

An Englishwoman approached Denning from behind the bar. "Why, if it isn't Captain Denning. I heard the *Sally* came in. Looking for a little fun tonight?"

Denning knew the part-time maid, part-time prostitute. "Not now, Mame. I'm looking for someone."

"Don't I know it, love." She winked. "In the corner. He's been waiting for yuh." She nudged Denning with her shoulder. "Brandy, Jack!" she called out, over the throng of voices.

Denning took his brandy, strolled deep into the crowd, and came upon a white-faced, squat of a man. His two rings and gold chain left Denning with the impression of one quite well off.

The man stood, his palm out. "Good day, Captain Denning. Jason Litchfield, representing the firm of Litchfield-Deats Manufacturing."

Denning forced himself to extend his hand. "Good day to you, sir."

"I trust you had a good trip?"

"I did, thank you. What can I do for you?"

"Have a seat, captain."

The accent was unmistakable to Denning. New York, for sure. "Northerner, eh? Looking for cotton?" He pulled up a chair.

"Why, yes. As a matter of fact, I am. How ever did you know?"

"Intuition."

"I saw your blockade runner come into port. I inspected the quality of your Sea Island cotton. Excellent. The best. Maybe we can cut a deal that will be to your advantage. I need cotton, the Sea Island and Georgia Bowed variety, and I'm willing to pay handsomely for it. What do you say?"

Denning was suspicious. "I suggest you take the official route. Cotton passes through the Mason-Dixon line are easy to obtain if you know the right people. Why come all the way out here to Nassau? I thought the Davis and Lincoln governments had come to an understanding. You need cotton. Lee needs meat. I don't think I need to explain more. You do know what I'm talking about?"

"Of course, sir. I am well aware of the cotton passes. I've been using them up until recently, with the help of a Wall Street cotton broker."

"Well, then. I don't understand. What is it you want from me?"

"Let me explain. Since last month millions of dollars of meat and other foods and goods have been hoarded by the National Detective Police in Washington and Maryland. They are being seized as contraband Rebel commodities. Some high-ups in Washington are engaged in some black market activity."

"Hoarding, you say?"

"Yes, captain." Litchfield bobbed his head like a bird drinking water. "And we have reason to believe it's being perpetrated by Baker."

"Who?"

"The NDP chief. Colonel Lafayette Baker. With the help of radical businessmen in Washington and New York. Baker and his friends also run guns into the Confederacy."

"I've known about some gun-running. So . . . Washington's behind it, are they?"

"They are, but nothing has been moving. Because the Northerners refuse to deal, the South won't ship their cotton to us. And now both armies are smack in the middle of Virginia. On the move and with the snipers and all, it's too dangerous. No rail line north is safe."

"So," Denning assumed, "you want me to take care of your own cotton needs as long as the seizure is in place."

"Yes. I'll make it worth your while."

Denning laughed. "Oh, you will, will you?"

"Certainly, my good man."

Denning was aware of the irony of the situation. It was the way of Nassau, the center for under-the-table Civil War commerce. Here were the two of them, enemies, sitting in a smelly tavern on a sun-baked tropical island, making a business transaction that was highly irregular, while their two armies were fighting it out on American soil.

"I'm not interested." Denning got up.

Litchfield jumped up to stop him leaving.

"But I'm willing to pay five percent above what the British agents are paying."

"So that's it. You must take me for an idiot."

"Excuse me?"

"I deal with the British," Denning replied. "How can I sell them out? You get the cotton and I suddenly leave the British empty-handed. Not likely. If word got around these islands, I'd be finished. Tell me, how do you expect to ship the cotton out of here?"

"I already have a contact in the harbor."

Denning had dealt with con men before. They always wanted something. He had chosen not to deal with the enemy for that reason. There were too many more people he had to trust, too many new deals, handshakes, agreements in bars. Too many risks. "I told you I'm not interested. Now, if you'll kindly step aside, I'll be on my way."

"Ten percent, then. Tops!"

"Don't be a fool," Denning said. "I don't deal with Northerners." He ignored Litchfield and began to move slowly toward the front entrance.

"You will!"

Denning stopped some few feet away and swung around. "Would you kindly repeat that?"

"Oh, come, now. You're a blockade runner," Litchfield said, as if to sway Denning. "Anything for profit, right? Money, that's what runs the world. Money and cotton right now."

Denning lunged at Litchfield and grabbed him around his collar with both hands, lifting him several inches off the ground. "I said I don't deal with Northerners. It's a policy of mine." Their faces were only inches apart. "I'm a Southerner with an *all* Southern crew."

"Stop! You're choking. . . me," Litchfield protested, looking to the crowd for support. But his pleas fell on unconcerned ears. They didn't care. He was a Yankee. Yankees weren't welcome in Nassau.

Denning finally dropped Litchfield in a heap. The man gripped his throat, gasping to catch his breath. He wobbled on one knee and dusted himself off, then disappeared through the entrance door.

"What are you looking at?" Denning asked, a sly grin forming, his eyes hitting on Cogswell, Woodson and Balsinger, who quickly looked away to continue nursing their liquid refreshments.

The crowd parted for him as he too left the tavern.

Denning's attention focused on business as he took an alleyway short-cut to the warehouse district. He stopped, paused, and looked up at the swinging sign over a long, open sliding door. L. LOCKERBIE AND COMPANY, LONDON, ENGLAND was printed in neat white letters several feet long and three feet high on a black background.

"Ah, Captain Denning."

Denning saw British cotton agent William Freeman in the shadows. This time the captain extended his hand more readily. "Freeman," he said.

"How are you this fine evening?"

"As well as can be expected," Denning answered sharply. He stepped inside. Spread out before him were hundreds of wood crates, in organized rows, piled to the high ceiling. Southern and English customers in naval uniforms and local clerks with clipboards were all over the open crates, examining the contents.

Freeman waved for a clerk. "Captain Denning will need some help."

"Yes, sir, Mr. Freeman."

Denning remembered the young English clerk from the last transaction in Nassau, and nodded at him.

"Hello again, Captain Denning," the clerk said. "I'll be right with you." He returned with a small cardboard box. "Complimentary, sir, to all skippers. Cuban cigars."

"Thank you."

Denning never refused a good cigar. He slit open the package with his nails. The cigar he removed was thick and smelled different from the Virginia brands he was used to.

The clerk lit a match and put the flame to the cigar end. "What do you think?"

Denning puffed. They were tasty, stronger than Virginia cigars. "Not bad at all. Well, what do you have for me today, Freeman?"

"Right this way," Freeman replied.

The clerk gestured for the three of them to proceed down the first row. "The latest ladies fashions from Paris. Hats and dresses. They just came in yesterday."

Denning pulled out one of the hats. It was made of brown suede with a wide chin ribbon. The other bonnets in the crate were the same style but different colors. Paris fashions were highly sought after by the Southern well-to-do who could still afford them. Such non-military goods always had the highest markup in Wilmington, more than six or seven times what he paid for them here in Nassau. "It's not exactly anything that Bobby Lee could use. How much?"

Freeman answered, "Eleven dollars per dozen."

"I'll take ten cases."

The delighted clerk wrote the figure down on his board. The ten cases were only the beginning. By the time the sun had gone down, he had filled the sheet with a tally of numbers. Army shoes. Lead bars. Small arms. Gunpowder. Dresses. It was another full load, worth thousands of dollars.

"I want everything loaded up tomorrow," Denning said, after the clerk read out the final quantities.

Freeman cleared his throat. He saw that Denning was serious. "Good grief. So soon? You just arrived."

"There's a quarter moon for a few days. I've got to return while I can still take advantage of it."

"Certainly. First thing then." Freeman looked to the clerk for confirmation.

"We have two other orders tomorrow, sir. But we can fit it in by mid-afternoon, providing the cotton's unloaded."

Denning blew out a rich cloud of cigar smoke. "It'll be off, I guarantee it. My thanks. Now, if you'll excuse me, I'll be on my way. Good evening. And thank you for the cigars."

"You are quite welcome."

Denning spun around to leave, then turned back. "Oh. . . one other thing. Three, no, make it four cases of these," he said, eying the cigar in his hand. "They just might go over quite well in Wilmington."

Seven

Chancellorsville, Virginia

Franklin Taylor climbed the telegraph pole effortlessly. At the peak, he wound his arm over the top wire and scanned the horizon in every direction. The dense wilderness lay before him, far to his left. There, in that mass of forest only a few miles away, were the two greatest armies on the continent, perhaps the world, separated only by timber and ground soon to be spotted with blood.

He hoped this line of telegraph wires was within distance of Hooker's army.

Would they receive the message of the sneak attack in time?

Taylor reached inside the pouch slung over his shoulder and clutched the pocket telegraph relay in his hand. He opened it and placed it carefully on the flat top of the pole. His hands moved deftly, as he removed the rest of his equipment, a rubber insulated telegraph wire, an encoding disc, and a pocket knife. He held his wire along the pole wire, then gently cut into it and wound the metal together, thus connecting his wire to the relay. He wrote on a piece of paper what he wanted to send. Using the preselected secret cipher code, he turned the disc for each letter and tapped the corresponding letter on the key. When he completed the message, he sweated out the long seconds.

The seconds became minutes.

He looked around nervously, saw no one, and sent the same message again, quicker this time. He waited. Nothing.

Had the lines gone dead? Had they been cut?

Major Luke Keating didn't know what the hell was going on.

Since breaking camp in the morning, he and twenty-eight thousand men of Jackson's II Corps complete with ambulances had taken to a rough dirt way called the Plank Road, on a loose-formation march through the western end of the Wilderness to position themselves behind Hooker's army in the woods. Jackson had never marched in a loose formation before. Keating wondered if it was to simulate a retreat. They had been marching for several hours and had covered more than ten miles. They needed a rest. Now, only a few short hours of daylight remained. Would they make camp? What if the Union pickets saw them? Was Union General Hooker laying an ambush in the meantime?

Keating rode upright in the saddle. He coughed hard. Autumn leaves of the previous year crackled under his horse's hooves. Even though his field glasses were powerful, his view failed to penetrate the gloomy pine and oak undergrowth. No snipers, at least.

They stopped. He saw a gray river of men with shouldered rifles directly ahead, being herded in formation, a potent combination of infantry and cavalry. A low mutter of voices swept the woods. Metal clanged.

The word came to him. *Fix bayonets.*

Supper sparked hot on the campfires this clear evening for the XI Corps Union soldiers in the trenches and breastworks at the edge of the Wilderness. The men were relaxing and playing cards between the baggage wagons, others drinking coffee, eating their meals. Suddenly, birds, deer, rabbits, and squirrels sprang from the woods. And right behind the animals came the sound of high-pitched bugles piercing the air, along with a mighty roar of men.

"*Charge!*"

Nearly thirty thousand of Stonewall Jackson's men descended on the Union soldiers like a huge ocean wave, guns and gleaming swords drawn, bayonets fixed, battle flags flapping, screaming the frightening Rebel yell.

Keating sensed the horrifying sight of panic written on the faces of the enemy. Suddenly, the war became very personal. He felt for a moment that it was almost unfair. But Jackson was never fair. Outnumbered as he was today, he had decided to use surprise to his favor. He had outflanked the flankers. Near the forefront of the thunderbolt, Keating and hundreds of others in the cavalry shot and slashed through the supper line before the Union men could run for their guns. Some men were caught in their tents, their camp kettles still red hot, warm meals in their bellies.

Keating shot one bluecoat in the heart with his Colt pistol. He shot another in the shoulder. A gush of blood speckled Keating's uniform. He had to shoot a third man—a big man—twice to bring him down. The first ball got him below the neck, the second in the stomach. Keating turned and saw a Union carbine aimed right at him. Twenty feet away! He saw the smoke, and winced, but in the overwhelming thunder of noise didn't hear the gun fire. The shot had gone wide. Keating removed his saber, ran up, and laid open the Union man's scalp.

Keating flowed with the human Rebel storm towards the center of the clearing beyond the breastworks and trenches. Line after line ran forward, sweeping over the bluecoats, mowing them down like a tornado in a forest.

Eight

Wilmington, North Carolina

The *Silver Sally* slipped through the new inlet shoals without incident on her return run, and steamed the twenty-five miles north to port under the cover of darkness and a constant light rain.

It was still raining at eleven o'clock the next morning when Captain Denning left his ship following his best rest since leaving Nassau. He hailed a carriage driver who took him to the Prince Hotel. The rain was beginning to let up.

Outside the lobby, Denning bought a freshly printed *Wilmington Daily News* and buried himself in the reading of it, leaning against one of the hotel's great stone pillars. The front-page headlines exploded at him. A lot had transpired in his absence. The murder of a Wilmington widow, the second widow in three weeks. Wilmington was becoming a wild town. Far away, Vicksburg, Mississippi, was under siege by Union general Ulysses Grant. Closer to North Carolina, Robert E. Lee had crushed Joe Hooker with a lightning flank assault at a junction called Chancellorsville, Virginia.

Denning pushed himself away from the pillar. *Chancellorsville.* General Stonewall Jackson had been seriously wounded. Although the majority of businessmen snapping up the papers most likely had never heard of Chancellorsville, Denning could picture the place in an instant. He had been brought up in the surrounding countryside. His father still farmed near there. The crowd gathered about the newsboy, buying up his papers until they were all gone. Under the hotel canopy,

Denning took out one of his Cuban cigars and eyed the murky street as the sky began to clear to the west.

A tall lanky man strode up and struck the match for him. "Captain Denning?" The man removed his hat and flicked the water off it.

"That's right." Denning puffed on his cigar. "Thanks for the light."

"You're welcome, sir. I just missed you at the dock. One of your ship-mates said you'd be here."

"And who are you?"

"Maxwell Toland. From the mayor's office. My father—the mayor—was wondering if you might be so kind as to help out a group who are doing all they can for the war effort?"

"Goodwill? That sort of thing?"

"Yes, sir."

"For the Cause?"

"You might say that, yes."

Denning put his arm around the man. "Maxwell, I never like to talk business without a drink. I know it's early but can I buy you one?"

"Well—"

"What's your fancy, son? Whiskey? Brandy? Wine?"

Toland stalled. "I reckon I better not."

"Why not? I'm sure your father won't mind too terribly. Tell him you were with me. I'll vouch for you."

Toland shook his head. "It's not that. I'm due back. We're very busy. What with the war on, we're short of manpower and all. I wrote out the information. Let's see. . ." He pulled up his cape clumsily, searched his pockets, then held out a small card with a hand-written name and address on it.

Denning took the card. "The Lads of the Liberty. And who might they be? A veteran's group?"

"Oh, no. A women's organization that sends clothing to the boys at the front. They're working out of an old print shop, not far from here. On Market and Third."

"What do they want with me?"

"I think you might have to go there to find out."

"I see." Denning was amused more than anything. All of a sudden he was in great demand. "Women? Ah, why not? Tell your father I'm on my way."

43

"Much obliged, sir. And give my special regards to Marie, would you please?"

"Who's Marie?" asked Denning.

"You'll find that out, too."

Denning held his Panama hat and the newspaper in his hand and wiped his boots on the mat inside the old print shop lobby. He stuck his head through the doorway and was met by a flurry of activity. Twenty or so women between the ages of twenty and sixty were busy either sewing by hand or packing and unpacking boxes. And half of them seemed to be talking all at the same time. A few of the ladies were somewhat wide. Three or four were younger and rather charming. Two women in the center of the room were sewing stars on the biggest Confederate flag he had ever seen.

"May I help you, sir?"

Denning turned to one side to see an old woman, her white hair tied in a bun. She was sorting some used socks and did not look overjoyed at doing it. Denning cleared his throat and said, "Begging your pardon, ma'am. I wish to see the woman in charge, Miss Keating."

The woman huffed. "Oh, *her.* The Gypsy."

"I beg your pardon, ma'am?"

"Across the aisle." She lowered her voice. "The one in the blue dress. And it's *Mrs.* Keating. Not miss, like many of the young men in town would wish." She went back to her work.

"Sorry," he whispered back, hiding a grin. "I didn't know she was married."

"Go and get yourself in there, if you must."

"Thank you, ma'am."

Denning stepped through the doorway, his eyes on the young woman. She was wearing a hooped, medium-blue dress, her back to him. He cleared his throat for a second time and slowly made his way into the open, the newspaper tucked under his arm. He was the only man in the large room and soon drew the stares of the women. It was obvious to them that he was not a common man, but one of distinction, spotlessly groomed, with a self-assured manner. They looked with appreciation on his wavy reddish-blond hair and bronze skin, firm mouth and curious grin. He nodded at a few of the younger women as he moved along.

Denning was conscious of the silence, except for the rain on the roof and his own footsteps on the plank floor. He stopped the instant the woman in the blue dress spun around.

"Good morning, monsieur. May I help you?" Her voice was clear. She pronounced her words perfectly, a slight spark of Carolina drawl mingled with a French accent.

"Mrs. Keating?"

"Yes." Her eyes locked onto his.

Denning quickly realized that this was a lady of means, and he couldn't take his eyes off her. She appeared to be in her early twenties; her clear skin was light brown, almost like a pale Indian. She was tall for a woman—five-foot-seven for sure. Her curly hair was long, in ringlets, and as black as a moonless Cape Fear night. Her high cheek bones and fine features gave her a certain wild beauty that set her apart from other Southern women. She had a slim nose, slightly turned up, with interesting green eyes. She reminded him of someone else at that age, a few years ago. Even the ribbon in her hair and her scent of freshly cut flowers were almost the same. Up close, Denning saw that Mrs. Keating's dress was slightly faded, a common sight among Southern women now after the two-year blockade. Even metal hairpins were luxuries and hard to find, as evidenced by the thick hand-made wooden pins in her hair.

"May I help you, monsieur?" she repeated curiously. "You do speak, do you not?"

Denning tipped his head. "Mrs. Keating. I'm Captain Joshua Denning. The mayor sent me to see you."

Her face broke with an alluring smile, her teeth a dazzling white. "Ah, yes. The captain of the *Silver Sally*."

He still couldn't take his eyes off her. "Yes, madam." He heard a few lowered voices behind him.

Mrs. Keating clapped her hands together. "*Ladies! Ladies, please!*" She waited for silence. "May I introduce to you Captain Joshua Denning, one of our daring blockade runners," she said, accenting his profession. "He and his crew of the *Silver Sally* have graciously offered to help us with our project."

Denning turned and bowed twice as the women clapped. "Thank you. Good ladies of the Confederacy, my crew and I are at your service.

45

We are ready to do what we can for the Cause." Whatever that is, he wanted to know.

Mrs. Keating motioned to a far corner of the room. "If you please, captain. I have an office where we can talk in private."

She gathered up her skirts with a pinch of her slender fingers. Her flat-heeled shoes barely made a sound as she whisked across the floor.

The small, musty-smelling office contained some shelves of boxes from which bulged worn cotton material. She closed the door. They both stood in the room, ignoring the wooden chairs.

"I'm impressed, Mrs. Keating. You have quite the operation here. Keeping the boys warm at the front, and all. Sometimes women don't receive the credit for their part in the war. Very commendable."

"Thank you, monsieur. That's very kind of you." Her face reddened. "We try."

"It seems you more than try. By the way, Maxwell Toland sends you his regards."

"That was nice of him."

"Now, madam, I would like to know what I'm supposed to help you with, seeing that you have already so boldly volunteered me for it."

"I'm sorry, captain, I did get carried away."

"What is it that you need?"

"Raw cotton material from the English factories. We want to buy as much as you can supply us with. The Army of Northern Virginia is badly clothed right now. It's a disgrace, it is. Naturally, though, price is a consideration. Our means are rather limited." Her eyes did not waver from him the entire time she spoke.

Denning laughed softly. How ironic. English fabric made from Southern cotton. The South couldn't do it themselves? He held her gaze. "Why should there be a price? Not all the skippers in my profession are from the same mold. We're not all a pack of money-grabbing hound-dogs like some local people make us out to be."

"That's good to know. I'll spread the word around."

"Don't be too kind, though," he joked. "I still have to do business around town."

"I understand."

"I'll bring back whatever I can for you. No charge. For the Cause."

She seemed surprised. "That is very generous of you, monsieur."

46

"My pleasure, madam."

Her eyes focused on the newspaper. "Is there good news, monsieur?"

"Pardon me?"

"Your newspaper. Is there good news from the front?"

Denning tried to be nonchalant. "The town is in a buzz. Lee defeated Hooker at Chancellorsville, Virginia." He handed her the paper, unfolded the front page for her. "But Jackson was wounded. Shot accidentally by his own pickets."

Her face went stiff with the news.

Denning saw the wedding ring on her finger. "Do you perhaps have a loved one in Lee's army?"

"Yes, I do. My husband is in Jackson's cavalry."

"Oh. The telegraph office is open, although it's probably crowded now. I hear the first of the casualty reports are out. I do hope your husband is safe."

"So do I." She paused, then said briskly, "I had really best get back to it."

"And I'd better see to my shipment. Until we meet again."

"I wish you many safe journeys, monsieur." She returned the paper to Denning and folded her hands at her waist. "Goodbye, captain. It's been a pleasure meeting you."

"The pleasure is all mine," Denning replied.

He tipped his hat, bowed slightly and withdrew, thinking that he did not leave her with a good impression of him. But had he looked back, he would have caught Marie Keating standing at the door frame, smiling, watching him curiously as he walked to the entrance.

Nine

Wilmington

Soon after Denning left, Marie grabbed her umbrella and headed out the old print shop to walk the two blocks to the telegraph office.

She looked around at the new Wilmington, far removed from the prewar version. The blockade had changed Wilmington from a quaint port into a frontier town lacking authority. It was now the base for Robert E. Lee's supply line to his Army of Northern Virginia. There was no peace or rest in the place, which seemed to be always on the go. It lingered with a high-spirited mixture of speculators, scallywags, prostitutes, drunkards, gunmen, and noisy British and Southern navy officers and enlisted men with strange accents and vulgar behavior. Money and riches flowed lavishly in Wilmington, "the city of champagne and oysters".

She turned the corner to the telegraph office, next to Beery's shipyard. She stopped and stared across the waterfront at the cotton bales stacked as high as houses, ready for shipment abroad. Prewar exports of resin, turpentine, tar, and grains had been taken over by cotton, cotton, and more cotton. To one side of the shipyard stood the incoming goods that had been run through the blockade, crated and guarded by men with shotguns.

The porch of the telegraph office was crowded with men in Confederate uniforms that bore the insignia of all the services. Civilian men were also present in large numbers. Everyone was there for a purpose. The Chancellorsville casualty notices were out.

"Good morning, Mrs. Keating," a man greeted Marie formally, his gray eyes intent on her. "Not such a pleasant day, is it?"

"It could be better, certainly, Mr. Jacoby," Marie replied, smiling. "The sun wants to break through, though."

Eli Jacoby had been a good friend of the Keating family for many years. He was a charming man, she thought, recently widowed, always polite to her without overdoing it. A cotton and tobacco trader, she remembered. He was supposed to be handling government military contracts now. She hadn't heard many good things about people in that venture. They often took advantage of the government military traders, selling them defective material. She hoped Jacoby wasn't one of the bad dealers.

Some of the men, including Jacoby, graciously gave her room at the wall. Without stopping to see if she knew anyone else, she made her way to the long white sheets posted on the outside wall. Under the roof, with the rain sprinkling overhead, Marie read down the names printed in fresh dark ink. When she came to the Ks, she held her hand to her stomach.

KAMM, EDWARD, SERGEANT
KAHLE, ALLAN, LIEUTENANT
KAISER, CHARLES, LIEUTENANT
KAY, WILLIAM, CAPTAIN
KAZAK, DEREK, SERGEANT
KEARNS, DAVID, MAJOR
KEARSE, JUSTIN, LIEUTENANT
KEENAN, GEORGE, MAJOR

She looked again. Her husband's name was not on the list. *Thank God!* He was still alive. She sighed out loud, ignoring the commotion around her. He had survived Chancellorsville.

Jacoby came up to Marie and removed his hat. "Luke? Is he—?" his voice trailed off.

"He's not on it."

"That's good to hear," he said.

"Oui."

Catching her breath, Marie relaxed and began to pick out her neighbors and acquaintances in the crowd. Their faces told the story of either joy or grief. However, as always, the sight and sound of death dominated. The widow Rogell was crying. Her son was in Lee's cavalry. Mrs. Elmsey too was crying, her face flushed a deep red. She had two boys in the infantry. Were they both dead? Mr. and Mrs. McAleer, Mrs. Corbett, Mr. and Mrs. Potter—they were all affected.

Marie didn't know what to say to them. Their boys were so young, not more than nineteen or twenty. She could tell them that the best die young, but she knew it was trite and false. The passing of life had come to rest violently on several Wilmington homes this noon hour. She turned and walked back to her office.

Marie Keating had come to America at fourteen. Her father, a wine and champagne agent for a large French winery near Paris, had been sent to the United States to establish overseas markets in North America. Four years later, after seeing their only child wed in an arranged alliance with the esteemed Keating family of North Carolina, Marie's parents had returned to France.

Marie tried to fit in as a Southern lady, but she felt so out of place in her adopted country. If it wasn't for her husband, and his friends and relatives, she would have been rejected by most good families of Wilmington. Her casual outspokenness had brought her trouble soon after the newly married Keatings had made a honeymoon tour throughout the state.

"Oh, you people," she had told a party group, referring to the South's dependence on slavery. "Why do Southerners do such things? France did away with slavery centuries ago. We survived."

Most had taken it in stride, but others at the party had never forgiven her. She had insulted the South. They believed that women shouldn't have political opinions. The only excuse they could make for her was that she was a foreigner, a French woman. And French women were ignorant of the cherished Southern ways. They resented her accent, her barely concealed disrespect for Southern formality, her opinions, her European ways and expressions, her suntanned skin and the fact that she was left-handed. The list of imperfections was long. Marie knew that people were gossiping about her and she accepted it with honor. She didn't mind that much. In fact, she was pleased that she was a subject of conversation.

But oddly enough her most serious imperfection in her critics' eyes was her mild devotion to the Rebel Cause. And the harder she worked for the Cause, the more suspect she became. For a time a foolish rumor ran rampant that she was a Northern spy. However, Marie's position regarding the war was passively neutral, the way France and England felt about it. While the people of Wilmington were hoping and praying daily that England and France would step in as official Confederate allies, Marie knew it was unlikely that either country ever would. *Why should they?* Europe only wanted the South's cotton. If they couldn't squeeze enough out of ports like Wilmington and Charleston, they'd search out other foreign markets. She knew they were doing this already. Dixie wasn't the only cotton producer. Southern cotton wasn't worth losing young English and French lives over in some idiotic foreign war.

Marie was astonished at how the South was still winning victories on the battlefield but losing the foodstuff war on the home front. The prices of such household commodities as bacon, flour, sugar, coffee, butter, and soap had increased ten times or more since the last year of peace. The true value of the Confederate dollar was quickly dwindling to virtually nothing. Last heard, it was worth less than ten cents. Credit was nonexistent. Cash the only policy. She was intelligent enough to realize that the Old South would not survive another year or two, unless it took the war to the North.

It was its only chance to win.

Ten

Washington, D.C.

The next morning, a livid Secretary of War Edwin Stanton threw the day's copy of the *Washington Post* at Colonel Baker.

"There! Take a good look," Stanton hollered, watching the paper fall to his office floor. "What does your spy have to say in his defense?"

Baker looked down at the pages by his feet. "What do you mean, sir?"

"Our reports say we lost twice as many men as Lee did. And we went into the spring campaign outnumbering him two to one!"

"Maybe my man couldn't get a dispatch through." Baker replied. He bent over and picked up the scattered papers, carefully.

"That's not good enough!" Stanton stood. He leaned over his desk and glared at Baker. "What good is a spy in Lee's army who can't tell us of Jackson's sneak attack that took most of the day to arrange? Good grief, almost half a day of marching! Doesn't he have eyes? How much time did your boy want?"

"The telegraph might have gone down."

"Forget the telegraph. Why didn't he send a note through our pickets? The president has been ill over all this. Do you know what he said to me? '*My God, my God. What will the country say? Where can I find a leader?*' He's thinking of relieving Hooker of command. If Lincoln had only known that we could have bagged Jackson, Lee, and the whole rotten bunch of them. If your spy had come through."

Baker knew that because of Stanton, Lincoln knew very little of the inner workings of his own cabinet. Only what he was supposed to know.

"I wouldn't necessarily believe the reports that we outnumbered Lee two to one. He's stronger than that, sir."

"I have my own sources. Lee's forces have always been greatly exaggerated."

Baker swallowed hard and said nothing.

Stanton sat down. He took a deep breath and fingered some paperwork on his desk. "Go on. Get back to work."

"Very good, sir."

Chancellorsville, Virginia

Luke Keating rode his horse into the compound of hospital tents.

"Major!"

Keating turned in the direction of the voice.

"Major! Over here!"

Keating saw a sergeant in his unit lying on the ground outside one of the tents, ignored by the scurry of others around him. Keating knew the sergeant's family. He was a fine boy, a good soldier who never gave anyone trouble. He had just celebrated his twentieth birthday in April. He was supporting himself on one elbow, his sunburned face and blond hair damp with sweat. His right boot had been removed and his pant leg was torn up to a large, bleeding, infected scab below the knee.

Keating dismounted and squatted over him. "Hank. Is there anything I can do for you?"

"Don't let them take me in there, Mr. Keating, Major. . . sir," the sergeant pleaded.

"What can I do, Hank?" Keating could see that the sergeant's leg was in terrible shape. He reeked of liquor, but that had to be anesthetic. There was never any proper anesthetic around. Only whiskey.

"Please. They told me they're going to take my leg off."

Keating knew why. "Hank! Gangrene's set in. Why didn't you get attention earlier?"

The frantic sergeant winced. "I was hoping it weren't too bad. They dug the powder out and patched me up. Now look at it. I'm scared, Major!"

"Did you write your mamma, today?"

"Yes, sir. I did, major."

53

Keating tried to make Hank relax. They talked of North Carolina, Cape Fear, and Wilmington. The boy's speech was becoming slurred. The whiskey was taking effect. Keating let him go on talking in his drunken state. It was then the major noticed another soldier, on the other side of the nearest tent, sitting off to one side, shivering and holding his blood-stained arm. He couldn't have been more than seventeen, probably not old enough to shave or vote. A doctor and two orderlies were speaking to each other in the open medical tent. Keating caught part of the dialogue, something about the *last two*. He sniffed, suddenly catching a whiff of the sweet-and-sour scent of blood and flesh in the air. Off to the side of the tent was a stack of arms and legs. Keating stared at them and comprehended the dreadful reality of what would soon happen to Hank.

The doctor came out and wiped his hands on his long, white cape splashed with fresh and dried-up blood stains. "You there," he called out to a bearded orderly outside the tent. "Bring that man in."

Hank cringed. He crept backwards on his hands, cowering like a child. "No!"

"You have to," Keating begged. "You'll die for sure if you don't."

"I'm as good as dead ifin I do go in that there tent. My girlfriend back home won't want me with one leg. What good will I be?"

The boy's hysterical, Keating told himself. "I'll write her, Hank, and explain. What's her name?"

"Excuse me, major," the heavy-set orderly said, as he put his arm around the sergeant's shoulders and dragged him into the tent. "In you go, fella."

From outside, Keating watched the struggle to contain Hank on the table. He was gagged, and two men sat on him. Keating froze, fighting his urge to burst in and rescue poor Hank. He saw him shaking violently, then heard the awful sawing sound. Keating wanted to cry, but no tears would come. He wanted to throw up, but couldn't do that either. He was too appalled. The horror of it seemed to paralyze his eyes, forcing him to keep looking. Luckily, Hank passed out, allowing the doctor to finish his grizzly work. The sergeant would now have a fifty-fifty chance of surviving an infection, so people have said, providing he could deal with the shock. Keating finally looked away, his eyes locking with those of the other soldier.

"Send in the last man!" the doctor cried harshly, poking his head out of the tent and throwing the sergeant's leg into the pile of human parts. Keating burned inside. Had the doctor no compassion? No mercy? Throwing Hank's leg out like that! Keating stared at the shivering soldier, then at the waiting doctor. This was the youth of the nation.

Such a pathetic waste.

Near Cape Fear

The mouth of the Cape Fear River posed a problem for Captain Robert Carlisle of the USS *Connecticut*. The river's two openings were only six miles apart, but due to the Frying Pan Shoals off Smith Island jutting ten miles into the ocean, the Union patrolling area spanned a staggering forty miles to cover both inlets. And all the forty miles of hiding places had to be patrolled, requiring a much larger force of Union ships than could properly be deployed. At least fifty at any one time were needed to cover the two inlets. The Union knew they were at a disadvantage and was doing its utmost to increase the quality of patrolling.

Carlisle felt the hollow reverberation of the *Connecticut*'s engines as he paced the deck of his five-hundred-ton gunboat, telescope in hand. The delay had been longer than expected, waiting an additional week for engine parts to be shipped to Hatteras. The ship was now on an eight-knot course adjacent to the shore. They were on the late-night watch for this patrol. It was a relief to be at sea again. Carlisle's assignment was to undertake an inside-line, two-day patrol of the Cape, then steam for the neutral waters off Nassau. An extra load of coal and enough provisions were on ship to keep them going for a week, making it unnecessary to send a foraging party to shore in that time. Carlisle always kept these foraging trips to a minimum, anyway, for fear of desertion.

A stiff westerly evening breeze cracked the sails. He glanced in the direction of the Confederate stronghold of Fort Fisher, guarding the New Inlet approach to the Cape Fear River. Based on experience, he stayed out of the range of the twenty guns in the earthen traverses and the additional twenty-four-gun wall that ended at the Mound Battery overlooking the Atlantic Ocean. Befriended by the partial moonlight, someone on the Mound could probably see the Union steamer right now. Without a doubt they were monitoring the ship's moves. Carlisle had tangled with the guns once before when his ship chased a blockade runner too near the shore. As a result, he had come very close to being blown clear out of the water. Nature favored the Rebels, for New Inlet was shallow, even at high water. Only specially constructed blockade runners could conquer it.

Carlisle's careful eye monitored the senior officer's ship in the center of his squadron, identified only by the white lantern on the bridge. Flanked by his fellow gunboats either anchored or cruising off the mouth, Carlisle always had his guns trained on the inlet. All it would take would be a flick of light, a sniff of burning coal, or the faintest noise. At any of these a cascade of shells from his eleven-inch pivot gun and eight twenty-pound howitzers would descend on the unsuspecting Rebel ship. The deck crew, composed mainly of petty officers, stood motionless, their penetrating eyes on the open water. The petty officers were the multi-purpose sailors who actually ran the ship. They manned the powerful guns aboard the USS *Connecticut* and were held together by a strong fraternity.

As Carlisle made his way past the men, a voice in the darkness boasted, "The men are ready for a fight, captain."

"Are they?" Carlisle replied absently. He stopped pacing to let his first-mate, Commander Stephen Farley, catch up to him. They continued in a slow promenade of the deck.

Carlisle stopped again and held the telescope to his right eye. He searched the New Inlet entrance for any sign of his adversaries. With the wind coming off shore, he and Farley were always alert to sounds and smells out of the ordinary. Anthracite coal, the enemy's lifeline, had a distinct but hard-to-detect smell. Nevertheless, it was not impossible to pick it up, given the right wind conditions.

"Keep a steady lookout, commander," Carlisle said to Farley.

"Aye, aye, sir."

Eleven

The Bahamas

The next return run out, the *Silver Sally* steamed through the channel at a constant eight knots, north by west. Leaning over the port rail, Captain Denning made a mental note of Boulder Island, a nautical mile or more off starboard. The island, nicknamed by pilots earlier in the war, was actually a large, high rock. It was surrounded by sand and was nearly two hundred yards long, protruding defiantly above the deep waters off Nassau to a height of fifty feet at its center. Pilots were in the habit of sailing within a few hundred yards of it in order to follow a particular channel leading to and from Nassau.

"Put up the British flag," Denning ordered Balsinger.

"Aye, aye, sir."

Denning looked the deck over, full of wood crates bound for Wilmington. Inside the crates were ladies fashions, French champagne, lead bars, guns, and raw British cotton for Marie Keating's Lads of Liberty. The captain turned and headed to his cabin in the aft quarter. Inside, he looked at the calendar—May 29.

Suddenly, he was stunned by the buzz of a cannon shot that just missed his cabin. The second shot—right behind the first—hit near the starboard bow, sending up a wall of sputtering water against the hull of his ship. He knew by the sound they were shots from two different guns—one light, one heavy. Denning lunged for the porthole and saw a Union warship, the sunlight glinting off her white sails. He had yet to see one in this close to port. A whistle came down the voice tube. Denning grabbed for it.

"Captain!" Matthew Balsinger's voice boomed.

"I see it," Denning answered. "How come no one spotted it sooner?"

"It was hiding behind the rock, with her stacks and sails down."

"Any battle damage?"

"None. But if the first shot was any closer to the smokestacks, we'd be going the rest of the way on one engine. If at all."

"I'll be right up."

On deck, Denning didn't need his telescope because they were close enough to the well-armed Union gunboat. A deadly foe, she had several howitzers and a formidable eleven-inch Dahlgren. Denning considered the range and decided that the two shells were warning shots. There was no doubt the Union captain could have hit the *Sally* if he had wanted to.

"We've been ambushed. What do we do?" Balsinger asked, his voice tight and high.

Denning cleared his throat as he went to the rail for a closer look. "There's not much we can do—can't outrun her." He looked to the *Sally*'s stern and saw the flag. "At least we're flying the British flag. That's all we have going for us."

From the gunboat came a clear voice. "Avast! Or I will blast you out of the water!"

Denning quickly looked to his crew up and down the rail. No one had panicked and they now waited on his orders, fearlessly. A damn good crew, they were. "We'll have to stop the engines," Denning said to Balsinger.

"Then what?"

"Bluff them."

As the *Silver Sally* slowed, the gunboat was able to edge closer. Denning continued to watch as the enemy swiftly decreased the distance between them. He ordered the engines stopped, and he heard a similar order given on the gunboat.

When the two boats were within thirty yards of each other, a second order rang out. "Prepare to be boarded!"

Denning considered the cruiser's cannon and howitzer barrels pointed in his direction. Capable Union men with hostile expressions stood behind each heavy gun. Denning knew he couldn't refuse the command. "Steady as she goes, men," he said in a low voice to Balsinger and those sailors nearest him. "I think I know how to deal with this."

"I was hoping you might, captain." Balsinger did not look relieved.

Denning cupped his hands to his mouth. "You have permission to board!"

A small craft was launched beside the gunboat. Six men, three of them officers, climbed down the laid-out Jacob's ladder ropes and slid into the tossing craft. Two men paddled the craft to the *Sally*. Denning took a few steps back in a line abreast with his men. He heard the boarding party crawling up the *Sally*'s ropes and waited.

Over they came.

Denning saw that each of the six Feds was armed with a cutlass and a Navy revolver. The captain stood out from the group, his polished sword gleaming in the sun. His eyes quickly observed Denning's men at their assigned places. He looked to be taken aback at the armed crew. "Who's in charge, here?" he demanded.

Denning detached himself from his men. "I am. Who are you?"

"Captain Carlisle, United States Navy."

Denning looked at the captain with great interest. He knew the man. What a coincidence! The son-of-a-bitch Carlisle had not changed much since their days at Annapolis. He had the same long neck, the same broad nose, and the same untidy hair out the sides of the cap, and the same bow-legged limp. But now he had a stringy moustache and different shaped spectacles that were stronger than Denning remembered, making Carlisle's eyes seem larger.

"Your name, sir?"

"Old King Cole," said Denning distinctly, convinced that Carlisle had not recognized him.

A few of his crew laughed.

A flush of red spread across Carlisle's cheeks. "Very funny. You have quite the sense of humor considering the pickle you're in."

"Me?"

"That's right! You!"

"You're the one in the pickle. What's the meaning of boarding my ship?"

"That British flag doesn't fool me. This is a Rebel blockade runner!"

Commander Farley leaned toward Carlisle and whispered, "It's the *Sally*."

"Eh?" Carlisle whispered back, looking annoyed that he was interrupted.

"The *Silver Sally*," the first mate said out of the side of his mouth. "The fastest ship in the Rebel fleet."

"Is it now?"

Farley nodded. "Yes, sir."

Carlisle turned back to Denning. "What is your cargo? As if I don't know. They can't be implements of war, can they?" Carlisle's eyes darted here and there, to Denning's face, to his own men, and back to Denning.

Denning replied, "None of your damn business."

"You might be flying the Union Jack, but you're no Britisher, that's for hell sure. The only uniforms I see here are Reb gray. We have reason to believe this is the Rebel blockade runner *Silver Sally*. Under authority of the United States Navy in Washington I have every right to search your ship for contraband material heading for the Confederacy."

Denning clasped his hands behind his back and firmly planted his legs. "These are neutral waters. This is not the open sea. Neither the United States nor its Navy has any authority here."

"We'll see about that, Reb." Carlisle withdrew his loaded pistol from his holster and swung it at one of the hundreds of long wooden cases on the deck. "I'll trouble you to open that yonder case there."

Denning nodded at one of his deck hands. "Do as he says. Let the. . . esteemed Captain Carlisle get it out of his system."

A reluctant sailor took a bar to the lid. With a loud creak, the contents were revealed, a stack of long, thick-barreled rifles.

"British Enfields. I knew it," Carlisle said.

Denning turned behind him. "Show your guns, men." Across the deck, guns clicked. More than a dozen barrels pointed at the small Union force. Other Rebel armed sailors appeared from below the deck to increase the Rebel squad.

It was a standoff.

Red-faced, Carlisle stared at Denning, taking the pistols into consideration. "I can order my men on ship to open up with a volley."

Denning shook his head. "But you won't, Bobby." He saw the Union captain fidget. "Don't be a fool. You'll go down too. You know, you're not all that smart coming aboard. Still as hot-tempered as ever."

"You know my first name. Hold on there." When the Rebel skipper removed his broad-brimmed hat and bowed, Carlisle's memory journeyed back to Maryland. "Joshua Denning," he muttered.

"Bobby Carlisle," Denning replied. "My old friend."

"So, we meet again. Friend, my eye!"

"Listen to me good, Carlisle. Order your ship to back off, or else. . ."

"Or else what? You're in no position—"

"Shut up!" Denning cut him short.

"How dare you!"

"Matt?"

"Aye, sir," Balsinger replied, caught unaware.

"Start the engines."

"Aye, sir." Balsinger yelled across the deck, "Start engines!"

"Here now, what do you think you're doing!" Carlisle pounded toward Denning. "What's the meaning of this? My men also own weaponry, in case you hadn't noticed."

"I urge you to keep a civil tongue, Bobby. On this ship you are out-gunned." On Carlisle's face he saw a hint of the eleven years of hate the Union officer had for him. "I give the orders now." The engines started and the ship began to move. "Matt, half-steam."

"Aye, aye, sir." Balsinger turned. "Half-steam!"

"You heard me, Bobby. I'll let one of your crew go to inform the rest on your steamer. But he can't take the boat. Leave it tied up to ours. Let him swim. You!" He gun-pointed at the lowest-ranked Union sailor. "Once you board your ship, your orders are to stay where you are until these five others return. Is that clear?"

The sailor glanced at Carlisle, then back at Denning. "I suppose it is."

"Well, shove off, lad," Denning demanded. "Do it!" Denning watched the sailor jump over the side and swim for the cruiser, then he ordered the *Silver Sally* to turn to port and pull away.

Balsinger approached his skipper and whispered, "This is your plan?"

"Quiet. I'm not finished yet."

"Oh."

The *Connecticut* did nothing. The gap widened to six hundred yards. The ship still remained motionless. The distance stretched to one mile. Two miles. Then three. The silence was profound, as Carlisle and Denning played a waiting game.

Carlisle finally broke down and accosted Denning. "What do you aim to do with us? Are we prisoners?" he asked, his eyes full of bitterness.

"We could hang you or make you walk the plank and let the sharks have you for dinner, like in the old days of the Spanish Main. Or we could let you go." In truth, the last thing Denning wanted was Union prisoners. They were trouble. They'd have to be guarded, fed, looked after, and gagged and tied going into shore at night. He estimated the *Sally* was five miles away from the *Connecticut*. He ordered the engines stopped, and they were soon drifting on the open Atlantic Ocean water, the waves lapping against the hull.

Calling to a junior officer, Denning smiled and said, "Launch the boat for our fine men of Lincoln's Navy." He walked over to Carlisle. "I hope your boarding party is in good physical condition because now you can row back. Lower away!" Denning ordered, turning to face Carlisle. "So long, Bobby."

Minutes later, in the boat with his men, Carlisle stared across the open water at the *Silver Sally*, too incensed to speak. Burned into his memory forever would be the sight of Denning on the *Sally*'s rail, his face lit with an expression of pleasure that he had embarrassed Carlisle in front of his Union boarding party. But deep down, Carlisle knew Denning had made a fatal error letting him go.

He'd get even with Denning somehow, somewhere.

Denning drew on his Havana cigar, licking the end of it, gazing out at the expanse of ocean water. The *Silver Sally* held a twelve-knot course, heading north by northwest for Cape Fear. The boat containing the six Union Navy men was more than a mile away and the *Connecticut* was steaming towards the officers. Boulder Island was blending into the mist.

Balsinger walked up. "Now, just who is this Bobby Carlisle? He's no relation to the famous Navy Carlisles, is he?"

"He is."

"He is?"

"We were in the same graduating class at Annapolis," Denning said.

"You were?"

Denning nodded. "His picture is on the wall in my cabin with the other officers." He shook his head. "Although he's crossed my mind lately, I didn't think I'd ever see him again. You know, we had a nickname in college for him."

"What was it?"

"Four Eyes."

"Applicable, I'd say," Balsinger observed with a smile.

"He detested it."

"No doubt."

The two laughed.

"It seemed pretty clear to me you weren't too fond of him."

Denning nodded. The corner of his mouth quivered. "It's not surprising. The bastard stole the only woman I ever loved."

"So that's it."

Denning fell silent, thinking of Marie Keating and how she reminded him of the woman from his past. She had brought back bittersweet memories of Clara and now Carlisle had done the same. He didn't like the odd coincidence. It spooked him. At the academy he had beaten Carlisle at everything, including marks. Denning finished second in the class, Carlisle somewhere in the middle. Classwork was a struggle for Carlisle. Funny thing. He never looked like navy material. Except, in the end he got Clara. And Denning let it happen. He gave in.

Clara was from Annapolis. Her family was steeped in Navy tradition. Pickled in tradition, more like it. Denning bumped into her in a store in the town and helped her carry two bags of flour to her buggy. They struck up a friendship that developed into something that neither of them expected. He never did ask her to marry him. He wanted to, and he thought she wanted him to. Denning was sure Carlisle was jealous that he was courting the prettiest girl in town. And she really was the prettiest.

Then Carlisle got in the way. He used his influence. Her parents never took to Denning. He wasn't from a Navy family like Clara and Bobby were. It was tough for Denning's father to even raise the money to send him to the academy, which was something Bobby's family never had trouble with. In fine fashion, the families arranged the marriage. Denning had heard the two fathers had sailed together in the Mexican War. He often wondered all these years if Bobby and Clara were ever happy. It was a typical marriage, by American standards, he thought, cynically. A self-centered, vain man, living up to the Carlisle name, matched oddly with a decent, probably self-sacrificing, woman.

Denning saw the craft and the gunboat on the horizon. He remembered Clara that last painful day, the day she broke off their relationship.

They were looking across the blue waters of Chesapeake Bay. The sun was shining, the birds were singing.

It was the worst day of Denning's life.

"And there he goes," he said to Balsinger. "He thought he was so clever, pulling a fast one on a Southerner, stealing his woman. How he detested us Southerners. The Southern race, he called us. I really got under his skin." Especially after the knife fight, Denning remembered.

It was the last year at the academy, only a few days before graduation. A group of cadets were in a tavern, all drinking, naturally. Some of them right heavy, including Denning and Carlisle, who were at opposite ends of the establishment. Carlisle and Clara had already made plans to marry. Denning and Carlisle shouted at each other. They went out into the street. The other cadets followed. They pulled out knives, and by the time it was over, Denning had stabbed Carlisle in the knee. The other cadets pulled them apart. The two sobered up in a hurry.

Their superiors never did find out what happened because it was all hushed up or they both would have been expelled from the academy. Their careers at stake, Carlisle told his superiors that some drunk in town did it. The rest of the cadets confirmed it. After graduation, Carlisle and Denning went their separate ways, Carlisle with a permanent limp. Now the two faced each other on opposite sides in a war.

"I'm glad he's still around," Denning finally said after the lengthy silence.

"You are? Why?"

"He's bound to make things right interesting. Now we'll see who's the better man."

"The better man? What the hell you talking about! With all the ships out there, our side and theirs, you'll probably never cross paths again."

Denning disagreed. "I think we'll meet again. Next time it won't be as cordial. Give Homer a new order," Denning said, putting his long telescope to his eye to watch Carlisle and his party boarding the *Connecticut*. "From now on we'll take a wide berth around Boulder Island. That channel is off limits."

"Aye, aye, sir."

Twelve

Northern Virginia, off Chesapeake Bay

A cricket chirped. In the moonlight, two sets of footsteps creaked the boards of the narrow old bridge. Off the ocean's horizon to the south, miles away, lightning flashed, reflecting off the water. Then came the rumble of distant thunder, like a band of bass drums.

Eli Jacoby saw the figure converge towards him on the bridge. He went for his concealed pistol, looked for identifying features, then relaxed. The figure seemed the right height and build. The same slow walk.

The man stopped four feet away. "Jacoby?"

"Wheeler. I see you made it. It's almost ten o'clock." Jacoby stopped too, his arms resting by his sides.

"Sorry we're late, old boy," said Wheeler, not sounding that apologetic. "I couldn't help it. We had to scramble to get the shipment going once we got the all-clear."

Jacoby looked over the bridge to his right. Three hundred yards away, along the shore, floated four barge loads of cotton bales. Alongside the barges were two large steamboats, bulging with Northern goods, rocking on the water. "Anybody follow you?" he asked.

"Nah. You?"

"Not a chance."

Lightning flashed and thunder cracked. The storm appeared to be heading their way.

"What a time for a storm."

"Don't worry," Jacoby said. "We've been watching it. By the direction of it, it'll go right by."

"I hope so, or else we won't be able to load."

"We'll load, no matter what," Jacoby said firmly. "We can't be hanging around here at daybreak."

"No, guess we can't."

"How's the boss in Washington?"

"Lincoln?"

Jacoby chuckled. "You know who I'm talking about."

"Ah, you mean Baker boy."

"Yeah, good ol' Baker boy."

"Cranky as ever," Wheeler grunted.

Jacoby laughed. "What's his problem? Is he not making enough money?"

"Yeah, that's about it."

"Nothing's changed then."

"Nah. But he's glad we're back in business."

"He ain't the only one," Jacoby said.

"Baker boy sends his compliments. The rest of the town isn't too happy. They could strangle Hooker, the dope. Sonofabitch. Imagine, losing nearly his entire army at Chancellorsville. Word is out. Lincoln will get rid of him and try another commander."

"Another one! How many idiot generals is that now?"

"I can't keep track of 'em," Wheeler said. "Scott. McClellan. Burnside. Hooker."

They laughed together. Neither had any respect for the Union field leadership so far in the war. Whoever was running the Army of the Potomac was not their concern. Dealing in war contraband and profits were.

"So, what's the word on the fighting? Are we going to be able to keep our line open for a while?"

Wheeler paused. "I think so. Just heard from a good source. Robert E. Lee's sent scouts into Maryland. So this side of Virginia should be safe for now."

"Maryland! Lee's going to try it again, is he? An invasion of the North."

"Oh, yeah. Looks like 'er. Washington is right scared this time, believe me. They are *real* scared."

"So, what do you got for me, Wheeler?"

"Beef. Pork. Colt revolvers. Fresh bandages."

"Just dandy."

"Any trouble coming down?"

Jacoby shook his head. "No. Not with the new set of passes. How about you?"

"Nothing. I'm with Baker. I'm just glad we're back in business and the rail lines are free again with the armies out of our way. I don't think we could have lasted much longer. Too much dissension amongst our. . . investors."

Jacoby nodded in agreement. "Same with us. The barge pilots are getting a little greedy, though. Any more trouble from them and I might consider rail all the way."

"They're your problem," Wheeler grunted. "Just keep them in check. We don't want anybody or anything to break the line now that it's finally freed up."

"I'll look after it." Jacoby turned and waved to a man behind him, off the bridge. "Let's tally up," he said back to Wheeler, "I've got my own people in Wilmington anxiously waiting for this stuff."

"I bet yuh do, Jacoby boy."

Thirteen

Outside Wilmington—June 1863

The long letter from her husband was unlike any previous letter Marie had received from him. She had been expecting something like this sooner or later. Still, it upset her. It wasn't so much what Luke said in the letter that bothered Marie. It was what he didn't say. She had known her husband long enough to sense that although he was pleased with the Chancellorsville victory, even he now saw the Cause in serious jeopardy.

He stated that not only could the Yankee army replace its casualties quickly, it was actually increasing in size every time they met. The Union was recruiting foreigners from Canada, France, England, Germany, and other European countries. Too many of the South's youngsters, the heart of the nation, were dying or going home minus a leg or arm. Their replacements weren't coming in fast enough, if it all. The South just didn't have the manpower. The Yankees had more modern weapons that were manufactured in the North, with matching ammunition. They didn't have to rely on the imported guns from Europe that the South was so dependent on. The Northern boys were better fed and better clothed. They were healthier and stronger. And the Union cavalry had a weapon called a Spencer repeater rifle which, according to Luke, could be loaded on Sunday and fired all week.

Marie folded the letter and looked to Luke's framed portrait over the fireplace mantle. The letter was no great shock to her. In fact, she was glad her husband had finally admitted it. How long would it take the others, including the bull-headed people around her in Wilmington?

Damn it all, the South was going to lose the war!

She thought of the people she knew. Even families in her social order, including Luke's parents, were now finding it difficult to survive with the current prices of everyday items. Inflation had hit the poorest families first in the summer of the first year of war, closely followed by the middle class. Some women and young girls, she had learned, were forced into prostitution just to survive and make ends meet. The economy was collapsing. What was left in Marie's bank account was slowly decreasing due to the devalued currency—one hundred dollars Confederate was worth only six dollars in gold.

How much longer would she and Luke be able to keep this house on this sprawling property, a mile north of town, with the fine silver and crystal displayed in expensive sideboards? How much longer would the Persian rug be under their feet? There were reports of uprisings in the South. In Richmond, stores had been looted by bitter women, incensed at the soaring domestic prices of goods. President Davis himself ordered the crowd to disperse or they would be fired on. He was successful and the crowd went their way, but the event left a sour taste in the mouths of the participants. She wondered if such an uprising could occur in Wilmington, and what would be the consequences if it did. Wilmington would be ripe for it. Soon. Very soon.

The war was bringing change faster than most people realized. It was believed in the South that women were put on this earth to do little else than look pretty, make their husbands happy, devote all their energies to domestic tasks at hand, and in her own case to make her husband look more important than he really was. Southern women were to smile, arrange parties, make love to their important husbands when called upon, produce the children, and to leave the talk of politics to the men. Marie always knew what was expected of her. It was so shallow.

Marie didn't want to think about such things any more. It was too depressing. She knew the cure for temporarily ridding herself of these worries. She changed into her riding dress and gear, and darted out the rear door for the sanctity of her stable. She flipped her sun hat off, straddled her horse, and rode like the wind through the long, open field beyond the trees. After an hour, she switched to the side-saddle position, the approved style for decent Southern women, and steered in the direction of the stable.

She had the horse in a controlled trot around the smokehouse, when she saw a tall man in an open carriage by the paddock. He jumped to the ground, holding his hat in his hand. She rode closer and straightened her back, squeezing her heels into the horse. "Whoa. Good girl, Lavender." She took off her gloves, and patted the dark-brown mare on the neck. "Why, Captain Denning. This is a pleasant surprise. How very nice to see you."

"Mrs. Keating." He smiled up at her. "May I help you down, madam?"

She hesitated, then flirtatiously cocked her head. "*Oui, monsieur.*"

He reached out for her. She was amazed at the gentleness with which the solid, handsome captain gripped her waist and brought her down in one graceful motion.

"I have what you asked for."

"Really? Oh, the cloth?"

Denning smiled. "Yes. Courtesy of the blockade." She followed him over to the carriage. "It's all here." He slid back a tarp to show her yards of cotton blankets, all gray, piled to the top of the side planks. "The best English quality. Heavy and thick."

"Yes. It surely is." She plunged her hands into the pile to feel some of the material in her tanned hands. "*Magnifique. Merci.* Thank you, so much." Then she realized how she appeared and tried to tuck some strands of hair under her sun hat. The inside band felt damp with perspiration. "I'm sorry. You didn't really catch me at my best." She mopped her brow. "Hot, *oui?*"

"Yes, it is hot. So, you're a rider. You seem comfortable in the saddle."

"My papa put me on my first horse when I was five. I've been riding ever since."

"Five. Good age to learn." Denning drew closer to the shiny, well-groomed horse and stroked her on the shoulder. "Fine looking Morgan you got here. She's slimmer than most I've seen, almost like an Arabian. Does she have any Arabian blood?"

Marie nodded. "Yes, she does."

"A little taller too. A good jumper, I would venture to say."

She felt at ease with Denning. "You know your horses, monsieur."

He glanced back at her. "I was raised in Virginia. You know what they say. How many Virginians can't ride?" he grinned.

"Touché. My husband agrees. He says that Virginian cavalry units are the best riders in Lee's army."

"Speaking of your husband, I take it that your trip to the telegraph office brought you good news?"

"He was not on the list," she sighed. "He wrote me after the battle at Chancellorsville." She didn't see a wedding ring on his finger. He was too good looking a man to be a bachelor. "Has anyone heard about Jackson?"

"He died, I'm afraid. Pneumonia."

"He'll be a great loss to the Confederate hopes," she said.

"I would think so."

A stable hand appeared and took the reins from Marie. She and Denning walked to the shade of the stable wall.

"Our hopes are running out, oui?" she said, leaning her back on a paddock post. "I've heard people say that one firm Rebel victory on Northern soil might bring England and France to our side. If that's the case, loans could be obtained on Southern securities. Then, perhaps, a European fleet could be established to reopen Southern ports to ship our cotton abroad. Could any of this be true?"

"It's possible," Denning answered, caught off guard by her topic of conversation. "We'll have to see what happens now that it's rumored Lee is on the move."

"A second invasion?"

Denning nodded. "My father's last letter confirmed it. When Lee pulled out of Chancellorsville, he headed north. Not south. I wonder if it'll work this time."

"This time?"

"The battle at Sharpsburg didn't budge Europe to recognize Southern independence, as the South had hoped it might."

"But Sharpsburg wasn't a clear-cut victory," she countered. "Lee had retreated. And Lincoln's Emancipation Proclamation didn't help. It made us appear as if we were fighting for slavery."

"True. But aren't we, in fact, though very few want to admit it?"

"That might be the case," she acknowledged.

Marie regarded Denning with amusement and wondered what he was thinking. He probably hadn't carried on too many political discussions with Southern women.

"This time, Lee's destination is either Maryland or Pennsylvania," Denning continued. "However, if England and France enter the war on the Confederate side, they would most certainly be supporting slavery, whether they wanted to or not. I don't think they are prepared to take that chance. They might recognize the Confederate States, that's all, and continue to purchase our cotton as long as it's advantageous to them."

"And while this goes on, the English and French send troops over to fight for the North."

"Then you've been hearing the same things I have. What hypocrisy." He paused. "I spent the first year and a half of the war overseas in Europe, then some time in Canada. Nova Scotia. I learned a few things from people. Do you know there are thousands of Canadians fighting in the Union Army for Lincoln, while their relatives and friends back home are selling their goods to the Confederacy where they get more money for them? Munitions, hospital supplies, medicines, saltpeter—you name it. Does any foreign country send their boys to fight for us in the South? Not on your life. But they are sure there with their hands out. There's money to be made in war, Madam Keating."

"Oui." She agreed with Denning. "I hear the North is growing quickly with European immigrants coming in and moving west. Despite the war, America is still the land of opportunity."

"To the North, anyway." Denning smiled. "You seem to have a good insight into the political scene," he finally said. "You should be a politician. You make more sense than they do."

"You are a gentleman, *monsieur.* It does one good to study politics, regardless of gender. No?"

"Yes."

She considered his suggestion. "But a woman politician, born in France. Who'd listen?"

"If the South had leaders like you, they wouldn't be in the mess they're in now."

"Thank you again," she said, flushing.

"The South has to change. You, madam, are one of the few people in Wilmington who I sense is smart enough to see it, as well as admit it."

She gave a quick nod of confirmation. They were of like views.

"The survival of slavery and cotton—that's what this war is all about," Denning said. "Independence is secondary. The South has hung onto its archaic institution of slavery for too long. It's hurting the same businesses they're trying to establish."

"What do you mean?" She slanted her head to one side, frowning.

Denning collected his thoughts. "Slavery has prevented the Confederacy from developing a class of skilled workers, which the North now has and has been developing for years. I saw it with my own eyes even before the war. At this very moment men are employed in Northern factories manufacturing guns, powder, bullets, cannons, and wagons by the thousands while the South has to import such hardware through the blockade, which is getting tougher by the month. After only one year of the war, the North practically stopped buying any munitions abroad. They didn't need to because their own manufacturers can make them everything they want. The North is booming right now—a technological empire."

Marie nodded her head. Luke had seen the Union weaponry at the front, and now Denning had confirmed it.

"Northern farmers are producing grain like never before," he went on. "A great portion of their wheat and flour is shipped to Great Britain, the same Great Britain buying up our cotton and pretending to be our ally. It's a farce. The South has rejected the industrial revolution for a hundred years and is now faced with a war where the same industrial revolution embraced by the North will be the deciding factor. The North has everything in its power to win, all the resources, except field leadership and a series of hard victories. And Europe is merely waiting to see who gains the upper hand. The South or the North."

"And it doesn't appear bright for the South, I must say," Marie said, Luke's letter coming to mind.

"No, it doesn't. And I think we both know it." He sighed, changing the subject. "Madam, your accent"—he smiled at her—"is so French but yet your English is excellent."

"My papa thought it best that I learn English. I believe it was about the same time he put me on a horse."

"Ah, I see. A smart man. Tell me, what made you ever settle in America?"

She told him the details, including her marriage to Luke Keating.

"Your father was getting you ready for America, then. An arranged marriage?" Denning joked.

"By your tone, I take it you don't approve of such unions."

"So it was arranged, then. It's not necessarily that, although arranged marriages are brutal."

"Brutal!" exclaimed Marie.

"It's. . . well, it's marriage in general, I guess."

"Oh, good Lord. What do you have against marriage?"

"I have my reasons. It's a good institution for some individuals. Some marry for convenience more so than love, however. I, for one, could never marry for convenience, which most marriages are."

"And what's wrong with marrying for convenience sake, monsieur?"

"Nothing, I suppose. Providing a person gets what he or she wants from it."

Marie fell silent. They walked across the yard to the shade of the back porch veranda. A long flowerbed spread out from that side of the house. The fragrance of the plants filled the porch.

A black female servant brought them some French spirits on a large tray. They sat down, and Denning accepted some wine in a crystal glass.

"Mrs. Keating, aren't you worried about your reputation? You're a married women. What if someone should see us? What if your servants should talk?" He leaned forward in his chair.

"What am I doing wrong?" She shrugged her shoulders, a glass of cherry brandy in her hand. She appreciated the company. "Besides, monsieur, I'm not too well liked as it is. So, what difference does it make?"

"In town, they call you the Gypsy woman."

"Oh, do they?" She laughed. "What else are they saying about me?"

He lowered his eyes, and looking straight at her said, "That you're a Union spy."

She laughed harder. "Is that one still going around? Do you believe it?"

"No, I don't. Besides, I'm in somewhat ill repute myself. If you know what I mean?"

"Oui. One of those nasty blockade skippers." She deepened her voice. "The scourge of the South! I hear the stories." She rested her head against the back of the chair. Her face was serious. She gently moved her glass back and forth, watching the rich liquid catch the light. "Tell me one thing, captain. Are you happy blockade running?"

"I'm doing my best," he answered her, looking surprised that she would ask such a question. "It's a business."

"Then I take it you are not happy. Are you?"

His eyes penetrated hers. "This is war, madam. Few are happy in a war, regardless of what they do. For me, it sure beats being a chicken farmer in Virginia, like my father is. And it beats fighting for Lee. How about you? Are you happy in your arranged marriage?"

An awkward pause set in. She looked away and chose not to answer at first.

"I'm sorry. I shouldn't have asked you that. Did I insult you?"

"No," she snapped. "It's the war. I never see my husband. That's what makes it difficult."

Denning backed off. "I can understand that, of course." He downed the last of his wine and stood up. Flipping the cover of his gold pocket watch, he took note of the time. "Thank you for your company, the chat and the wine. I should get back into town."

She came to her feet. "I'm sure you are busy."

"Yes. I must deliver the blankets to your office, and I have to make ready for this evening's auction. This has been one interesting afternoon. And I'm serious—you should go into politics. You have the knowledge for it. If you do, I'll be your running mate." He smiled and tipped his hat. "If not, you could always make a good spy."

He made her laugh once more. "Oh, go on," she said, glad they were parting in good humor.

Watching him stride to the carriage, Marie saw Denning as a mysterious man. She wondered if the other Rebel skippers were like him.

But probably none of them were as handsome as he was.

Fourteen

Wilmington

The sunny conditions did not keep up for the auction later that day.

Denning focused his attention on the hundreds of businessmen in the crowd. Most of the men were well-dressed. By the size of some stomachs, many were obviously well-fed, too, lacking very little in the way of daily necessities. These were men of leisure, professional merchants, blockade skippers turned speculators, and fancy low-lives, vowing to outbid each other for the recent blockaded goods imported from Bermuda and the Bahamas. Some individuals were trustworthy, others were of dubious honesty. The rest were out-and-out cheats. There could even be a Union spy or two in there. A few ladies were sprinkled through the crowd, clinging to their escorts. Denning quickly picked out the *Silver Sally*'s overseas contraband, opposite the wide platform occupied by the middle-aged, obese crier and his young clerk.

Under the now darkening sky, the crier took the side steps, approached the crowd, and held his hands up for silence. "Ladies and gentlemen," he began in a strong voice. "The sale is about to commence. The condition is cash. No issue of the Hoyer and Ludwig Confederate plate will be taken. The shipment first on the list is from the *Silver Sally*."

Denning felt a tap on his shoulder, and turned. "Mr. Jacoby."

Denning didn't trust Eli Jacoby. He had the same air of vanity that Denning saw in the Virginia secessionists he knew. Jacoby was a frequent spectator at the auctions and claimed to have a son aboard one of the blockade runners based in Charleston. Recent talk from a source revealed that he had been bartering with secret contacts through the Mason-Dixon line for the sought-after modern Northern hand weapons and munitions. How he was doing it, no one seemed to know for sure. The story Denning had heard implied that Jacoby had good friends in high places. He also was a more-than-frequent visitor to Wilmington's best brothels, where some of these friends in high places congregated.

"Captain Denning. Congratulations on one more successful trip. My son tells me it's not as easy as it once was."

"It's certainly not."

"Tell me, captain, how is it that they are auctioning off your goods in only a few days, while other in-coming cargoes sit for days or weeks on the docks?"

"None of your business," Denning said calmly.

Jacoby cleared his throat. "Please, captain, I didn't mean to be insulting."

"No, of course not. But you tried anyway."

"It's just that I'd like to know how it's done, for future reference."

Denning didn't believe him. "Like you, I know people," he said. *The mayor, for one*, he reminded himself.

Jacoby tipped his hat. "Good luck today."

"Thank you," Denning said, forcing the words out.

The *Silver Sally*'s high markup, nonmilitary items disappeared first. They were the latest in female fashions from Paris—dresses, hats, boots, and perfumes. The Cuban cigars, soaps, and other toiletries followed in a flurry. Although the profit was lower, the military articles saw the hardest of competition. Denning watched as they went before the bidders. Fifteen cases of lead bars. Twenty cases of army boots. Thirty cases of leather. More than three thousand Enfield rifles. Twenty-five hundred Austrian rifles. Three hundred barrels of gunpowder. One million cartridges. Two million percussion caps. Denning had made his way near the platform as the last case of guns vanished with the raising of a customer's arm. There, he checked the assistant's tally sheet. Four hundred and fifty thousand gross in gold was the result of the three-day run through the Union blockade. After expenses, about one-quarter of that would be clear profit.

Denning nodded, pleased. *Pretty damn good haul.*

Later, as night fell, Captain Denning took a long walk down Market and Chestnut Streets, finishing up at his ship. Stars poked through the cloud overhead. It would be a cool evening. He thought back to the auction, and shook his head. The heart of the Confederacy was in the hands of a gang of greedy profiteers, holders of government agreements, men like Eli Jacoby, using Wilmington as their home base. They were cold, heartless men who paid gunmen to guard the blockaded goods until prices rose. Their profits helped them buy more shipments. Denning hadn't expected the war to wind down into such a fierce fight for revenue. But it had. And it was getting worse. The whole world was going money crazy. And he was caught in the middle of it.

For the first time, Denning didn't like what he saw.

Fifteen

Three days later, off New Inlet

The two officers aboard the cruising gunboat USS *Connecticut* thought they caught sight of a man-made object outlined against the Atlantic beach.

"What does it look like to you?" Captain Carlisle asked Commander Stephen Farley. Carlisle wiped his brow and gave the telescope to his first mate. It was a warm and sticky night with no moon. He dreaded these Carolina summers.

Farley looked through the eyepiece for about ten seconds, methodically checking the shore. Sure enough, there she was, the pilot house and bow of a ship at anchor peeking through the mist, six or seven hundred yards off port. He couldn't see any smokestacks or masts, which were undoubtedly lowered to prevent being spotted.

"She's a blockade runner," Farley said, excitedly.

"Smell that?"

Farley nodded. He caught the weak scent of anthracite coal, the blockade runners' fuel. He also smelled brandy on Carlisle's breath. "Aye, sir. I do."

"We got one coming out of the gate! All we have to do is throw out the net." Carlisle grabbed the telescope back. He couldn't believe his luck. From this distance, the enemy side-wheel steamer bore a close similarity to the *Silver Sally*. She had the length, close to three hundred feet.

"We'll have to wait for her to make a move, sir. We can't go in. Fort Fisher will be in range."

"Right you are," Carlisle admitted. "No sense getting shot at. Especially if I can get the pirate to come to us. Let's give her some slack. All ahead one-third. Let's see what she's going to do, eh?"

"Aye, aye, sir."

The *Connecticut* slid out to sea, on a course away from the beach. The enemy made the maneuver Carlisle had hoped for. From a distance of more than a thousand yards out from shore, the runner steered north, leaving the inlet and the high-powered guns at Fort Fisher to the rear, still using the beach as her camouflage.

Now she was out of range of the fort's guns, exactly what Carlisle wanted. "Slow to one-quarter speed," ordered Carlisle. It still looked to him like the *Silver Sally*. His heart beat faster just thinking of another chance at that bastard Denning.

"Aye, sir."

As the gunboat skimmed across the waves, Carlisle was confident the blockade runner was at his mercy. "Swing the ship completely around, and come up on her stern!"

"Aye, sir. Should I shoot off a flare to alert the other boats?"

"No, dammit! I want her for myself!"

"Right. Yes, of course, sir."

The *Connecticut* veered starboard and bore down on the enemy vessel. By blocking her return to New Inlet, Carlisle had forced her into the open. The captain's pulse quickened. Nothing could go wrong now. Nothing.

The distance narrowed to five hundred yards. And closing.

"What's she doing now, sir?"

"He's one tough customer," Carlisle said, squinting through the eyepiece. "He's hugging close to the beach. The smokestacks and masts still haven't gone up. I don't think the skipper knows we're behind him. Come with me."

Farley followed his skipper to the cabin.

"Starboard a little," Carlisle whispered to the pilot. "Steady. . . steady."

"Aye, aye, sir," the pilot replied, comprehending his skipper's strategy to come along the enemy's starboard side.

"Full speed ahead! And have the gun crews on this side on full alert. Go!"

"Aye, sir," Farley barked. Then he sent his orders down the chain of command. The words raced across the ship in an instant.

"You heard it, men," said the nearest pivot-gun officer to his four subordinates, as Farley pointed in the direction of the runner. The gun officer's responsibility was the pivot-mounted, eleven-inch Dahlgren smoothbore, affectionately nicknamed Big Bear. The biggest gun on the cruiser, weighing in at sixteen thousand pounds, Big Bear could fire a 130-pound shell more than four thousand feet.

"Swing her around," Farley gasped.

One deck hand released the screw-compressor clamps on the gun's two sides. Another hand pushed the barrel onto the circular rails. Once in position, they locked it with two snaps of the clamps. The crew were poised, awaiting their next order.

At two hundred yards to the enemy's rear, Carlisle saw three smoke-stacks and two masts suddenly whip into position. Was it the *Sally*? Carlisle was forced to do something now. "Aim and fire, Big Bear!" he cried loudly, not worrying about keeping his voice down.

The gun flashed a red flame, illuminating the water for a radius of a hundred yards. The whistling projectile crashed down off the enemy's stern, and a high spout of water sprayed into the air. They had missed.

"Reload!" Carlisle knew it would take a while for Big Bear to be ready for round two. "Fire howitzer one and two!" he yelled.

The first howitzer shell missed too, but the second one sliced one of the smokestacks in half. Sparks and steel fragments spewed onto the ship's deck, and several men cried out in agony as the long cylindrical stack landed over the side rail, hissing as it hit the water. Steam rose over midships. A triumphant cheer shook Carlisle's gunboat.

"Fetch me my megaphone," Carlisle ordered Farley.

"Aye, sir."

A small fire had broken out on the crippled Rebel ship, but was quickly snuffed out by her men. By now, the two war vessels were only fifty yards apart. Already three nearby Union gunboats were heading to the action to give support. Carlisle was determined to beat them there. The enemy ship didn't have a chance with only one funnel to draw a proper draft. Without a healthy fire there would be no steam. She could go no farther. That much was certain.

Carlisle plunked the megaphone to his mouth. "Surrender your ship!" he screamed, his voice whipping across the water to the enemy ship. "There are three back-ups on the way!"

"We surrender," came the reply. "We have injured men aboard who need medical assistance."

"Prepare to be boarded!" Carlisle shouted. "We will shoot to kill if provoked."

"There will be no resistance. The ship is yours."

Carlisle turned to his first mate. "Farley, grab a lantern, form a boarding detail and launch a lifeboat. Look lively."

"Aye, aye, sir."

Carlisle and Farley took an armed party of seven men up the boat's side. Carlisle limped aboard the blockade runner. He saw a short, bearded man in a foreign uniform, and an array of officers. The pungent smell of burning destruction hovered in the air. Carlisle faced the skipper at close range. With a flick of his arm, he sent Farley and two sailors off to check the contraband merchandise.

"You the skipper?" Carlisle snorted, raising the lantern to shoulder level.

"I am, sir," the bearded man said stiffly, squinting at the light. "Captain Andrew Luddenworth of Her Majesty Queen Victoria's Royal Navy."

Carlisle doubted the name the skipper gave. Many runner captains used aliases, although he had to be English with that accent. "The name of your ship, sir?" The creaking and banging of wood crates competed with the skippers voices.

"*Princess Ann.*"

"What is your destination and cargo?"

The British skipper didn't answer.

"Cat got your tongue, eh?" Carlisle said. "Ah, never mind. Bermuda or Bahamas, it doesn't matter. It won't get there."

Farley appeared at his captain's side. "What did you find?" Carlisle asked, lowering the lantern to his knee.

"Four injured men. One dead. Crates of turpentine. Bags of rice and tobacco. At least eight hundred bales of cotton, sir. The brand, I couldn't tell you. And there—"

"Sea Island, sir. I only haul the better quality," the British skipper answered, having no fear of the Union captors. He knew the law. It was a joke. He'd be set free.

"Oh, you only haul the better quality," Carlisle said, mocking the Englishman. "Your ship is now the property of the United States Navy. What do you think of that? How many Southerners are aboard?"

"That's for you to find out."

"We will. When we do, it's prison for them all. Where they belong."

"Sir," Farley said to Carlisle. "That's not all she has. There's a young lady aboard."

"A lady?" Carlisle stared at Farley.

"Aye, sir. A real good-looker, if you don't mind me saying so."

"She a stowaway?"

"I doubt it, sir."

Carlisle thought about, then huffed a reply. "Think she may be a lady of the evening?"

Farley chuckled. "Too good looking and too well dressed for that, sir."

"Never mind her. Just take her in custody with the rest."

"Yes, sir."

"Well, we did it, Farley."

"Congratulations, sir, on your first capture."

Carlisle smiled. Although it wasn't the *Silver Sally*, it was still a blockade runner. "When we get to shore, we celebrate."

Sixteen

Maryland

On the sixteenth of June, Robert E. Lee's forward column crossed the Potomac into the open, green fields of Maryland. The Union army followed along a wide parallel line, careful to stay between Washington and Lee. The preliminary reports reaching Wilmington of Lee's invasion of the North were apparently true. Franklin Taylor, for one, saw with his own eyes how swift the advance was.

Fear spread throughout the state as the seventy-thousand-strong Rebel force devoured unripe corn crops. They seized horses, cattle, clothing, food, grain, and wagons from civilians, paying for them in useless Confederate scrip. Taylor remembered the first, less-aggressive invasion of the North in 1862, when Lee was hoping for allies in Maryland. This time the soldiers showed no mercy. They viciously bound free blacks and sent them south into slavery. The raid seemed to intensify once the soldiers had heard that the extreme western portion of Virginia had voted that week to break away from the state and the Confederacy to form West Virginia, the newest state of the Union.

It was a terrible blow to most Virginians in Lee's army.

Taylor was occupied with his own fears after his Signal Corps had waded through the Potomac with the rest of the army's rear. He didn't feel a traitor any longer, if he ever had. His home soil of West Virginia had sided with the Union. What better reason to be a Union informer. In the late afternoon, he split away from camp on horseback, his destination the newly-laid telegraph wires. Having failed in his attempt to notify the Union force of Stonewall Jackson's flank movement at Chancellorsville, Taylor was determined he would advise his base about Lee's proposed destination.

Coming out in a clearing of tall green weeds, he saw a path winding into a heavily wooded forest. Beyond that, on a hill, stood the poles and lines, six or seven hundred yards to the right. By now he had traveled several miles. Snipers from either side could be in the woods.

He urged his horse into a moderate trot, and set out on the path.

Washington, D.C.

The telegraph officer at the Treasury Department jerked as his machine came to life with a steady stream of clicks. The young man grabbed his note pad and copied the letters down as they came over the wires.

"Colonel, it's from *Yankee*," he cried out to Lafayette Baker, not taking his eyes from the machine.

Baker stepped into the telegraph room. "Are you certain?"

"I can tell by his fist."

Following a lengthy series of ticks, the line went dead. With Baker glaring intently over his shoulder, the young man took the jumbled blocks of letters and decoded them using his book. "There it is, sir," he said, finished, giving the sheet of paper to Baker.

LEE DESPERATELY NEEDS SUPPLIES DESTINATION GETTYSBURG PENNSYLVANIA RUMORS OF SHOE FACTORY YANKEE

Baker smiled. He had good news for Stanton. "Now we know where Lee's heading."

"God almighty, sir! Lee's going to invade Pennsylvania."

"Yeah. Fancy that. Fine man that Taylor." Baker was jubilant. "Nice work," he said to the telegraph officer.

Maryland

Taylor jumped when he heard the twig crack. He dismounted and withdrew his pistol slowly. He could hear a distinct rustle of leaves. He could barely see a hundred feet in any direction. The rustle came closer. Was it an animal? A soldier? Where was it? Then he heard a muffled cough.

85

Was it a Yank or a Reb?

Taylor obeyed his first impulse, which was to hide. He slung the horse's reins around a tree, then dodged away, squatting down behind a thick trunk. A few seconds later he realized the sound was to his left, leaving him between the unidentified person and his horse. He held his gun up and cocked it. If it was a Union soldier, what would he do? He was on their side, but they wouldn't know that. He could be shot before he was able to stammer a word in his own defense.

Then, across the thicket, a Reb on horseback came into view.

Taylor's heart hammered all the way up to his throat. Peering around the trunk, he saw the Reb officer on foot, his horse by his side, held loosely by the reins. Taylor relaxed. As the Reb came within twenty feet of the tree, Taylor uncocked his gun and put it away, then slipped out from behind the trunk, careful not to startle the officer.

"Easy, friend. That's my horse." Taylor saw that he was a cavalry major, quite possibly searching for Reb deserters.

The officer aimed his pistol directly at Taylor. "And who are you?"

"Lieutenant Franklin Taylor." Taylor rubbed his shoulder patch. "Signal Corps. You?"

"Major Luke Keating." Keating looked curiously at the young soldier with the uniform nearly as tattered as his own. "Signal Corps? Out here?"

Taylor pointed in the direction of the telegraph wires on the other side of the trees. "Keeping in communication with Richmond."

"Then you don't mind none if I check your knapsack?"

"No, not at all."

Without taking his eyes off the lieutenant, Keating fumbled inside Taylor's baggage strapped to the saddle. He pulled out the pocket telegraph relay and coding disk, looked at them, then put them back. "Empty your pockets."

"My pockets?"

"Yes, lieutenant. Your pockets. And be mighty quick about it."

Taylor threw to the ground what he had in his possession, a pouch of chewing tobacco and some Reb money in small bills.

"Now your boots, lieutenant."

"My boots?"

"Yes, your boots! Take off your boots!"

It was what Taylor did not want to hear. He cursed himself for not burning the message or burying it immediately after he was done. He sat on the ground and tugged at his boots one at a time, throwing them at the major's feet. To Taylor's horror, a piece of paper dropped out, the same message he had sent to Baker.

The major read it. At first he just stood there, looking at the sheet, then down at Taylor, as if the words were not intelligible. "Get up!" The major's voice cracked like a whip.

"What's the matter?"

"I said, get up!"

A fire burned in the cavalry officer's eyes. "I'm getting awfully tired of having to repeat myself, lieutenant." He kicked Taylor hard in the ribs. "Get up, spy! General Lee would like to speak to you!"

Taylor tried to stand, but fell down to a crouched position, the pain in his ribs too great.

"Get up, I say!"

Taylor had to do something. *Fast.* With a rapid movement, he went for his Colt revolver and fired before the major could react. Both horses jumped. Keating tumbled backwards, his head smacking the ground. Taylor crawled over. The Rebel officer's face was an open wound of gaping flesh and black gunpowder burns. There was no movement from him.

Taylor crouched, his eyes darting, searching the woods. Were there any more?

Wilmington

Five days later in the peace of the morning, Marie Keating casually thumbed through the mail after returning from one of her rides. Under the shadow of the veranda, still in her riding dress and gear, she threw her hat on the white table and sat down. One of the letters was from the War Department in Richmond.

She feared the worst. Without opening the envelope, she imagined what she would do if it turned out to be what she expected. Would she burst out crying? Would she pass out? She clutched the letter in her shaking hands. She opened the letter. While she was reading it, Captain Denning surprised her by driving up in a carriage. She did not focus on Denning as he ascended the wood steps. Instead, she was far off in a blood-stained battlefield, strewn with dead and dying men.

Denning removed his Panama hat. "Mrs. Keating?" He looked down at the piece of paper Marie had dropped to the floor and saw the War Department letterhead.

She didn't say a word. She didn't have to. He knew now.

"I'm sorry... Mrs. Keating." He bent to pick the letter up. "Your husband?"

She nodded at him with a heavy, drawn face and he didn't know what to do. He slipped the letter onto the table. She lowered her head, got up from her chair and began to make her way to the door. Then the unexpected happened. She tripped on one of the boards. Falling forward, she reached for his arms and he reached out and caught her. His grip was strong. She struggled to free herself. But Denning wouldn't release her and she eventually gave up. There, on the veranda, they held each other in a strong embrace, while she finally sobbed.

After a few moments, she wiped her tears with her hand. Marie hadn't held a man in over a year, not since Luke on his last furlough. Then she started to pull back, realizing what she was doing. "*Mon Dieu*! I don't know what you must think of me? Let me go, please," she gasped.

"You tripped. You couldn't help it," said Denning, still holding her.

"I know. But—"

But Denning didn't want to release her. With one arm around her waist and his other hand on her neck, he kissed her with such passion that Marie felt a brief twinge of pain in her shoulders and back.

Marie had never been kissed like that in her life. Not by Luke. Not by any man. She was stunned by a feeling of fearful elation... an unexpected... *pleasure*. She had the urge to push him away, but she didn't. She had no willpower. Instead, she went limp in his arms then responded with short kisses on his lips, while she swept her fingers across his face, over his jaw, and down his strong neck. His hold on her tightened. She tried to bring her breathing under control. In a sudden reverse, her flesh revolted.

What was she doing?

She finally struggled away from Denning's tense grip and lowered herself into a veranda chair, her head in her hands, her legs trembling.

What had she done?

Denning stood over her. "I love you Marie Keating. I think you're the most beautiful woman I've ever laid eyes on."

Marie shot a menacing stare at the daring blockade skipper. The sincerity in his gray-blue eyes left her with the impression that he had meant those words. Did he really love her? But how could he? They hardly knew each other.

"Please, Captain Denning," she choked, as she tried to gather herself together. She was suddenly worried that the servants could see them. "You must forget this ever happened. It's all my fault. Everything happened too suddenly. My husband—"

"No, it's not your fault," he said gently, before she could speak about her husband. "And I shan't think the worse of you or myself for it."

Denning looked back at the wagon-full of blockade supplies he had snuck through the Cape for her. Marie saw that the wagon was full of cloth and canvas. The supplies must've been for her. Marie dropped her head and did not look up. She found she didn't have the strength. She didn't look up again until she heard the captain's boots pounding on the wood steps. He was leaving.

She suddenly felt cheated. The news of Luke's death made her feel she had lost her youth. Suddenly widowed at twenty-two, she didn't even have children as a solace. She hated the sound of the word *widow* and knew her life would change because of it. Southern custom dictated that she must wear a black mourning dress, a black veil, and black boots for years. She must never smile, or laugh, or talk, or flirt with men in public.

She pictured Luke. . . and Denning. . . She closed her eyes.

This was awful.

Seventeen

Hatteras Inlet, North Carolina

Captain Carlisle crawled out of bed on the fourth day in port, dizzy from a wicked hangover. He managed to focus his blurry eyes on the framed picture of his wife and son on the dresser, while his vision cleared. Jonathan was just a baby then. And Clara was so pretty.

Carlisle stumbled to the second-story bedroom window of the officer quarters overlooking the sun-drenched Cape and watched his new ship, the old *Princess Ann*, with fascination. She was receiving the final coat of dark blue paint, one of the last stages of its conversion to Union gunboat duty. Carlisle and the crew of the USS *Connecticut* had returned to Hatteras with their prize, the *Princess Ann*, in tow. They were compensated by Squadron Leader Baines with a prompt, well-deserved leave. And they took advantage of it by celebrating for three days.

Carlisle had finally been rewarded. Eighteen months of grueling patrol duty in freezing winters and deathly hot summers had netted him his first seizure. He had to admit it was better than fighting in a stinking hell-hole like the Chancellorsville battle he had read stories about. His thirty-dollars-a-month pay was now a pittance compared to his share of the booty after the cargo had been quickly auctioned away by his government. By the rules, the Union government skimmed half the money right off. The commander of the squadron received five percent. Baines, the local squadron commander, took one percent. The rest was sliced into twenty equal shares. Carlisle happily took three shares. The officers and midshipmen divided up ten. The remaining crew took the rest. Carlisle was now nearly three thousand dollars richer for it, and some of it had already been spent on the best liquor money could buy.

Carlisle also received special commendation from Squadron Leader Baines for the capture of the Confederate spy Beatrice "Dixie" Blair, a woman as well known in the North as she was in the South. The arrangements she had made to meet with members of the British government in Nassau had been spoiled by Carlisle, according to Baines, who had her interrogated.

Carlisle bent down stiffly and picked up the Philadelphia newspaper on the floor. The story of the capture graced the front page and had caused quite a commotion throughout the continent. Dixie Blair was behind bars! And he had put her there. What a stroke of luck she was aboard—all the more reason for Carlisle to go on a seventy-two-hour bender. The *Princess Ann*, renamed the USS *Annapolis*, was the reward for a job well done. And it would be ready to sail in forty-eight hours.

"Proud of me now, *Daddy*," Carlisle grunted to himself.

Smithville, North Carolina

Mae Keating opened the front door of her two-story clapboard house and browsed through the side flower garden. Her flowers were the largest, the brightest, and the neatest in the neighborhood. As she looked on them with pride, a covered carriage jolted to a halt in the dusty street. To her astonishment, she saw her nephew's wife step out with a piece of luggage in her hand.

Luke's spinster Aunt Mae was considered an odd sort. In her fifties, barely five feet tall, she was round in body, face, and eyes. She had very few friends, but somehow seemed to know everyone in town, and the everyday gossip about every one of them.

When Marie saw Mae, she knew that a few days with the spinster was probably enough to send her back to Wilmington with a different, maybe even a cheerful, attitude. Marie had not been able to bring herself to wear black. At least not immediately. She couldn't stand to act the way the South expected her to act; the black clothes and all that went with appropriate Southern widowhood. She was French. She just couldn't wear black, not after what had happened with Captain

Denning, although she promised herself she would hold that secret deep in her heart.

"Oh, my word, look who it is. Marie! Oh, my!" said Aunt Mae rapidly in her shrill tone. "Oh, what a treat. Dear girl, come into the house and I'll put on some tea. I don't get too many visitors, you know. At least not from Wilmington, anyway. Tell me all about Wilmington these days," she gabbled on. "These murders. Three widows in one month and they were from such well-to-do families. All stabbed, I hear. How dreadful." She held her hand to her chest. "You must be careful. No woman is safe anymore. I watch the blockade runners sail by every so often in the twilight. There really isn't much else to do here. Except, I was invited to a wedding. Last week. Priscilla Blackford. I don't believe you know the family. She was married off to a navy blockade officer. They sure marry quickly nowadays, with no proper courting and all."

Marie remembered what annoyed her most about Mae. She had the curse of the mouth. Once she started with her chitter-chatter she wouldn't shut up. Marie smiled suitably for the occasion, remembering that Luke had always treated Mae with the deepest respect. Marie needed some extra strength now.

"It's nice to see you again, Aunt Mae."

Mae's baby face warmed. "Oh, dear me. I am so excited. You look. . . so. . ." She stopped.

"So, what?"

Mae noticed Marie's rich skin color. "What have you been doing? You've been in the sun. You look like some darkie field worker!"

"Horseback riding, Auntie. Just riding."

"Riding without a hat, I bet. Mercy."

"I confess. Oui."

"Anyway, I'm glad you're here," said Mae.

Marie held onto Mae's arm, listening to the woman prattle on about no one visiting her. They took the stone steps together up to the front entrance. Before they arrived at the porch, Marie suddenly interrupted the one-sided conversation. "Aunt Mae, I have something to tell you. About Luke." She paused to see Aunt Mae's smile shrink away.

"And what's that? How is he?"

"I'm afraid the news isn't good." She grimaced, shaking her head, trying to prepare the woman.

"Is he not well?"

"I wish it were that."

"I don't understand. What is it? What is it?"

"You see, auntie. . . he's dead." Before Marie could explain why she wore her favorite pale-blue dress instead of mourning clothes, her aunt fainted.

"I was afraid this would happen," Marie said to herself, catching the woman before she fell.

Eighteen

Hatteras Inlet, North Carolina

Carlisle stood on the bridge of his new Union warship, the converted USS *Annapolis*, as the crew in navy blues were preparing for their first firing exercise. According to the chief engineer, the English engines were stronger and more reliable than her American counterparts, capable of fifteen or sixteen knots given the right conditions, even with the massive weight of deck guns. Carlisle had smiled at that. The best way to catch a blockade runner was with another blockade runner.

Carlisle surveyed the sea, then gave his attention to the ship as he took a turn about the deck. The three tall smokestacks and two masts seemed to reach for the sky. The sixteen-thousand pound Big Bear was the only gun transplanted from the *Connecticut* and would again be the king of the firing fleet. The Big Bear powder monkeys were proud of her. The other gun men were positioned in teams by the smaller and less deadly twenty-pound howitzers.

"It's all yours," he said to Stephen Farley, as the two met near the port rail.

Farley's concentration shifted from the youngsters controlling the biggest gun to the three flat wood rafts about three hundred yards off the ship's bow. The crew would fire first with two shots, quickly followed by the stationary howitzers on the port side, the closest to the distant rafts, followed up by the starboard howitzers.

"Aim and fire Big Bear!" yelled Farley.

He plugged his ears as a blast echoed throughout the ship. The high-explosive one-hundred-pound shell flew from the muzzle in a flurry of smoke and flame. . . and splashed into the water fifty feet beyond the intended targets.

"Aim and fire two when ready!"

Farley and Carlisle watched the men racing to the order of a second shot. The smoke cleared. To direct his fire on target, the aimer made his distance and barrel-height adjustment, then he pulled the rope on the firing mechanism. The second missile splashed off to the right, but closer than the first shot. Then the howitzers opened up one at a time. Although some projectiles were closer than the giant Dahlgren smoothbore shell, none found their mark.

"Stop your firing!" Farley yelled. He was pleased with the men's work. Their teamwork was the best he had seen to date, although they had not hit a raft. It was not surprising—the rafts were much smaller and flatter than a blockade runner. All in all, it was decent shooting from the men on the port side.

Carlisle grunted. "Turn the ship around!" he ordered the pilot with a wave.

By the time the starboard howitzers finished firing, only one crew had managed to hit a raft.

"Could be better," Carlisle complained to Farley within earshot of several crews.

"But sir. . ."

"They have to be quicker and more accurate."

"Stupid ass!" someone said.

"I heard that!" Carlisle screamed, his face burning red. He saw who said it too. No one spoke as he pounded over to the man, a wiry, dark-haired petty officer named Britts. "For that, you will be doused with water. Farley?"

"Aye, sir," Farley answered, taking a deep breath.

"See to it. I want all available men on deck. I'll be back." Carlisle looked hard at Britts. "There'll be the devil to pay for you, lad."

When Carlisle returned from his cabin, reinforced by a flask shot of brandy, he saw the buckets on the deck, dozens of them, filled with water. The offending sailor was tied to the main mast and stripped to his waist exposing an array of vulgar tattoos.

"Proceed," Carlisle said.

Farley nodded at the six sailors to commence with the punishment. The shipmates threw bucket after bucket into Britts' face. At first the disciplinary action appeared to be quite comical, until Carlisle ordered the men to speed it up, leaving Britts little time to catch his breath between throws.

"Faster!" Carlisle screamed over Britts' choking. "Faster!"

Britts tried to turn away, but the ropes held his shoulders tight. His head rolled from side to side, then didn't move at all. Carlisle ordered the men to keep throwing, but Farley stepped in, his face betraying deep concern for the petty officer. "That's enough, men." The men stopped. "He's out cold, captain."

"I'll say when it's enough!" Carlisle bawled. "Keep it up. He could be faking. Three more buckets."

Reluctantly, Farley nodded at the sailors to continue. After three more buckets of water, he glanced over at Carlisle. "Is that enough now, captain?"

Carlisle twisted his mouth into an awkward smile. "Let that be a lesson to you all. Untie him and take him to his bunk. Commander Farley?"

"Aye, sir?" Farley glared at his skipper.

"Finish up, and then I want you to report to my cabin on the double."

Carlisle was occupied with the ship's log when Farley arrived and stood at attention. Carlisle flipped through the pages as if no one else were in the room. He ignored his subordinate for a solid minute, then he snapped the log closed and wiped his spectacles with a handkerchief.

"Mr. Farley, you embarrassed me out there. I want you to answer a question for me. Who is in command of this ship?" Carlisle looked up and slipped his spectacles on, his hands shaking.

"You are, sir." Farley avoided the captain, fixing his gaze on the wall.

"I'm glad we've established that. Look at me, damn you! I administer the punishment on this ship and I say when it stops. Not you! I find your conduct unseamanlike and un-American. This ship must submit to my authority. Any rebellious spirit aboard this ship must be broken." Carlisle stopped shouting to gulp for air. "You have a lot to learn about commanding a ship, Farley. Half these men couldn't pour piss out of a boot without directions on the heel. They need discipline, instruction. Understand?"

Farley clenched his fists tightly, then unclenched them. He had never felt so insulted. "Aye, aye, sir."

"If you want to run the ship, go ahead." Carlisle jumped to his feet. "It will be considered mutiny and I'll have you behind bars for the rest of your life."

Farley swallowed his anger and said as politely as he could, "Begging your pardon, captain. I should advise you that if Britts had choked to death, you, sir, would have been charged with murder and you'd be the one behind bars for the rest of your life. I only said what I did to protect you, sir, from any such legal complications."

Carlisle knew there was a certain amount of truth to what Farley had said. The two men stared at each other, while several cold seconds passed. "Dismiss, Commander Farley."

"Aye, sir." Farley saluted and left.

The salty air of the bridge was a relief for the *Annapolis*'s first mate. He had stood up to the captain, and he felt he was within his rights to do so. He hated the captain's rages. They were so childish, and so utterly stupid. Carlisle was a changed man since his wife died in the winter. And he was getting worse. His attitude. His drinking. Where would it stop? He used to be such a good officer. Not the best of leaders, but fair. No more. Farley had hoped that the capture of the *Princess Ann* would have made the captain easier to deal with.

But it hadn't.

Nineteen

Nassau, Bahamas

"Anything wrong, skipper?" Matthew Balsinger asked, downing a brandy, a barmaid in his lap.

"I'm fine," Denning answered, his reply clipped.

"You say so."

For Joshua Denning everything was not fine. He couldn't concentrate the way he used to. Outside of sitting at the tavern table with his first mate, who was becoming more intoxicated by the minute, Denning had been keeping to himself for days. Everything once familiar to him was now strange and distant. Food and liquor were tasteless. He couldn't sleep at night. The last few days his mind kept wandering back to Wilmington. . . and Marie. He thought for the hundredth time of how he had held her. He had been thrilled by the magic of her soft touch, the feel of her tumbling long hair in his hands. He hadn't thought it would ever happen again in his life. *Damn! He was in love. . . with her.* Or he thought he was. He had told her he was. But he doubted himself after saying it and he had been doubting it ever since. Was it a mistake? Could he love again? A week had passed since the kiss and the embrace. Up to now, he had been thinking only of himself. What about her? How was she feeling back in Wilmington? Did she love him? How could she? She was a widow.

Denning watched as the barmaid left Balsinger. Balsinger's hair seemed to have grayed in just a few months, and he was already doing honor to the bottle. His red eyes, shaky hands, flushed cheeks and slurred speech were the signals to Denning. Balsinger's steady diet of shore-leave liquor had often made him a mean drunk. The crew used to enjoy whooping it up with him, but those days were fewer and fewer.

Denning looked down at the opened *New York Times* on the scratched table. He leaned back in his chair, a glass of sherry in his hand. Earlier, a right-hand column on the front page had caught his eye. The Reb spy Dixie Blair had been captured aboard a blockade runner off Cape Fear, and by Captain Robert Carlisle of all people! Blair's exploits were already legendary. She was a Virginian, like himself, and an undercover informer for Stonewall Jackson, feeding him information on Yankee troop movements during the Valley Campaign. She had been caught by the Yankees once before and had escaped. Now she was in Northern hands for the second time. And Carlisle was responsible.

Balsinger tugged at his skipper's sleeve. "That's him, captain. At the door. The Englishman. The one who was asking for you at the hotel."

Balsinger waved the Englishman over to the table. Denning looked up at a man in a brownish-yellow checkered suit, brown tie and bowler hat. He seemed a boy really, with a shy smile and a sparkle in his eye.

"We meet again," said Balsinger.

The Englishman politely removed his hat. "Yes. Quite right." He turned to the captain. "Captain Denning?"

Denning put his glass of sherry down and folded the newspaper off to the side. "Yes, I am."

"How do you do, sir? I'm Charles Bishop of *The Times* of London."

"A newspaperman." Denning smiled. "Sit down, Mr. Bishop."

"Thank you, sir." Bishop pulled up a chair and lowered his slim body into it.

"Care for a drink?"

"Don't mind if I do, captain."

Denning ordered a brandy for the Englishman although he seemed too young to handle any strong liquor.

After the barmaid brought the drinks, Denning leaned forward. "Now, sonny, what's on your mind?"

Bishop grinned. "Well, sir, I'm on assignment actually. The Civil War is big news in our country."

"Is it really?"

"There's been a lot of coverage of the battles. But, so far, very little has been written about blockade running. As you know, blockade running is very close to our hearts because the ships are built in Great Britain. Many of the shipmates are British. The coal you use comes from Wales. British aristocracy is in favor of your cause up to a point, although—"

Denning interrupted, "Hold on. Do you have anything against the English language, lad?"

"Why, no, I don't, sir. Why?"

"Speak plainly then." Denning drank his sherry. "I have no doubt in my mind you are a wealth of information that I already know. Before you go any further, will you please kindly get to the point."

Bishop drew a breath. "I wish to take a run through the blockade with you."

"So, that's it," Balsinger said, slapping his knee.

"I guess that's plain enough. Then write about it, I take it?"

"Precisely, captain."

"I see. You realize it will probably make you famous."

Bishop smiled. "I should only hope it will. I'll gladly pay you for the privilege to come aboard, sir."

"Forget that. I don't want your money." Denning sighed. "Was this your idea or the paper's?"

"Mine."

"Are you sure you want to sail with us?"

"Oh, absolutely."

"It could be dangerous."

"I'm not afraid."

The more Denning talked to Bishop, the more he liked him. The youngster had the same innocent, adventurous spirit that he had possessed so many years ago when he left the farm in Virginia. "Tell me, how long have you been with the *Times*?"

"About a year now, sir. This is my first assignment outside the country. If I do well, then I will stay on in a new capacity, quite possibly as a correspondent covering the war."

"Starting off with a bang, aren't you?" Denning took a moment to think about it. "All right, you can sail with us."

"Splendid. You're not shooting me a line now, are you?"

Denning remembered the slang term commonly used in Great Britain. "No," he said. "I'm not shooting you a line."

100

"But, captain. He might get in the way," Balsinger complained, downing his brandy.

Denning faced Bishop. "You don't aim to get in the way, do you?"

"Oh, no. I won't. Promise."

"Well, be sure you don't. We're leaving day after tomorrow, at noon. Be at the dock on time. We don't want to come looking for you."

"I'll be there."

"A toast," Denning declared, holding up the last drop of liquid in his glass. "To another safe cotton run."

"Hear hear," said Bishop. The brandy stung his throat. "Whew! What is this?"

Balsinger and Denning laughed. The local rum had struck again.

"Nassau Navy Rum," Balsinger said. "My favorite. Puts a curl in yer tail, don't it?"

Denning handed out Cuban cigars and the three lit up. "How is England these days?"

"In what way, sir?"

"How badly are they hurting for our cotton now?" Denning wanted to know. He never avoided a political conversation, no matter the place.

"We had a surplus before the war, which has since run out. Now my country is making do with the little Southern cotton getting through while we establish other markets in the West Indies, India, and Egypt. If the blockade tightens any more, England won't have to seek any more Southern cotton at all. Where does that put the Confederacy, sir? Cotton is the only negotiable commodity they can use overseas, what with their shrinking dollar."

Denning had to admit that despite his youth, the Englishman knew the situation. "Mr. Bishop, how long have you been in town?"

"Since yesterday, sir."

"Do you have a gun on your person?"

"Why. . . no. I don't."

Denning reached inside the breast pocket of his jacket and slid the Englishman a loaded one-shot derringer across the table. "In that case, here. You should leastwise have some protection. You might need this, especially if you set foot outside tonight."

Bishop touched the small weapon without lifting it. "Gad. I've never carried a gun in my life, sir."

"Well, this isn't England. Welcome to the free world, or what's left of it," Balsinger said.

Denning smiled.

"Nassau is not that safe of a place."

"Really, captain? I think it's rather kind of fun."

"Fun, eh?" Denning snickered. "You won't feel that way the first time you're robbed. Stick it in your belt," he insisted.

"What about you, sir? Is this your only piece of protection?" he said, taking the derringer and concealing it beneath his coat.

Denning flipped back his own coat and exposed his holster. He removed his eight-inch-barreled revolver. Bishop's eyes bulged. "I have another," said Denning, standing, putting the gun away. "Now, I have an appointment. Would you accompany me?"

"If you don't mind me tagging along?"

"Not at all."

The captain left Balsinger to his drinking with a gentle warning to sober up in time for the return run. Then he walked out of the tavern, Bishop at his heels.

Denning greeted the British cotton agent and his clerk inside the warehouse door. "Did the Paris fashions arrive?"

"Indeed, they did, captain," said William Freeman. "Come with me." The white-haired Englishman recognized Bishop as a fellow country-man by the cut of his clothes. "Is he with you, captain?"

"Yes, he is. A correspondent with *The Times*."

"How do you do? Charles Bishop is my name." Bishop held out his hand and Freeman was forced to shake it.

"William Freeman," said the older Englishman uncomfortably.

Freeman took Denning aside and said, "*The Times*? I don't like it one bit."

"We're taking him into Wilmington with us."

"But why does this. . . young buck have to come here?" he whispered.

"What's the matter, Freeman? Got something to hide?"

"Me? Well, no. It's just we don't want him—"

"Snooping around," Denning answered for him. "If you're running an honest venture here, then you have nothing to worry about. Listen to me, Freeman. This boy is a glory seeker. He wants to do a story on a run through the blockade. What the hell does he care how we make a deal? Now, where are those fashions? I want to see them. *Now.*"

"I don't trust him."

"But I do. Do you want me to go elsewhere? To a competitor?"

"No, captain, I do not."

"The fashions then."

"Very well. Follow me."

On the far side of the wood floor were three open crates. One of them stood out with the gaudiest of dresses, different cuts and shapes but all of them either bright red or pink. Only women of ill repute would dare wear such garments. The two other crates contained hats.

"I'll take all three," Denning said. He knew of two wicked establishments in town that might be interested. "And some more cases of perfume. To go with the dresses," he chuckled.

"How many?" Freeman watched Bishop studying the open crates.

"Six. And that should be it. See you at the dock tomorrow morning. Bright and early."

"Yes, sir," Freeman replied, watching Bishop depart with Denning.

Outside the sliding door, Bishop pulled out a note pad and a sharp pencil. "What are you hauling on this trip, captain?"

"Oh. . . champagne, crystal glasses, rifles, lead bars, pistols, ammunition, percussion caps. I can give you the exact figures on board."

"I'd appreciate that, sir."

"And don't forget the dresses, the hats, and the perfume. And last but not least, our main shipment, badly needed in the Confederacy."

"And what is that?"

"Five hundred and fifty barrels of gunpowder."

"Pardon me? Did you say gunpowder?"

"That's right. One well-aimed shot at us on the open sea and we'll all be goners. It'll take hours to put the fire out. You don't look well, Mr. Bishop. It must be the air."

The Englishman put his pad and pencil in his trousers pocket. He looked ill. "I think I could use another of those Nassau Navy brandies."

"Now, now, Mr. Bishop. You're not thinking of backing out, are you?"

Twenty

Atlantic Ocean

The *Sally*'s navigator stood by the rail. He positioned his sextant to his eye and peered into the telescope, his white beard and heavy jowls pressed to the instrument. He picked out the horizon on the horizon glass. He adjusted the index arm until the sun's bright image reflected in the index glass and grazed the horizon line. He then read the altitude of the sun off the graduated arc.

Ben Woodson was doing what he did best, reducing the most difficult aspects of navigation down to the simplest of terms. The sun by day, the stars by night. The readings had to be exact. When it was cloudy, he went by compass. Cloud and fog together posed the biggest problem. Woodson was a patient, organized man, always seeking perfection. Denning did not demand it of Woodson. Woodson expected it of himself.

He returned with the information he had collected to the pilot house, where he read from his book to compare the sun's altitude as he had measured it thirty minutes ago. Woodson then bent over his Atlantic charts in the pilot house, plotting his course. The chart sheets were long, made of thick, crisp paper, yellowed and dog-eared with age. Using his own symbols, he penciled in an extension of a crooked line to the left of Nassau which he had started on his plotting sheet three days earlier. He measured the next point with dividers, then called out to Cogswell to turn three points south for a correction. Woodson was already determining the distance to the next point in his mind. Then he double-checked his present position on the compass... *north by northwest.* It was crucial now, coming into shore. Relying on instruments offshore from the inlets was the toughest. Often hit or miss.

"We're on course, Homer," he said.

Cogswell nodded.

Woodson recorded several figures into a log, already catalogued with speeds, distances, weather conditions, and high and low water marks for the day. The high water mark was coming up. He reached into a shelf below the table and pulled out a map marked with the Cape Fear region, her reefs, her shoals, and her beaches. Now came the tricky part.

Landfall.

The first two days at sea for Bishop were the worst. He did not count on rough waters and his own untimely seasickness. It bothered him that the rolling blockade runner was not as stable as the wide ocean liner on which he had sailed to Nassau. By the third day, however, his stomach, along with the weather, had settled down.

Captain Denning slid up to Bishop at the starboard stern this sunny afternoon, a few hours from the North Carolina coast. The shore was still beyond the horizon. The dying wind was barely measurable, the sparkling waters down to ripples. Denning looked across at the wood float in the water and the connecting rope to the ship. Woodson appeared and waited for the hourglass to empty before he made his measurement on the rope for the ship's speed.

Denning slapped the Englishman gently on the back. "Well, how is our landlubber doing?"

Bishop steadied himself against the roll of the ship. He glanced up at the tall, tanned captain. "Much better, thank you, sir."

"I noticed you're looking chipper today. Couldn't come at a better time. Now the strategy begins. Got your note pad?"

"Yes, sir."

Denning cast a glance fore and aft, then pointed to the western horizon. "Out there is our destination. Cape Fear, North Carolina. Our gateway to Wilmington. Cape Fear has two entrances. New Inlet and Old Inlet. Old Inlet faces south. New Inlet faces west. Each one is unique. Off Old Inlet are the Frying Pan Shoals. They jut out several miles into the ocean. The Feds hate them because they prevent the force from cruising in too close. New Inlet got her name a hundred years ago. She was created by a hurricane in 1761. The winds dug a gorge right through the sand, up to the river. She fills up at high tide. It's shallow, even then. She's perfect for blockade runners. The deeper draft Union ships would never make it. What I also like about it is that Fort Fisher is just up the coast from it—the strongest earthwork fortification on the continent. Breech-loading cannons capable of firing seven-thousand yards. That's four miles. That's damn good cover. The Feds stay away."

Bishop nodded, as he wrote in shorthand. "I'm sure they do."

"I know the man who had the guns installed. Colonel William Lamb, a journalist by trade."

"I say. Really?"

"Lives right at the fort in a cottage with his wife. Nice lady. I've dined with them."

"Why do they call it Cape Fear? Is it as dangerous as it sounds?"

"During different times of year it can be—the storms, the treacherous waters, the shoals—"

"Shoals?" Bishop asked, as he continued to write.

"Shoals are underwater sandbars. They are our enemies to the same degree the Federal gunboats are. Without a good pilot like Homer Cogswell we wouldn't stand a chance. He knows the Cape Fear waters better than any man I know. He was raised near there. What we have to do now is sneak our way through the outer patrols of Union gunboats to the shore somewhere in the vicinity of either opening. Then we hide and wait until nightfall and high tide to make our final run through the inner line of ships. Hmm, we must be coming into shore now."

"How can you tell, sir?"

"Thataway." Denning pointed. "The belt of mist rising up to the northwest. You only get that kind of mist close to shore."

"Where did that come from so fast?"

"SHIPS AHOY! SHIPS AHOY!"

Denning looked up at the youngest member of his crew, freckle-faced Jimmy Parkens, stationed up the foremast. "What is it, Jimmy?"

Parkens pointed aft of the runner. His eye was to the lens of his strong telescope. "Two ships, sir. To the stern. Both gunboats. One of them is. . . is a converted runner, sir. She's a big one. Three stacks. A Union blue, it is."

Bishop leaped with Denning on top of a row of crates on the bridge. Two black marks dotted the horizon, a long way off.

Balsinger walked up. "Do you think they've spotted us?"

"I don't know with any certainty," Denning replied. "But my guess would be they have. We'll have to take precautions and give them the slip." Denning looked to sea. An important decision had to be made now, and his ship's survival would depend on it. Which opening would they take? Denning waited for several minutes and finally saw that the two gunboats were heading toward Smith Island to cut off the *Silver Sally*'s path south. They had made the first move.

"They did spot us," Denning said calmly to Balsinger. "Let's take a wide sweep to port and try for one of the beaches south of New Inlet." He looked back to the rolling mist, now collecting swiftly. "Let's hope we lose them completely."

"Aye, aye, sir."

Fog quickly consumed the *Silver Sally*, and visibility shrunk to about two hundred yards. They came out of the gray uncertainty after thirty minutes to see not only land, but also another gunboat, this one patrolling the beach inlets.

Denning cursed his bad luck. The gunboat was blocking the *Sally*'s path to one of her favorite hideaway beaches. From three-quarters of a mile away, the Union boat fired a shell that struck the water short of its mark. Denning knew that it was getting tougher each trip to split the blockade. There were just too many ships patrolling up and down the North Carolina coast. Denning made up his mind that New Inlet was out of the question. His only hope was Smith Island, as long as the first two blockaders were not ahead of him.

"It has to be Smith Island now, Homer," Denning said to Cogswell at the pilot house. "We can hide there till nightfall. The Feds are starting to cut off some of our hideouts. Swing around. Head her out to sea. Stay away from the coast until I give the order."

In their change of course, the fog blanketed the *Sally* for the second time. Despite the lowered visibility, Denning had seen two Union gunboats appear, then vanish without a trace. Neither enemy ship had shot a shell. As a precaution, Denning called for his sailors to put up the North's Stars and Stripes flag.

* * * *

The sun burned brightly off starboard. Across the water, the strange fog was keeping pace with the *Sally* on its southerly course. More than two hours of sunlight remained, too long for Denning's liking. How could they shake the warships for that length of time?

"Head for shore," Denning ordered, guided by his instincts.

Denning, Balsinger and Bishop stood on the bridge, perched on gunpowder barrels. Suddenly there was a break in the fog. The men now had a clear view of the Cape, and the lighthouse on low-lying Smith Island, ten miles and several points off the starboard bow.

"Enemy gunboat at one thousand yards!" Parkens called out. "Two points off the starboard stern!"

Denning saw the converted runner and two other ships in close proximity, close enough to shoot. Denning had to make a choice. The only sensible thing to do was to turn and head back farther out to sea, outrun the gunboats in neutral waters, hope to slip back into the fog, and wait until nightfall.

"Hard a-port!" he shouted, his voice echoing off the deck.

The crew responded to his frantic order. During the swift maneuver, Denning clung to the edge of a gunpowder barrel to steady himself. He raised his brass telescope to focus on the nearest ship, the converted runner. She was heavily armed with a Dahlgren smoothbore, eleven-inch pivot gun, and at least six twenty-pound howitzers. She was bearing down on him, but still hadn't fired. The skipper had to be lining up for a perfect shot. It couldn't be anything else.

At first, Denning smiled ruefully at what he saw through the strong lens. A man limped to the rail. But it wasn't just any man. The bow-legged gait had given him away. At six hundred yards Denning could tell it was his old adversary. *That bastard Carlisle!* He didn't give up easily. So it was him who had the converted runner, the big ship with three stacks, and she was turning to cut the *Sally* off. The two other warships saw what was happening and swung around to form a triangle about the runner. All the Union ships had to do was send up a dense column of black smoke as a signal to all the other cruisers, then proceed to tighten the grip about him, to wedge him.

Bolstered by the sight of Carlisle, Denning had an idea. With such an opportunity, he would revise his plan of attack. He ran for the pilot house before the turn finished. Partway, he stopped to rethink. Yes, the opportunity was there, but it had never been tried before, that he knew of. The ship was in good trim. She could do it. He broke into a run the rest of the way before he could talk himself out of it.

In the pilot house, Cogswell had his weathered hands on the helm, his warm pipe clenched between his teeth. He looked over at Woodson. They were in a pickle.

Denning flew into the cabin. "Homer! Head for shore."

"What?"

"We're going in! Old Inlet. Now!"

"Are you sure?"

"Never more sure in my life."

"But captain!" Woodson said, his cool, dark eyes on Denning.

"You're not at the helm, Ben. You heard me, Homer! Turn her to starboard! My old friend Carlisle is out there. And I know he won't leave me alone."

"But in *daylight?*"

"Yes, in daylight." Denning couldn't believe he was saying it. "You have to hit the channel dead-on, Homer. You can do it. What do you say?"

"Well, I'll be damned," Cogswell said. No matter how bizarre the order, he would give his all. "Yeah, we can do it. I think."

"Good man," said Denning.

Cogswell shot the wheel around in his calloused hands. Beneath the deck the ship's engines and rudder beat in unison, causing the ship to vibrate for a moment.

"You're both crazy!" said Woodson, shaking his head.

"You don't have to do anything," Denning laughed. "Get down on the floor. We'll let you know when it's over."

Balsinger ran up, his face glistening with sweat. "What are you doing, skipper?"

"What does it look like?"

"You're heading into shore!"

"Talk him out of it," Woodson urged Balsinger.

"You're not?" said Balsinger, astonished. "Don't!"

"Carlisle is commanding one of those ships," Denning snapped, his eyes heavy on the pursuing Federal ships. "He won't give up. We're going in, Matt."

"I don't believe this is happening."

"Believe it," Denning said gruffly. "I told you we'd meet up with Carlisle again."

"But skipper," Balsinger argued. "This is only the outer line of ships. It's going to get hotter than this at the mouth of the Cape!"

"Not necessarily. They'll never suspect it. The inner line will be at anchor this time of day."

"Supposing they aren't at anchor?"

"If we make our move now, no one has time to alert anybody. Besides, it takes a number of minutes for them to get up a head of steam." Denning checked his pocket watch. Coming on to eight. About an hour of sunlight remained. He was losing patience with his first officer. "With high tide in fifteen minutes, we have the advantage. Don't you get the picture? Hell, a blind man can see it!"

"Some advantage." Balsinger's voice rose. "Remember what we're hauling. Gunpowder. Five hundred barrels of it. Carlisle and his Blue-bellies will blow us clear out of the water!"

Denning held Balsinger's stare for a moment, long enough that Balsinger thought he had persuaded the captain to reconsider. The sight of the gunboats ahead convinced him that Denning was wrong. But for Denning it was too late for either the danger of the volatile gunpowder or the daylight to make a difference. His sense of adventure was stronger than his fear of getting caught and being sent to a Yankee prison. "All the more reason to go like hell to shore. We have to stand and fight with what we have at our disposal."

"But, skipper, you call this a fight? It's more like suicide."

"Never mind!" Denning yelled, with finality. "Hop to it. Call the engine room. Tell Jackson I want all the steam he can muster up. And I want the sails up for more speed. Go!" Balsinger was too stricken to move. He acknowledged what was demanded of him, but balked. "Carry out my orders, Mr. Balsinger, or you will be replaced on the next run!"

"Aye, aye, sir," Balsinger complied, his voice shaky. He reached for the tube in the pilot house. He held it to his mouth and let out a piercing whistle. The chief engineer answered. "Jackson!" Balsinger thundered into the voice tube. "The captain wants full steam!"

"What!"

Balsinger looked back at Denning conferring with Cogswell. "I said full steam! We're going in!"

"Now?"

"Yeah, dammit! Give her all she's got!"

Balsinger caught the attention of two sailors outside the house. "Get those sails up, on the double! Move!"

Denning patted Cogswell on the shoulder.

"That's it, steady," Denning said, guiding his pilot through the starboard shift. "Straighten her out and cut the seam through the two of them. Right. . . there." He pointed through the opening in front of Cogswell. "Get us through, Homer."

"Aye, sir," Cogswell replied, making a determined sign of the cross, his fist thumping his chest. At least in the early evening hours he would be able to tell exactly where the Frying Pan Shoals were off Smith Island. And there would still be enough of the high tide left to be an advantage to the runner.

Denning withdrew, then came back. He was out of breath. "One more thing. Make an extra sign of the cross for me."

Cogswell smiled. "I will, sir."

Denning flew out of the pilot house, nearly knocking Bishop down. "Bishop," he said, his eyes full of mischief. "You are going to be a party to history in the making. You are going to write the greatest story *The Times* has ever seen. You are about to see the first daylight cotton run of the war. What do you say to that, boy?"

"Good grief. I hope I live to tell of it."

"Don't talk like that."

On the bridge of the USS *Annapolis*, Commander Farley lowered his telescope and smiled at Captain Carlisle. He wasn't fooled by the Stars and Stripes of the escaping runner. The size and the three stacks gave her away. Only one other runner was that big—theirs.

"Sir, it's the *Silver Sally*."

"I'll be a horned devil," Carlisle said swiftly. "Are you sure?"

"Yes, sir. A couple of clear shots, sir, will do 'er."

"The crazy fool thinks he can get away. Well, he's not going to make it. You're right, Farley. Order the Big Bear gunners to fire at will. This is a job for them."

"Aye, aye, sir."

"I. . . want. . . Denning," Carlisle said slowly, his fist pounding into his open hand. He looked upon the *Sally* with venomous contempt. He could see a promotion. "May God have mercy on your soul, Denning."

Carlisle waddled to the engineer's hatchway in the deck, only fifteen feet away. "I want maximum pressure," he yelled down to the sooty faces in the hot one-hundred-degree-plus depths. "This ship better be doing sixteen knots or more!"

"HIT THE DECK!" Denning shouted, as he heard the first heavy shell fired from Carlisle's runner.

Denning reached across to Bishop and pulled him down. The ball whistled over the starboard paddle-box. So far, his ship seemed to be outrunning the three gunboats, but he was still well in range of their guns. The walls of Fort Caswell, at the base of Oak Island, were coming into view. So were four inner-line warships, directly in his path. The fort needed to be alerted to the Sally's predicament before the inner line of Fed boats could move. But, how could he do that?

Denning looked up at his two men exposed on the masts. They didn't flinch. Brave men they were, disciplined. "Bishop. Get up. Do you remember where the crates of Paris dresses are?"

"*Dresses*? At a time like this?"

"I need the red dresses! Help me find them. You watched them being loaded, remember. The lids weren't hammered down. Yank them all up if you have to." Then he heard another shell. "Get down!"

The next shell splashed so close that Denning and Bishop felt the turbulence from the projectile. It struck the water off the ship's bow, and the spray that shot up rocked the boat. Another missile followed, this one from a different ship. It missed by fifty feet. One of the other ships had closed to less than five hundred yards, trying to catch the *Sally* in a cross fire.

"Be quick about it, Bishop. Help me find those dresses."

The two men worked frantically, pulling the tops off crates.

"Here, captain," Bishop said, propping open his sixth crate. "Here they are!"

Denning stumbled over to Bishop. He removed three of the red garments and plunked two of them into the young man's trembling arms.

"What am I to do with these?"

112

"Take one up to Jimmy aloft, on the foremast. Give the other to the man on the other mast. Tell them to wave the things like madmen. They'll know why. Got it?"

"I suppose so."

"Now, up the mast with you!"

Denning hurried down a row of crates and scrambled to the port paddle-box. He waved the gaudy red dress over his head, thanking his maker for the good fortune to purchase the merchandise when he did. The inner line of gunboats still looked to be at anchor. But for how much longer? "Pour on the coal! We need more steam!" he cried to a sailor who relayed the order to the engineer's hatch.

"You heard the captain! More steam!"

Marie and Mae Keating were out on a buggy ride that early evening. Near the beach, they heard the distant echo of cannon bursts on the water and out of curiosity decided to follow the sounds. Marie took the covered carriage along a dirt trail to the tip of Oak Island, more than a hundred feet across from Fort Caswell. They looked over at the closest battery to them, draped over the stone wall. One of the soldiers slumped against the long smoothbore waved to her. Marie waved back.

Mae jerked Marie's hand down. "Now, remember your condition." She spoke rapidly, her chin high. "You're a widow. If you're not going to dress like one, then kindly act like one."

Marie didn't reply. In spite of her aunt's constant badgering during the stay, Marie had steadfastly refused to wear black. For one thing, she hadn't brought any such attire with her to Smithville, giving the excuse that she had left in too great haste to even think of purchasing mourning clothes. On the beach, Mae brought up the subject of proper mourning procedures for the third time that day until the boom of more cannon and howitzer fire in the distance drew their attention away.

Marie dropped the reins and studied the line of dark Union gunboats with their bright white sails on the ocean horizon. Suddenly, to her disbelief, she saw a vessel off Smith Island. It was a different ship than the others. She was long, sleek, slate gray in color, not Union dark. Was Marie seeing things? It was a blockade runner! She shot a glance at Luke's aunt. Aunt Mae saw it too. The ship was under full steam in a race for port. No Reb runner had ever tried to take on the Union gunboats in daylight before. They had to be out of their minds!

Marie was fascinated. "They're trying to make a run for it!"

"No!" Mae's mouth dropped open.

"Oh, yes. Where are those field glasses?"

Mae found them under the seat and handed them to Marie.

"They'll never make it. They'll just never make it." Mae touched her hand to her breast. "Oh, my. Oh, my! Those dear brave men. What would make them do such a foolhardy thing?"

Marie slung the leather connecting strap of the heavy binoculars around her neck, as her gloved hands played with the focuser. Through the strong lenses, she caught a better look at what was unfolding before her. More than ten ships were converging on the fleeing, defenseless runner. She saw a figure on the paddle-box nearest her waving what looked like a large red flag. It seemed to be waving in her direction. That was strange. Two other figures on the two masts were doing the same thing. Three red flags? Why? It had to be a signal of some sort.

Then it dawned on her. Of course. The ship was trying to signal to the fort. She looked back at the dark cannon barrels protruding over the walls of Fort Caswell. They were ghostly silent. Why weren't they covering the runner by firing on the Federals? The guns across the water at Fort Holmes hadn't fired either. Strange. Very strange.

Marie squeezed Mae's arm. "Jump down. Quickly!"

"Why?"

"Get down!"

"But why?"

"The ship, she's in trouble." Marie helped Mae to the sandy beach. "We have to yell to those men to get their attention."

"Yell? Me?" the old woman clucked, her nostrils swelling.

"All right, then. I will."

"Widows don't do that. What would people say?"

Marie held her breath, then blew up. "Out here? *Mon Dieu!* This is *stupide*. Do you see anybody out here?"

"Well, no. . . except for the men. . ."

"*Excuse moi!*" Marie ignored Mae and lifted her skirts up to her ankles. "Like my papa used to say," she muttered to herself, "if you want something done right, you might as well do it yourself."

She set the binoculars down in the buggy, then ran thirty feet or so up the shoreline, her heels digging into the soft sand. She stopped, screamed and waved her arms, shawl, and bonnet at the soldiers beside the nearest cannon. The men looked over, and she pointed at the runner. "Over there! A runner, she's in trouble!"

"We know. They're not close enough!" came the reply in a slow, drawling voice that carried across the weeds and sand. "We might hit the runner!"

Marie understood. They did see it after all. These men knew what they were doing. Why waste shells. Or worse, sink the runner. Marie ran back to the buggy. The two women continued to sit and watch the incredible chase, flinching at every Federal shell raining down on the runner. The volley of firepower became intense. Then the ship came within a mile of the fort's walls. Three of the fort's guns erupted in blasts that reverberated over the water and beach, a devastating explosion of sound, accompanied by fierce yellow-orange flames. The ground shook beneath the carriage, startling the women and Mae's horse. Huge puffs of smoke quickly blanketed the men and their guns. Then, across the water, the battery of guns at Fort Holmes opened up.

Marie fought the horse to bring it under control. "Easy, easy."

"We had better remove ourselves from here, Marie." The exploding shore cannons so near frightened Mae. Two more heavy guns fired. She winced and plugged her ears. The horse jumped again and neighed.

"I'm not moving one inch, Aunt Mae."

The cannons kept up a steady stream of firing. Frightened, Mae began to scream and wouldn't stop. Marie turned to her and shook her by the shoulders. "Stop it." When that didn't work, Marie slapped her hard across the face.

Mae was stunned. "You slapped me."

"*Oui.* I had to do something. Control yourself. I'm staying right here. You are too."

Marie retrieved the field glasses. With one hand on the reins, the other on the glasses, Marie watched through the lenses. She wasn't going to miss this for anything. The ship was closer, much closer. She saw a bare-headed figure on the paddle-box. He was tall, light-haired. He was wearing a white shirt rolled to the elbows and unbuttoned in the front, exposing the top portion of a muscled chest. "*Mon Dieu!*"

"What's the matter?" Mae said.

"I think she's the *Silver Sally*."

"Are you sure? How do you know?"

"I recognize her captain, Joshua Denning."

Mae was taken aback. "I know the pilot."

"You do?"

They gawked at each other, surprised at what the other knew.

"Homer Cogswell," Mae said. "His family lives in town. He has two of the most darling girls."

Marie slid the glasses down from her eyes, then raised them to her face again. It *was* him. Joshua Denning. She saw that one of the enemy ships was in closer pursuit than the others, in a position to perhaps fire at and capture the runner. Shell after shell hit the water nearby. She urged the runner on.

Go, Joshua, go. You can do it.

Then she closed her eyes, reopening them moments later. The air filled with a continuous pounding thunder from the fort's guns. A steady stream of smoke engulfed the beach, until the women were breathing in the sulfur.

Captain Carlisle realized he was going to lose the race and his promotion, unless he did something. By now the cannon balls from the Rebel shore were landing in the center of the Union fleet. Although caught in a crossfire from the two forts, he wasn't about to turn back. Not yet. He removed his pistol from his holster and stormed over to the engineer's pit.

He pointed the barrel at the terrified chief engineer below. "I need more steam," he wailed. "If you can't get this ship moving any faster, I'll blow your damn head off! Do I make myself clear?"

"Yes, sir!"

Carlisle looked to the rear of the *Sally* and back to his Big Bear crew. He lifted his arm into the air. "Fire!"

On command, a Big Bear shell was on its way.

Commander Farley tried to catch his superior's attention. "Sir, they're shooting at us. Look out! Here comes one!" His next words were lost as a blast of water lashed the hull and tumbled along the deck, forcing both officers to their knees.

Carlisle scrambled to rise. "Confound it. Denning's going to get away."

"Captain, turn her around!" Farley cried.

"No!"

"Sir, give it up!"

Another shot landed in the ship's path, sending the bow up and down over the turbulence.

"All right! All right!" Carlisle cupped his hands around his mouth and cried, "Hard to port!" He cursed. Denning got away again.

The shore cannonade ceased. The *Sally* was out of danger.

Denning shook hands with Parkens coming down the foremast. "We did it, Jimmy. A day-lighter."

The youngster's bronzed, freckled face shone with sweat and pride. He was always eager to please his boss. "We sure did, sir. Wait till my friends in town hear about this. And waving a whore's dress." He looked at the garment in his hand and laughed at the idea of it. It was ludicrous. But who cared? It worked.

Denning turned to the others on deck. "Well done, men! Well done!"

"I don't believe it," Balsinger said, glancing back at the retreating Union ships. Denning said they were supposed to be at anchor. They weren't. They were on patrol. Their guns were now silent, but his ears still buzzed from the sound of shells.

"Nothing to it," Denning replied, laughing, collecting the dresses from the men and throwing them into the open crate on deck. He gave Balsinger an *I-knew-it-all-the-time* smile. "Break open the victory champagne."

"I could use a good belt, skipper," Balsinger admitted.

"Me too," Bishop laughed, nervously. "Now that was a bit of all right."

The smoky mist over the beach lifted.

Marie watched the men celebrating through the eyepiece as the *Sally* steamed by the tip of Oak Island. She could hear the men's voices raised in a victory song. The runner absorbed the last golden rays of the day, until it took on the color of the sun now dropping below the western sky. She saw Denning near the rail, holding a dark bottle. The singing stopped. She waved to him with enthusiastic arms.

"Joshua!" She saw him look to the beach. "Joshua!"

"He can't hear you," Mae said.

"He sees me. He's looking."

"Do you know him that well?" Mae asked, shocked. "And by his first name?"

"He did it! He did it!"

"You seem happy to see him."

"I am." To Marie, Denning was a real Reb hero and she felt a part of his success. Marie and Denning exchanged looks through the glasses. Marie knew he had recognized her. Then the ship's bell rang three times. Her heart was in her throat. The bell was for her.

He *had* recognized her.

Twenty-one

Oak Island

Marie turned the buggy around. She watched the *Sally* sail up the Cape Fear River with Joshua Denning aboard, still waving. In another twenty-five miles the runner would be docking in Wilmington. She wanted to be there, to share in the excitement. Wilmington would celebrate for days. Then she looked over at Mae.

"I'm sorry I had to slap you," Marie apologized, stifling an outright laugh. "You were becoming hysterical."

"That's not what concerns me."

"Meaning?"

"That is not becoming a woman in your condition."

"What isn't?" Marie clucked the horse into a trot, onto the main road into Smithville.

"That display of emotion. Waving and screaming. Oh, my dear." Mae stopped herself and wiped a drop of perspiration from her forehead.

"Emotion! I'm not dead just because my husband is."

"That's disrespectful. If only. . . oh, my."

For a moment Marie thought Mae was going to faint again. "What?"

"Ever since you've arrived you don't seem very remorseful over Luke's death. I haven't seen any tears."

"That's not so," Marie replied, avoiding Mae's eyes. "You have it all wrong. I did all the crying I could before I got here, thank you very much."

"Oh, you did?"

"*Oui.*"

"What does that man on the *Sally* have to do with you?"

"He's. . . he's a patriot," Marie said. "He's supplied The Lads of Liberty with blockaded blankets."

"You're a widow. You must conduct yourself accordingly. You must wear the proper clothes. You must behave yourself. What are you going to do when you go back to work? If you do not wear black, the town will ruin you. As if they are not saying enough things about you now. Don't look at me like that. I know! And to think that Luke loved you so."

Marie heaved on the reins and stopped the buggy on the dirt road. They tried to stare each other down. "Oh, did he?"

"Didn't he?"

"You want to hear the truth?" she said to Mae.

"Yes," Mae paused. "Of course."

"He didn't love me."

Mae put her hand to her mouth. "Whatever do you mean, girl?"

Marie took a deep breath to say what she had never told anyone else. "For the three years I'd been married to Luke, I played the perfect Southern wife. I did what was expected of me, with dignity. The Southern way. I was expected to be quiet and unassuming in political discussions at parties, even though I felt my opinions were just as important as any man's, and oftentimes made more sense. I had to be silent or talk about nothings, look sweet and innocent, and play dumb.

"He never once told me that he loved me," she continued, taking a well-deserved breath. "I was there to. . . impress his friends, his family, you, his associates. What else? I never had any say in the matter of marriage and neither did he. Our parents thought it best that we bridge the two international businesses—cotton and wine. He was never mean to me or anything. I was just bored. I've been bored for three years. What I saw today was. . . was the most exciting thing I've seen in years. Now you know why I can't wear black. Why I can't mourn for Luke. I didn't love him." Marie put the horse in a trot.

Mae's smile was half-warm, half-cynical. "Are you in love with that captain?"

Marie was not prepared for that. Her palms hurt from gripping the reins so hard. "And what if I am?"

"So, you are in love with him."

"I didn't say that. You did."

Mae was flabbergasted. "Those captains have the nastiest of reputations, you know. They frequent with low-lives. They sleep in brothels. They have a woman in every port. And the orgies! No street in Wilmington is safe when their sailors are let loose in town. I've seen them on leave in Smithville. . ."

Mae prattled on with gossip of brawls in town. Marie scarcely gave ear to Mae's tales. She looked ahead in a daze, thinking only of Joshua. It's true, he had complimented her on her knowledge of politics and the war, but was he like the other captains? He was a bachelor, a handsome one, too. Did he have a wicked woman in Nassau, another one in Bermuda, a third or fourth in the red-light district of Wilmington where no decent woman would be caught? And worse, was he a drinker like Luke? Did he beat his women? Did he throw his money in the streets, as one drunken captain did last week in Wilmington?

Suddenly, Marie was looking at Joshua Denning through new eyes, as if her perspective had suddenly shifted. And why not? She hardly knew the man. Had she been blinded by that aura of mystery about him? Right now she felt as if a knife had sliced right through her heart. How could she have been so taken by him?

For once, maybe gabby Aunt Mae was right about something.

Cape Fear River

The sun dipped below the horizon. The walls of Fort Anderson, to port, formed ahead in the twilight.

Denning watched Marie on the shore, until she faded from sight around a turn in the river. What was she doing out here? And who was that with her?

"Who was that woman calling your name?" Bishop asked.

Denning smiled. "A friend from Wilmington." He turned to the Englishman. "You were pretty clear-headed under fire, Mr. Bishop."

"On the contrary. I was quite scared," Bishop admitted.

"But you didn't panic. Now, how are you going to send your story to England?"

Bishop downed his second glass of champagne. He was enjoying himself. "Actually. . . I. . ."

"You didn't think it through that well, did you?"

"Not precisely, no," Bishop confessed.

"Do you mind if I give you some advice?"

"Not at all. Please do."

"If you wish to stay in the Confederacy for some time and continue to do stories for the *Times*, you'll have to come up with an organized system of sending your work out quickly. While it's still news. Maybe I can be of help."

"Anything would be appreciated, captain."

"Wire is the only way," Denning advised Bishop. "I know someone at the Wilmington telegraph office. Perhaps we can talk to him together. If your dispatches can be wired to him, he could send them out by runners to Bermuda and Nassau. Sending out on two different ships might be a good idea, just in case one ship gets, well, you know."

"Caught."

Denning nodded. "The captains would only have to transfer your work to a British cotton steamer and there you go. Your story could be home a week after it's written."

"I must say, captain, that's splendid."

"I'd be more than happy to be a part of the courier service and deliver when I'm able. What do you say, Bishop?"

"I rather like it."

"Just say a few good things about me in your first dispatch."

"Oh, I will. Certainly."

Washington, D.C.

Edwin Stanton was in one of his customary black moods two days later at his office.

"I want *Yankee* removed from Lee's army," he ordered Colonel Baker.

"But. . . how else can we get the inside information on Lee's progress?"

"He didn't do anything for us at Chancellorsville."

"What about Gettysburg?"

"Too late. It's out of his hands. We have our army between Lee and Washington. Any movement can now be reported by our army scouts. Yankee has outlived his usefulness. I have a new job for him in Wilmington."

"Wilmington?"

"Yes, Wilmington. The Navy Department has been pressuring Lincoln to put a stop to blockade running completely, to lessen the threat of England and France entering the war on the side of the Rebs. No one wants to hear of any more daylight runs either. It's giving our Navy a bad name."

"But, sir. It was only one run."

"One was sufficient. We need a direct contact in Wilmington, not through our spies in Richmond."

"But, sir," Baker began, then stopped himself.

"But what?"

"Nothing."

"I know what you're going to say. You already have a man in Wilmington."

Baker's mouth quivered.

"I told you once before, Baker, that I have my own sources. You shouldn't keep things from me. I know about your border shipments. I know about your secret telegraph. And I know about your cotton and gun-runner friend in Wilmington, Eli Jacoby. I know everything that goes on in Washington, including what you've been doing. Not all your agents are loyal to you."

"Now that you know, what are you going to do?" Baker said, feeling out his boss.

"I don't know. I suppose that's up to you."

Baker confronted his superior. "Bring me up on charges and I'll take a bundle of people with me. It'll cause a scandal that could even rock your position here." *You arrogant ass.*

Baker expected Stanton to fly into a fit. He didn't.

Instead he said, "Listen to me, Baker. And listen good. The power base in Washington and across this country is not controlled by Lincoln and his cabinet or the House of Representatives or even the War Department. No sir, the real power in this country belongs to an inner group of Republicans from Wall Street, who run the nation lock, stock, and barrel. Do you want to jump on the band wagon, or be left in the dust? This group needs the support from your forces to carry out some of their plans. They also want total control of all telegraph communications and I'll run it for them. They can't allow anyone to stand in their way. That's where you come in with your people. As for your other operations, I don't care. Just do as I say and don't go off on any more spy operations without consulting me."

"All right," Baker said. Stanton had him.

Twenty-two

Wilmington

Word of Joshua Denning's daring daylight run to bring gunpowder to Lee's Army of Northern Virginia spread through the town like a fire fanned by a westerly. Denning was a celebrity. No Rebel or British skipper had done what he did. He basked in his newfound status as the most courageous of blockade running skippers. The mayor congratulated him before hundreds of well-wishers on the steps of City Hall. Newspapermen interviewed him. Men bought him drinks in taverns. And now the young and inexperienced Charles Bishop had his story ready for *The Times* of London, and it was sent out on the next two runners. Both Denning and Bishop were about to make a name for themselves in Great Britain.

Denning left the dock riding a chestnut Arabian horse, a gift from the City of Wilmington the day before. Cigar in mouth and a large flat package under his arm, he rode the mare through the assembly of workers and past the giant flagpole. Draped high on top was the largest Bars and Stars Confederate flag Denning had ever seen, and he had laid his eyes on a few flags in his career. The height and length of it made it a symbol of protection over the dock. Bright and glorious in the morning sunshine, it could be seen from a mile away or more.

Denning rode slowly through Market Street, enjoying the balmy and breezy afternoon. Several people greeted him. Arriving at the old print shop, the captain saw Eli Jacoby coming down the plank steps.

"Captain Denning."

"Mr. Jacoby. What brings you here?"

"A friendly, yet not so friendly matter. Giving my condolences to Mrs. Keating. I have to hand it to her, still working and all. But this is war. Every person counts in the effort. And you?" asked Jacoby.

"The same thing," Denning said. In all that had happened in the last forty-eight hours, he had forgotten that Marie was now a widow.

"Oh, yes. You know her, I'm told. Running cotton cloth for The Lads of Liberty."

"How is she?"

Jacoby shrugged. "As well as can be expected in these circumstances." He moved up to Denning and lowered his voice. "Captain. Someday, maybe we can make some transactions of our own. You and me, without auctions. Perhaps rifles? I have an excellent supplier."

Denning dismounted and tied the reins to the post in front of him. "You don't give up, do you? I already have a good supplier from whom I get guns that work."

Jacoby backed off. "I see. By the way, my congratulations to you. I didn't think running the Cape in daylight was possible."

"Neither did I until I was forced to try it."

"That must have been quite an exhibition you put on. You own the town. A good day to you, captain." Jacoby smiled and trotted off, in a hurry as usual.

Denning took the stairs to the back entrance to Marie's office. He debated for a moment whether to go further, for she was a widow in mourning, according to Southern ways, and he was to keep his distance. He stomped his cigar into the ground, thought about it, then continued. The window shutters were open. A woman was seated at a desk, her side to him. Her long hair was tied in a matronly bun and she wore a long, black mourning dress, buttoned to her neck. He poked his head and upper body through the high, wide window and leaned on the sill, removing his hat. The room was warm and sticky.

"Marie?"

The woman jumped and turned about. It was her.

"Oh. . . you scared me." She looked strangely at him. "Captain Denning. What are you doing here?" Her voice was cold and formal.

Denning was confused. Why hadn't she worn her all-black apparel on the beach at Smithville? Why now? Then again, she was widowed.

So, what did he expect? He had ridden off to see her like a schoolboy, and he had a present for her. He felt so stupid. What was he thinking?

"You still did not answer me. What are you doing here?"

"My name is Joshua. At Oak Island you called me by my first name. Remember? I heard you."

"I know. I'm sorry. I'm sorry for everything." Tears filled her eyes. "Please, Joshua. . . captain. I'm asking you to leave the premises." She held back, then blurted out the words that were painful to say. "And don't come back."

"Surely you don't mean that?"

"I do, monsieur."

"Why? What have I done?"

"Captain, if you please, do as I say. If you don't, people will talk about me more than they ever did. I don't want any further disgrace to fall upon my husband's family. We cannot see each. . . other. . . again. . ." She swallowed hard and turned her back to him.

It was useless for Denning to continue. "I see. Well, then, I must bow to the Southern code of honor and respect your widowhood," he said, betraying a hint of disrespect to the ways of the South he had grown up with. "As you wish, *ma'am*. Goodbye." His voice snapped like a whip. He shrank away and left the window.

Marie listened to the sound of Denning's boots until she could hear them no more. For two days she had battled within herself to put the words together to tell him that she didn't want to see him again, although her arms ached for him, despite her mourning attire and his rambling sea-faring reputation. She couldn't help recalling how passionately Denning had kissed her on the veranda. Never in her life had she felt like that. But she knew that if she struck up a relationship with him people would talk and she *would* be ruined, just as Aunt Mae had said. This was awful.

She dropped her head into her hands.

Twenty-three

Maryland, near the Pennsylvania Border

Lieutenant Franklin Taylor was in a deep sleep on his ground cot when he felt someone poke him in the shoulder.

"Rise and shine, lieutenant."

Taylor opened his eyes, slowly. It was pitch dark.

He looked up.

"Taylor, we have to talk," a man standing over him whispered, smelling of horseflesh and leather. "In private somewhere."

"Who are you?" Taylor asked, his throat dry.

"Never you mind, mister. Where can we go?"

Taylor rubbed his mouth and eyes, and threw off his blanket. "By the creek, yonder."

The two men slid away from the camp and found a path through some bushes to the creek bank.

Taylor stumbled and looked back. "This should be good enough."

"Keep your voice low. We safe here?"

"Yes. Who are you?"

"Washington sent me. Give me your code name."

Taylor hesitated. "*Yankee.* Yours?"

"*Chief.*"

"Colonel Baker?"

"In the flesh."

"We finally meet."

"Yeah."

"What are you doing here? How did you get through the lines? How did you get past the pickets?"

"Easy, boy. I have the right uniform and the right papers. The Rebs think I'm spying for them."

"They do? Since when?"

"It's a long story."

"Was my last message received?"

"Destination Gettysburg? Yeah, it was." Baker muffled a cough. "Washington has the situation in check. We're watching Lee. But we can't locate Jeb Stuart and his cavalry. Any word there?"

"Nothing. He's out foraging. That's all I know. Where? I couldn't tell you. Even Lee doesn't know and he's hotter than a skinned bear about it. Lee needs every man he can get."

"We'll find him."

"There's a battle a-brewing, maybe the biggest of the war. Lee has more men now than he's had in over a year."

"I know." Baker licked his lips, before going on. "Taylor, you're being discharged."

"Discharged?"

"Not so loud. Yes, you are, boy."

"How can I just walk out of here?"

"Don't worry. We have a high-ranking agent in Richmond who will arrange for you to leave with the best forged papers going. Your superior will receive them by tomorrow."

"Then what do you want me to do?" asked Taylor.

"Your next stop is Wilmington, North Carolina. Your orders are to take on the disguise of a Southern cotton dealer and work with an agent based in the town."

"A cotton dealer? You must be kidding? What do I know about cotton dealing?"

"You'll learn. Fast. Your job is to help put a stop to the blockade-running trade. Wilmington is the number one port, the biggest supplier for Lee. Once you leave here and you're through the lines—you'll find the pass cards in with the forged papers—get yourself a haircut. Fix yourself up. I can't see you well enough, but I sure as hell can smell you. You'll have to dress the part. Be ready to leave after sunup. Your orders should come through by then."

"How do I get clothes and everything else?"

"Here." Baker handed the spy a thick envelope. "There's some Rebel money in there. Your man in Wilmington will fix you up with the rest. He resides at the Fountain Hotel. His code name is *Banker*."

"Who is he? What's his name?" Taylor asked, tucking the envelope under his belt.

"Eli Jacoby."

"How good is he?"

"The best. Listen to him. One other thing."

"What's that?"

"Don't mess up. There's more at stake here than you realize. That's from the Secretary of War."

"Stanton?"

"Right you are."

Taylor took it at face value. *Mess up and no money in the bank account.* "I understand, perfectly."

Wilmington

Denning came into Marie's thoughts during the night. Two o'clock came and went and she couldn't sleep. *Three o'clock.* Still nothing. She shifted from one side to the other. To her front, then onto her back. No position seemed comfortable. *Four o'clock.* She lay awake until near dawn, then finally drifted off.

A few hours later, in the heat of the morning, Marie changed the direction of her carriage from the route to her office to that of the city's docks. Along the way, on Water Street, Maxwell Toland greeted her. He politely gave her his condolences. His was a good face for her to see. She always found him a gentleman. The two were on friendly first name terms, having first met at one of the mayor's political rallies when he was running for office.

"What good wind brings you out this way, Marie?" Toland gave his horse a pat as he regarded the dark-haired woman in mourning clothing.

"I thought I might ride down to the dock."

He was taken aback that a widow was driving around without accompaniment. "And what do you plan to do there?"

"I really must have a look at the *Silver Sally*." She smiled.

"You're not the only one this last little while." He adjusted his glasses. "May I escort you?"

"Yes, you may. That's kind of you, Maxwell."

Toland tied his horse to the rear of the carriage and jumped up beside her, taking the reins. "How is Captain Denning these days?"

Did the town know of her and Joshua? Then she caught the innocent intent of the question. "He's been a big help," she smiled. "Every time he's been through the blockade, he's brought something back that we can use. We're grateful. Why do you ask?"

"It was my idea to ask Denning, you know, once you and my father thought up the idea in the first place." Toland looked proud. "I just wanted to see how things were coming along."

"You made a good choice," she said.

"You know, Marie, you should not be riding your own carriage around the city dressed in black. It's not proper for a widow woman. People will talk."

"What other way is there for me, monsieur?"

"Hire someone. It's too dangerous alone. Don't you know about the murders?"

"Of course, I do."

"There was another one last night."

"Oh? Another widow?"

"Yes. That's four in two months. Please, you must promise me to never ride at night."

"I won't. I'm not supposed to talk to men, either, Maxwell, nor ride with them."

"That's right. You're not."

"People are looking at us right now."

He smiled. "We can't help it, can we? I'm your driver." He snapped the horse into a slow trot.

Marie looked down the street and saw Eli Jacoby. As they rode closer, he crossed directly in front of the carriage, and tipped his hat at her. She nodded, then turned the other way.

"What does Mr. Jacoby do?" she asked casually, noticing that Toland had seen him too.

"No one seems to know for sure. But I'll tell you one thing. He plays a lot of poker."

The mayor's son guided the carriage around a long row of cotton bales piled high. Then a view of the busy waterfront opened up to them. "There she is. There." He pointed to one of the blockade runners. They came to a halt alongside the ship a few moments later. Toland pulled on the horse's reins as dock workers and sailors busied themselves up and down the waterfront.

Marie examined the rakish, slate-gray runner, from her slanted smokestacks and hinged masts down to the port paddle-wheel. So this was the ship that had aroused so much attention. She seemed larger up close, and showed a few marks from her many dangerous voyages through the Union blockade.

"That's her," Toland said, relaxing the reins. "She's proved herself to be a good one. Never a more handsome craft in the Confederate fleet, I dare say."

In her mind she pictured the ship as it was that day off Oak Island with Joshua at the side paddle wheel, sleeves rolled up, shirt open, wet with perspiration.

"That Denning must be one interesting fellow."

It took Marie a long time to think about that and reply. "He is. Least-wise, from what I hear."

Why had she come here today, she wondered? Was it the right thing to do? Was it a final goodbye? When she discovered she couldn't answer her own questions, she took a long, enduring look at the *Sally* and said to Toland, "Would you take me to the office now, Maxwell?"

"Yes, ma'am," Toland replied.

Her eyes were on the throng of sweaty dock workers when she caught sight of a tall man, over six feet in height, in black, wearing a Panama hat. He was fifty feet away, walking away from her. When he turned left alongside a row of cotton bales, she saw his magnificent profile. It was Denning.

"Wait. Not yet." She had a sudden impulse and stepped down to the ground. "Stay here, Maxwell."

"Where are you going?"

Marie burrowed her way through the workers. She didn't want to call out his name. She turned where he had by the end of the line of bales. There were more men on the other side. Dozens of them. He was gone, lost in the workers and row upon row of cotton. Still, under the circumstances, she thought it might be better that she hadn't caught up to him.

What would she have said to him?

Twenty-four

Wilmington—July 1863

The sharp shift from the fighting front in Virginia to the blockade-running port in North Carolina was an eye-opener for Franklin Taylor. This was living. Here he was, soaking in a round metal bathtub inside a second-story Fountain Hotel room, his arms slung over the sides, a long, blockade-purchased Cuban cigar in his mouth. It was his second genuine hot bath in over a year. The first had been yesterday, in the same tub. Washing himself in a cold river with other soldiers didn't count. Those weren't real baths. But this was.

For the twenty-four hours since meeting Eli Jacoby, Taylor had been enjoying himself tremendously, eating the best of foods, and sleeping in clean sheets with a roof over his head. He was glad to get away from the starving, ill-clad, sickly Army of Northern Virginia, who were now engaged in the greatest battle of the war to date near a once-quiet little town in Pennsylvania called Gettysburg. This new assignment was going to be all right. What more could a Yankee informant ask for?

A knock at the door made Taylor sit upright in the tub. "Who is it?"

"Jacoby."

He relaxed. "Come in. The door's open."

Eli Jacoby entered the room. He was sporting a neatly trimmed beard, and a new dark suit with wide lapels, and he had a large parcel under his arm. "In the water. Again? Haven't you had enough? You're going to dry your pores right up," he joked.

"I thought I needed another soaking. I got dirty since yesterday."

Jacoby threw the package on the bed and opened it.

"There you are, Taylor. More clothes. Shirts, neckties, three pairs of trousers, two jackets. All in your size. I left a little room for you to fatten up some."

"Much obliged. Any word on Gettysburg?" asked Taylor, leaning back in the tub.

"Reports are sketchy. Lee took the first day, that appears certain. And I think the second day was a deadlock. There's been no updates since."

"You mean they're still at it?"

"That they are."

"They might go on for days."

"They could," Jacoby said. "But win or lose, Lee is on his last legs anyway. You know that. By what I've been seeing around here lately in Wilmington, the Confederacy will be lucky if she makes it through to next year. The docks are tied up with cotton and other supplies, unable to move. The Union blockade can take the credit for that. One runner should be sold soon. The *Silver Sally*."

"The one that did the daylight run?"

"That's her," Jacoby said. "I got her first mate plenty drunk this afternoon. He told me the captain is planning to sell the *Sally* off shortly. The Davis government is getting ready to pass legislation to run the blockade-running business with some stringent rules and Joshua Denning, her captain, wants to go out in a blaze of glory."

"After a daylight run is one way of doing it," Taylor laughed.

"The next run might be her last. Get dressed," Jacoby ordered. "I'll see you in the lounge."

Marie tolerated the wearing of black as long as she could. But she had to ride. She undressed, and threw on her usual riding gear and dashed from the house, anxious to relieve her tension on horseback. Inside the stable she greeted her horse, Lavender, with a pat on the mane, then strode to her saddle hanging on the wall and reached for it.

Her hand never made it. Someone grabbed her from behind so quickly that it knocked the wind out of her. She felt a tremor of panic as a hand pressed over her mouth while the other hand shoved her headfirst into the wall. Pain shot through her body. Looking down, she saw a hand against her chest. It was a man's hand, hairy, full of veins, holding a knife. The man shoved his body up against hers. She tried to scream but couldn't, nor could she move.

She struggled, but the more she did that the more the man jammed her to the wall until she was finding it hard to control her breathing. With his knife, he started cutting away at her blouse. She felt several cuts into her chest. She winced. The man was a pig. He was going to rape her. After a few moments the top of her breasts were exposed. Blood clung to what was left of her slashed blouse. The knife dropped to the straw-covered, plank floor. This was her chance to sneak a look. Craning her neck sideways, she saw that his face was covered in a black mask, two slits for the eyes. She wriggled her mouth free from his grasp and bit into the fleshy part of his hand as hard as she could.

"Help!" she screamed, her breath returning to her. "Help! Someone *help* me!"

"Shut up!" the man threatened, his hand firmly over her mouth again, "or I'll run you through with the knife."

Marie's horse kicked at the stall, aware that her owner was in trouble. Marie freed her mouth and screamed again, as the man held her and tried to muffle her while he stooped to pick up the knife. Then he threw Marie to the floor, where she banged her head. He was on top of her now. His hand slid to her mouth. The knife grazed her neck. He began to rip the front of her riding dress.

"One more sound and you die!" the man snorted.

Marie was too weak to reply, to argue, to scream, or to move. She wanted to beat her fists into his face, but she hadn't the energy. Then she thought she heard hooves in the yard. The stable and the dark figure over her started spinning around and around. . .

She came to.

She heard a pistol shot and realized she had been unconscious. She had no idea how much time had passed. Her vision was blurry, and she tried to focus. She caught the silhouette of someone at the door opening. What was he going to do? She heard the gallop of a horse far in the distance. What was happening? Had the man an accomplice? Had she been raped? No, she still had the dress and breeches on, although she had been stripped bare to the waist. Leaning on one elbow, she looked up to the figure, then frantically dragged herself along the floor to get away from him. The man moved slowly toward her, her vision still too fuzzy to see who it was.

She pulled herself to a support post and clung to it, as though it would protect her. "Leave me alone! Go away!" she said, frantically.

"Don't worry, Marie."

She wanted to scream, but held back. It was a different voice, not the man who had attacked her.

"It's me, Joshua."

"Joshua?"

She collapsed, barely conscious. She felt gentle hands and strong arms slide under her with tenderness and scoop her off the plank floor as if she were as light as a baby.

"Marie. You're safe now. He's gone. He can't harm you now," the kind voice whispered in her ear.

"Joshua! Oh, Joshua. Is that you?" His voice was a tonic to her. She slipped her arms around his neck.

"Yes, it's me. I'm taking you into the house."

The last thing she remembered before she passed out the second time was Denning's jacket going over her bare shoulders and breasts, and being carried out into the bright sunshine.

Once the doctor arrived, Denning left the house to check the stable for clues. The attacker had been dressed entirely in black, including a black mask covering his face. Denning had seen that much, but he had been more concerned for Marie's safety at the time or he would have chased the hooded attacker and killed him with no questions asked. Instead, he chased him off with a shot that must have missed the man by inches as he jumped on his horse and fled. Denning noted that the man was of average to medium height, maybe average build, with long hair escaping from beneath the mask.

Denning heard Marie's horse stir in the stall. He walked on the straw, kicking at it as he went, up to where Marie's English saddle was hanging. Bending down, he saw blood on the plank floor. Realizing it was probably her blood, he felt a spark of anger at the viciousness of the attack. He patted Marie's horse on the nose as the animal poked his head through the stall's opening.

"Fella," he said, softly, "if you could only talk."

He walked out the back door to where the killer's horse had been tied. In the red clay earth were hoof and boot prints, the latter made with a wide, flat heel and round toe. He knew the type of boot, a fashionable one. He returned to the stable. Then, in front of one of the empty stalls he saw a gold-colored handkerchief buried in the straw. Why hadn't he seen it before? He picked it up.

There were two initials embroidered on it.

Twenty-five

Wilmington

Doctor Stephens was leaving Marie's bedroom when Denning took the wide circular staircase to the upper floor of the Keating home.

"How is she?" Denning asked, hat in hand.

The doctor wiped his forehead before he spoke. "She's awake. Right off, I suspected a concussion, I did, but not now. However, she will have a nasty bump on her head for a spell. She's still in something of a state of shock."

"No wonder. The cuts to her chest, were they deep?"

"They've been taken care of and washed, sir. She's bandaged. Nothing serious there." He sighed, resting his hand on Denning's shoulder. "My friend, if you had not come to her aid, it's no telling what might have happened."

"May I see her?"

"Yes. She has been asking for you. Keep your visit short."

"Of course."

One of the servants approached. Denning took the doctor by the arm into the adjacent parlor. "Let's keep this incident to ourselves for the time being and not tell anyone," he whispered.

"But why?" the doctor whispered back. "Do you not want to see this madman apprehended?"

"We might be drawing some unpleasant and unnecessary attention to the Keating family at this time. Leave this to me. Trust me, doctor, please."

139

"As you wish, Captain Denning."

Denning left the parlor. He opened Marie's door. The room had a tranquil feeling. The window was open and a slight warm breeze stirred the curtains. The wallpaper was a soft blue. Marie was wearing a night-gown, laying on her back, eyes closed, a comforter up to her waist. She turned at the sound of Denning's footsteps.

"Joshua," she said weakly. She held out her hand and Denning gripped it, then let it go limp by her side.

"You do remember my first name," Denning remarked.

"Yes. I don't know what made you come to the house, but I'm glad you did. He was going to kill me!" She cried out, covering her face with her hands. "I'm so sorry for the way I treated you at the office."

He looked down at her watery eyes. Her delicate skin was pale, scarred from the attack, her former radiant color gone. "That's neither here nor there. You're safe now. That's what counts."

"Do you forgive me?"

"What's to forgive?"

"You really are a good man." She wiped her tears with the back of her hand. "What's that? Under your arm?"

"A little something. A present I had bought you in Nassau." He set the long flat box on the dresser. "I had it with me that day in Wilmington."

"You did?"

"I came to the house today to give it to you. Now I wonder if it's the right time after what happened. You can open it at your leisure."

"Merci."

He saw the stable through the open window. "I do hope you will continue your riding."

"I want to."

Denning pulled a chair close to her, and settled in it.

"Marie, I have to ask you some questions about what happened. Are you up to it?"

"Yes." She took a shaky breath. "I'll try."

"I know the person was hooded, but did you get a look at his face during the. . . the struggle?"

"No."

"Did you notice anything about him that might tell me who he was?"

"No," Marie replied, her breathing labored.

"You realize that it might have been the one who's murdered the Wilmington widows?"

"Oui. I thought about that."

"Did you know the other victims?"

She rubbed the back of her head and felt a lump. "I knew two of them. The other two, I knew of their families. That's all. Why?"

"Did Maxwell Toland know them?"

"Maxwell? Why would you ask that?"

He didn't answer.

"Why Maxwell?" she persisted. "Joshua, I want you to answer me. What does Maxwell Toland have to do with this?"

Denning pulled the handkerchief from his pocket.

When she saw the initials MT, her eyes widened, and her mouth quivered. "Joshua! But that still doesn't mean anything."

"It fits, though. The killer had long hair. So does Toland. They're about the same height. Around six feet."

"Oui, but how many other men, and women for that matter, have those initials? Oh—" her voice trailed off.

"What?"

"I bit his hand."

"Which hand? Left or right?"

Marie tried to recall. "Ah. . . right. No left."

"Left. Are you sure?"

"Oui. His left."

"Did you bite him hard?"

"Hard enough to bleed. I can still taste his blood in my mouth."

"Did you notice anything else about your attacker? Did he smell?"

"Smell?"

"Yes. Any unusual odors. Cologne? Leather?"

She couldn't remember.

Denning brushed his hand against her cheek. She reached up for his hand, squeezing it.

"Get some rest, Marie."

"What are you going to do?"

"Leave that to me. I'll check in on you tomorrow."

She tried to sit up but her head was too sore to even raise it a few inches off the pillow. "Do you really suspect Maxwell?"

"I'll have to find out."

"What if the killer comes back?"

"He won't."

"How do you know?"

Denning was determined. "He just won't. I guarantee it. Not ever again."

That evening, Denning waited patiently in the lobby of the Fountain Hotel. He had left a message at the mayor's office for Maxwell Toland to meet with him. When Toland finally walked through the wide entrance door, Denning gave him the handkerchief, monogrammed MT.

"Did you lose this?"

Surprised, Toland took it in his hands. "Why, yes I did. But you asked me here for that?"

Denning looked down at Toland's hands. Both were unmarked. He wasn't the killer. "I have something to tell you about Marie. She was attacked today."

"That's awful. By whom?"

"I don't know," Denning replied. "But I found your handkerchief there."

Toland went white. "You don't suspect me, do you?"

"No, I don't. Not now. Let's talk. How about we have that drink I promised back a while ago?"

"Now might be a good time. Yes, I'll take it."

They stepped inside the bar, had two brandies each, and after Denning had given Toland the details of the attack, they left an hour later. While standing in the lobby with Toland, Denning saw Eli Jacoby emerge from a staircase, talking with a young man. Denning had seen the two together the last few days. Jacoby left the young man and walked through the lobby to leave through the front entrance.

"Maxwell, I have to go," Denning said briskly.

Outside, he watched Jacoby take the stone steps to the busy street. The sidewalks were roaring with drunks. Denning heard a crowd of carousers on the other side of the road emerging from another hotel. Every night seemed to give rise to a celebration in Wilmington. The crowd would be a good cover for him.

Denning followed Jacoby down a long dark alley. Jacoby suddenly stopped and turned as if he had heard something. He picked up his pace and soon came to the end of the alley, adjacent to the Prince Hotel. Denning was right behind him, in the darkness.

"Jacoby."

Jacoby whipped around. "Who are you? Come out of there!"

Denning moved out from the shadows, into the light of the noisy street. "Don't be so jumpy," he said. "Compose yourself."

"Captain Denning. What are you doing? Why are you following me?"

"I want to do business. Right here and now."

"Here? The alley? What do you want?"

Denning reached for the speculator's sleeve and pulled him back to the alley. "Come with me."

"Unhand me." He flicked Denning's grip off. "I don't like people sneaking up on me."

"I didn't want to be seen. Let's talk business. I want rifles. You said you had a supplier. Where is he?"

Jacoby paused. "Bermuda. He can get you almost anything you fancy."

"How about Spencer repeaters?"

Jacoby didn't flinch. "You and everyone else."

"I said I want Spencers."

"They won't come cheap."

"Neither will my cotton. Sea Island for Spencers. What do you say?"

"Very well. It could be done."

"What's your associate's name?"

"Burns. Douglas Burns," Jacoby said.

"Northerner, I bet?"

"Ohio man."

Denning grinned. "It doesn't bother you, does it? Dealing on both sides, I mean."

"No. Why should it?"

"Whose side are you really on?" Denning asked.

"I was beginning to wonder that of you? And why the sudden change of heart? I never expected you, of all people, to deal directly with the North."

"I don't see it that way at all," Denning replied. "The South could use those Spencers. At least they'd have a fighting chance."

There was a long moment of silence between the two. On the street, the action didn't let up. "Is that it, Denning?"

Denning shrugged, dropping his hands into his pockets. Jacoby turned away.

"Yeah, except for a couple things."

Jacoby turned back to face Denning. "Well. . ."

"I watched you leaving the hotel. I was wondering about your boots. You wouldn't happen to have any red clay on them?"

"Why should that matter to you?"

Denning played with Jacoby's lapel, then grabbed him by his collar. "Your left hand. There's a bandage on it. There couldn't be any teeth marks under it, by chance?"

Jacoby stepped back and pulled a knife from his breast pocket.

"Hold on, Jacoby. I just asked a couple of simple questions."

"That's enough. How dare you handle me! You didn't want to make a deal at all. What do you want?" Catching Denning off guard, Jacoby took a quick swipe at him, cutting him across the right knuckle.

"It *was* you." Denning reached down into the top part of his boot for his knife, ignoring his bleeding knuckle. "And you probably killed those other widows, didn't you?"

Jacoby took another swipe that missed. He was fast with a knife and quick on his feet. "What are you talking about?"

Denning stepped back, knife in hand. His arms were out in front of him, ready to spar. "What's the matter? They couldn't stand the sight of your ugly face?"

In a lightning move, Jacoby kicked the knife from Denning's hand. As Jacoby rushed forward, Denning kicked him in the chest. Although he dropped quickly, Jacoby's knife was still in his hand. He faltered, then came back at Denning with even more strength. Denning kicked him down again, then grabbed him by his lapels and threw him across the alley into a wall. Once again, Jacoby got to his feet. Frantically, he looked about for his knife. Unable to find it, he took a run at Denning, who slid away and pushed Jacoby into a stack of empty barrels.

Denning kicked the barrels away as he jumped on Jacoby and held his face down, a knee crunching his back. He grabbed Jacoby by the hair and rubbed his face into the ground until he almost choked. In a rage, Denning flipped Jacoby around and punched him in the side of the head, then grabbed him by the throat and squeezed. "Admit it! It was you! I know you attacked Marie Keating today. You left a monogrammed handkerchief behind. MT. Maxwell Toland." He shook Jacoby. "You tried to blame it on him, but it didn't work." When Jacoby didn't answer, Denning got up, pulling Jacoby to his knees, then kneed him hard in the ribs.

Jacoby leaned over, coughed and spat out some dirt. "Why don't you just call the law, if you think it was me?"

Denning laughed. "The law you say. There's no law in this city. I'm the law for the moment." He pulled out his Navy revolver, and Jacoby looked up at it. "I'll shoot you right here and now. Confess! Or would you rather I break every bone in your body? Did you attack Marie Keating?"

"All right! All right! It was me. Pompous bitch!"

"Bastard!"

Jacoby then pulled Denning's feet out from under him. The gun fell away. Rolling over, they both scrambled for the weapon. Denning came up with it, threw it to one side, and kicked Jacoby in the midriff. Jacoby took the pain and bent over, which gave Denning the opportunity to kick him in the face. Then Denning punched him again, and again to the chest.

"Stop it, Denning!" Maxwell Toland ran up the alley. "Stop it, I said!" He grabbed hold of the captain's shoulders. "What are you doing?"

Denning pointed at Jacoby on the ground. "I have your. . . widow killer. Eli Jacoby."

"What!"

"He admitted it, at least to accosting Marie Keating this afternoon. I have the proof."

Toland looked down at the stumbling Jacoby rising to his feet, steadying himself against the wall. Finally, he fell back to the ground. There was no way he was going anywhere.

"What I can't understand, Toland," Denning said, as he held a handkerchief hard to his bleeding knuckles, "is his motive for murder."

Toland was still reeling from the shock, when he said, "The Chief of Police will find out. He has his ways." He shook his head. "This is crazy. Jacoby?"

"By the way, your chief of police can look into someone else, a sidekick of Jacoby," Denning sighed. "You never know what you might get out of him."

Twenty-six

Wilmington

The Monday, July 6 copy of the *New York Times* reported the battle
details of Robert E. Lee and his Army of Northern Virginia. Denning
knew by past experience that he'd read a clearer and less biased view
of the Gettysburg battle in the *Times* than he would in any propagan-
da-filled Southern paper. He chuckled to himself, in the privacy of his
top-floor room in the Prince Hotel. He knew that interested parties,
including military officers on both sides, would read each other's papers
for news of the political scene and battle fronts in Virginia and elsewhere. Censorship was nonexistent, which suited Denning fine.

He always sought the truth.

The first page announced the South's misfortunes. Off to the left in
bold print was—SPLENDID TRIUMPH OF THE ARMY OF THE
POTOMAC and ROUT OF LEE'S FORCES ON FRIDAY. Northern
correspondents were enthusiastic in their telegraph accounts of the
three-day Gettysburg battle which claimed tens of thousands of lives
from both armies. It was obviously a great victory for Lincoln. Denning
flipped to the back page to catch the Postscript section where he could
read the latest dispatch from Gettysburg.

> *...OFFICIAL INFORMATION LEAVES NO DOUBT THAT
> LEE'S ARMY IS IN FULL RETREAT. THE LINE OF RETREAT IS
> NOT DEFINITELY KNOWN. IT IS EITHER THROUGH CASH-
> TOWN OR FAIRFIELD...*

Back to the front page, he read that Vicksburg, Mississippi, after a two-month siege, had finally fallen victim to General Grant's forces. With the great shipping waters of the Mississippi River in the hands of the Union, the South had been split in two, the worst possible position for her to be in.

Denning whipped the paper closed and threw it on the desk. The Confederacy had reached its high-water mark after Chancellorsville and was now falling apart. This was a rich man's war and a poor man's fight. He thought of his own situation. The next cotton run would be his last, his thirteenth trip. He knew that now. After that, the crew would have to fend for themselves.

A few minutes later, Maxwell Toland knocked at the door. Denning let him in.

"How's Marie?"

"I saw her earlier this morning," Denning answered, closing the door. "She was. . . better. She's perked up since she knows you weren't involved."

"Good. Captain, I have some information for you about Jacoby. It's taken two days, but we put some of the pieces together, thanks to our Chief of Police. It's strange what you don't know about someone. My father still can't believe it was Jacoby. They used to dine and drink and play cards together. Well, after some. . . persuasive interrogation, Jacoby did admit to the four widow murders and attacking Marie Keating. All the four widows were young, under thirty, handsome, well-off, which made them—"

"Desirable," Denning said.

"Exactly, captain. And they'd all been widowed since the war began which left them somewhat vulnerable. From the details squeezed out of him, Jacoby was heavily in debt from his poker playing. *Big* stakes. Thousands of dollars in gold. It's not hard to read between the lines. Jacoby began by courting these women, undoubtedly after a part of their family fortune. Each woman rejected Jacoby's advances and he killed them. Remarrying so soon is not our custom here in the Carolinas, as you know. The women didn't want any part of that. Honor, you know."

"Why Marie? He wasn't courting her. Was he after the family money?"

"Eventually, maybe he was. He was after her and her alone, and wanted her bad. He's a womanizer. Since all this happened, the chief has heard some previously unreported complaints from the brothel owners in town of Jacoby's brutality towards some prostitutes. Personally, I think the man is sick."

"Sounds like it. I'm glad he's locked up."

"That's not all," Toland went on. "He's part of a Yankee spy organization. We found a cipher-code book in his hotel room. He was engaged in cotton scheming and gun-running along a line to Washington. Yes, sir, plenty."

Denning nodded. He had played poker with Jacoby twice and won. He knew he was gun-running, but the other things were still a shock. Spying! Murder! Toland had said it best; it's funny what you don't know about someone.

"As for his fancy-dressed friend, the one you had the hunch about," Toland continued, "he's a spy too. Franklin Taylor is his name. We raided his room at the Fountain and found a pocket telegraph, an encoding disk, rubber insulated wire, and coding books."

"So what's going to happen to them?"

"Taylor," he said, "I don't know. But Jacoby wants to cut a deal. If we let him go free, he promises to expose all the spies in the South he knows, along with the crooked government officials and all his contacts on his Washington supply line."

"Are you going to do it?"

"Yes," replied Toland.

"I can see why, I guess. You let one go to bag several more."

"Yes," Toland agreed.

"Why don't you let me have one last crack at him before you send him off?"

Toland laughed. "Sorry. I can't let you do that. Unless, of course, he doesn't come through with his end of the bargain. Then he's all yours. And I'll tell him that."

"Yes. Please do."

Later that day, Denning rode his mare down the dirt road past the Keating house to the stable beyond. He tied the animal to the fence and looked inside. No sign of life. Marie's horse was out. He made his way to the trail behind the stable, and heard hooves. Marie rode her horse through the trees towards him.

Marie smiled at Denning and brought Lavender to a smooth, square stop. She was wearing her present, the new riding dress and breeches. No sun hat. There was a light in her eyes, her dark hair was shiny and her skin glowed the color he best remembered.

"What are you doing out of bed?" He scolded her. "Aren't you afraid to be out here, by yourself?"

"No." She removed a pistol from a holster at her waist. "I have a friend with me."

"That's a Colt dragoon," Denning said, astonished. "Do you know how to load and fire that thing?"

"Oui." She returned the gun to its holster.

"I guess I shouldn't doubt it."

"I'm doing what you told me," she said, looking down at him as he patted Lavender's withers.

"What is that?"

"Continue my riding, in spite of what happened. I had to get over the fear of going to the stable."

"But so soon!" Denning said. "I guess I'd better help you down? Come along."

Marie tingled when Denning gripped her around the waist. It didn't matter that she could still feel the slight burning of the healing cuts and bruises to her body. He put her on the ground softly. Denning was as smooth and strong as ever in the way he handled her.

Unable to restrain herself, she dropped her crop to the ground and kissed Denning tenderly on the lips, her body pressed to his. This time she would not pull back out of fear or guilt. She was free to be herself on this path, hidden from the house and stable. He returned with a harder kiss. She moved her arms up to his powerful shoulders. As he seized her, the inhibition of their first embrace was gone.

"Joshua, I love you," she said, trembling between breaths. "I love you."

His hands moved up from her waist.

She closed her eyes and braced herself. Nothing would stop her. . . except her upbringing. . . ethics. . . morality. His face was on her breasts now. Stepping back, she lost her balance. She fell, taking Joshua with her to the ground with a thud. She laughed, unexpectedly, like a child. A silly laugh, giddy and high, a laugh free of tension.

Denning picked her up and propped her gently against the tree. "Are you all right?" He smiled into her eyes.

"I'm fine. I think."

"You're still in some pain. You crazy woman. Go back to bed and rest up."

"I got a little carried away."

"Yes. So did I."

She put her arms around him and squeezed. "Oh, Joshua. I didn't mind."

It was his turn to pull back. He suddenly appeared to be afraid of the woman. "I know."

"What's the matter?" she asked. She had never seen chaos so marked upon a man's face. It puzzled and saddened her at the same time. Only a moment ago, she had been ready to let him take her on the spot or in the bushes, despite what had occurred to her only days before in the stable.

He took her hands away. "It's just that with what you've been through, something isn't right."

"Let me be the judge of that. Don't you want me?"

"No. I mean, yes." He hesitated, then said, "I have to go in a few minutes."

"Now? Where?"

"The *Silver Sally* sails this evening. I came to tell you this will be my final run."

"This evening? Oh, Joshua. Don't. I fear for you."

"I just need to do this last one. Then I'm through with blockade running for good."

"Why one more?"

"I have to. This one is different from all the rest. Different from anybody else's."

"Then what? After the run."

"I don't know." He took her in his arms, one final time, and kissed her. "I'm not the marrying kind, remember." He studied her eyes. "You are. I'm not."

Something inside Marie wanted to snap. She didn't know if she should pity him or slap him. "What's the matter with you? Whose talking marriage, you damn fool?" she said, her voice rising in anger.

He said nothing. As he retreated to the paddock, she leaned against the tree, bewildered and shattered. She heard horse's hooves, the stable blocking her view of Denning's departure. She couldn't let him go like this. She jumped on Lavender and galloped past the paddock, through the yard, and onto the dusty road.

"Joshua, wait!"

This time he wouldn't get away. She would know what to say to him. Up the road, he turned his head and pulled on the reins. Marie rode up alongside and yanked her horse to a stop.

"I'm sorry," she apologized, shrugging. "It seems I'm always saying that, aren't I?"

"You do seem to be making it a habit."

"I lost my head. Forgive me. Kiss me one more time."

With that she reached over, holding his face in her hands. He removed his hat and slipped his hands around her shoulders, their horses nearly touching. They kissed long and hard on the road, surrounded by a cloud of dust.

Then Denning broke it off and left in a gallop, without saying a word.

She shook her head. *Captain Joshua Denning, if I didn't love you so, I could hate you.*

Twenty-seven

Wilmington

Denning climbed a row of cotton bales, lit a Cuban cigar and regarded the rugged faces of his loyal crew assembled on the deck. Thirty-three weathered expressions stared up at him, in small groups of twos and threes.

Most of the crew had anticipated what was coming from their captain this warm evening before the lines were cast. White-bearded, jowl-faced Ben Woodson, Denning's conscientious navigator from Savannah, had his head down. He had told Denning only yesterday that he was tired and war-weary. Denning looked to Homer Cogswell, the forty-year-old pilot from Smithville, the chunk of granite on legs, father of two, who knew every Cape Fear underwater sandbar by name. Cogswell was a wise man, experienced in life, fearless, steady, a real rock. He was playing with his moustache, smoking his pipe. He had taken them through many a tight spot. Denning knew that Cogswell had been saving most of his money and was considering his future. He was one of the few sensible ones. Freckled Jimmy Parkens, the able young officer who had clung bravely to the foremast and waved the red dress, looked around slowly. He had come to Denning as a journeyman, the son of a friend, an old Annapolis graduate of 1852. He was devoted to Denning, his first runner captain. The hard-drinking bachelor and first officer Matthew Balsinger, efficient on board, careless on shore, leaned on a stack of cotton bales, a picture of mixed emotion. He was shaking, hung over from the night before. He hadn't saved a dollar all year, too busy drinking and having a good time to think ahead.

They were such a varied bunch, Denning thought.

"Gather round, men, and listen up," Denning addressed them. "I called you all together here to tell you that the rumors you've been hearing in Wilmington are correct. This is our final run." His words evoked murmuring in the crowd. "Quiet, please. We're heading for Bermuda this time. I can't say enough good things about all of you. Some of you go back many years with me, some of you have been here only a short while. But all of you are important. The *Silver Sally* will be up for sale on our successful return to Wilmington. And you will be paid double for the final run. So, make the most of it. Thank you, men." Denning cleared his throat. "I couldn't have asked for a better crew. Dismiss."

Cogswell glanced at Woodson. "This'll be our thirteenth trip," the pilot said.

"Yeah, you're right."

"How do you feel about that?"

"I dunno," Woodson said, after a considerable pause. "I wonder if it crossed the skipper's mind."

They didn't need to elaborate. There was an unwritten superstition in the blockade-running trade. It was unlucky to quit voluntarily after your thirteenth run. Obviously, Denning chose to ignore it.

In the pilot house, Denning watched Cogswell make the turn to sea, carefully keeping the Marsh Islands and Zeke Island on the *Sally*'s left. The cool five-knot breeze blowing in from the water off New Inlet was a relief from the stifling heat and humidity earlier in the day.

"Stop engines," Denning called down the pilot's voice tube to the engineer's room.

"Aye, aye, sir."

Denning put the tube on its hook and turned to Balsinger. "Drop anchor."

Denning stood over the rail, threw his cigar in the water and checked his revolver strapped to the holster inside his coat. The *Sally* was drifting to the wharf off Federal Point, near Fort Buchanan. She was entering the zone where the crew were to go silent. They would wait for the fort's signal to move out. Denning extended his telescope to the beach off port where he caught an explosion far out to sea, five or six miles distant. The reflection off the water told of a runner in trouble. He saw three vulturous gunboats advancing on the kill. Too bad his men had to see this.

No one spoke as they waited for the flames to die. "Steady, men," he said to those who could hear—Balsinger, Woodson, Cogswell, and two petty officers. "It's not going to happen to us," he said firmly.

The tide was starting to ebb.

It took almost thirty-five minutes for Fort Buchanan to answer.

Denning spoke first. "There it is, Homer. The all-clear."

"We'll have to move straight out and avoid the beach in front of Fort Fisher, sir," Cogswell explained. "The shoals at this hour could be trouble."

"I agree, Homer. Besides, we'd be too close to the smoking runner."

The seamen pulled the anchor up as quietly as they could. The ship began to drift. Denning slapped Homer Cogswell on the shoulder. With the commotion far to port, Cogswell had no other option but to steer starboard.

"It's all yours, Homer. Keep your weather-eye open and get us through."

Cogswell smiled. "Aye, aye, sir," he said, as he took the helm, and crossed himself. The Caroline Shoal and a seam in the Union inner line was dead ahead.

He had been here before.

Twenty-eight

Hamilton, Bermuda

Denning was amazed at the amount of guns packed in wooden crates, strewn across the large warehouse floor. There were breech-loaders and muzzle-loaders. There were regular Army and Navy revolvers, pocket revolvers, dragoons, derringers, hammer pistols, shotguns, carbines, long arm rifles. He noted the company names: Allen & Wheelock, Colt, Remington, Marlin, Smith & Wesson, Whitney, and Spencer. They were all Union makes, from the strong manufacturing states of New Jersey, Massachusetts and New York.

"Quite the collection," Denning said to the gun dealer, Douglas Burns, a wiry Northerner in ordinary dock work clothes.

Burns smiled. "Business is booming, captain."

"I'll bet it is. It's the Spencers I'm after. Do you mind if I try one of them out?"

"Which one?"

"The carbine."

"That can be arranged right now."

On a breezy rise overlooking the blockade runners in Hamilton harbor, Burns handed Joshua Denning what was now the most controversial weapon of the Civil War, the fast-action, breech-loading Spencer repeater rifle. Thirty yards away was an upright crude wood plank outline of a man attached to a stick pounded into the ground. Denning examined the gun in his hands. He had heard great things about the

Spencer repeater, and wanted to see for himself what all the hoopla was about.

"It's light," he said, surprised. "And easy to handle."

"Here's how it works," Burns said. "A tube is in here, in the butt of the gun. It holds seven self-contained cartridges. Pulling the lever down opens the breech, which pushes a cartridge forward into the barrel by way of the spring-fed tubular magazine. Pull the hammer back and you're ready to fire. After firing, the lever action also spits the spent casing out."

Denning brought the loaded carbine-version Spencer to bear on the six-foot target across the high grass.

"Ready when you are," Burns said, stepping back several feet to the captain's right.

Denning squinted over the barrel sight, his open eye intent on the outline. He fired and pumped the lever each time for the next shell, until the chamber was empty. He had reeled off the full seven fifty-caliber shells in eighteen seconds without even trying to reload as fast as he could. The barrel was hardly warm. Denning was impressed. Its capabilities made it a gun to be reckoned with. Denning and Burns walked to the target to discover five holes in the chest and head area, two in the right leg.

"Pretty good shooting, captain."

"Thank you."

"The repeating rifle version is even more accurate. What do you think of her?"

"Quite the peashooter. When they said it could be loaded on Sunday and fired all week, they weren't kidding."

"Then you're happy with it."

"Naturally. I think this will be my personal one. How many others can we deal for?"

"Six thousand one hundred and twenty-four. That's the entire lot. If you're interested?"

"I am. Cartridge boxes for them too?"

"Yes, sir."

Denning knew that Bobby Lee could use them. Spencers would make the other rifles, especially the muzzle-loaders, obsolete.

In the harbor, during the next day or two, he'd have to supervise how the ship would be packed. Bermuda was a hundred and twenty miles farther from Wilmington than Nassau, and that meant more coal aboard to make the trip, and fewer guns and other supplies. He'd have to balance things. That was the trouble with Bermuda. Too far.

"Why?" Denning suddenly asked.

"Pardon me?"

"Why are you dealing with me? You know damn well the guns are headed for Bobby Lee and the Army of Northern Virginia."

"Pure economics, captain. The Rebs pay more for military items than any Northern agent would."

"But Spencers?" Denning hoisted the gun up and whipped the breech back with a click. "These things can end the war for the Union. Unless some people in high places don't want to end the war just yet."

Burns grinned and his eyes flashed. "I oftentimes get the feeling that certain people in Washington want the war prolonged."

"The ones who profit from this little North-South skirmish."

"That's only part of it. The North is a hard sell, captain. Many Union army traditionalists still believe that such guns will tempt soldiers to waste ammunition."

"I've experienced the traditionalists myself in the Navy," Denning observed, recalling his old-fashioned naval superiors and their battle tactics.

"But once they see what they have, they'll change their minds," said Burns. "I heard tell that Lincoln himself tested the gun this year during a demonstration probably much like this and had recommended it strongly for mass production. The South, in their situation, is a little more open because, you must admit, it's only a matter of time before the Union wins," Burns said slowly, bracing himself for Denning's reaction.

Denning was not offended. "I've been seeing the light on that matter for some time. The Confederacy is on its last legs. Vicksburg has fallen. Lee's retreated from Gettysburg. Leastwise, these Spencers can give Lee a fighting chance."

"I'll say this for Bobby Lee. If he would've had Stonewall Jackson and these guns at Gettysburg, the outcome might have been different. The Union would be the ones in full retreat. And all Washington would be running scared."

"You might have something there, Burns," Denning said, aiming the gun barrel toward the *Silver Sally* down in the harbor.

"By the way, captain. How is my friend, Mr. Jacoby?"

Denning dropped the gun to his side. "Oh. . . he's. . . tied up at the moment."

Denning pounded on the hotel room door. "Matt! Open up, Matt!"

"Yeah. . . yeah. Keep your shirt on."

Denning heard a loud bang in the room, as if someone had fallen to the floor. "Hurry up!"

When the door opened, Matthew Balsinger stood there staggering, much the worse for drink. Over his shoulder Denning could see a woman asleep in the bed, her arms and large, bare breasts outside the covers. A strong smell of brandy hung in the hall. Denning stared at his first mate. He was unshaven, stripped to the waist, his massive biceps and muscular chest heaving. His messy premature gray hair made him look like an old man.

"What do you think you're doing? We're sailing in two hours. You're drunk as a skunk!"

Balsinger belched. "Is that so?" he said. His eyes were bloodshot, his speech raspy. "Dealing with Bluebellies. Why did you do it?"

"Is that what's been eating you? Lee needs those rifles and medical supplies."

"Sure. Captain Joshua Denning will win the war for the South, all by himself."

"I never said that."

"The *Sally* won't make it. You should have. . . have given up sooner. You won't make it."

"After all we've been through. How can you say we won't make it?"

"You won't make it. You. . . you're going to get everybody killed. This is our thirteenth trip."

"So?"

"You can't quit after thirteen. Twelve or fourteen, maybe. Never thirteen."

"I don't run my ship according to silly superstitions."

"You're playing with our lives. What's the matter with you? It's that woman. . . and Carlisle. They're doing this to you."

"That's enough."

"It's a game to you, ain't it? Matching wits with Carlisle, so you can show off to that Gypsy woman. That damn spy!"

"Shut up, Matt. You're not making sense."

Balsinger swore at Denning and took a wild, awkward swing at his superior. Denning ducked easily and pushed Balsinger to the floor. Balsinger stayed there, unable to move. Although he outweighed his captain, Balsinger was in no condition to retaliate.

Denning shook his head, disgusted. Balsinger had finally gone too far. In peace time, he would have been court-martialed for such rebellion. Denning had seen the gradual change in the last few months and had ignored it, hoping that Balsinger would snap out of it. It was a shame that such a good officer had succumbed to drink. Denning didn't know whether to be angry at Balsinger or to feel sorry for him.

"I'll give you a second chance, Matt. Are you coming?" Denning said, waiting.

"No. I quit!"

"Suit yourself. We part company then."

"You won't make it. You've reached your limit. Your number's up."

Denning threw a handful of gold sovereigns on the wood floor. "There you go. Your pay in full for the trip. Don't spend them all in one place. You're a damn fool, Matthew Balsinger."

Denning left, knowing he would probably never see Balsinger again.

"You're the fool. I'll do just fine," Balsinger roared, kicking the door closed with an unsteady leg. "Don't worry about me!"

His bed creaked.

"Keep the racket down," the woman muttered, rubbing her eyes, placing the covers over her bare breasts.

"Ah, shut up!" Balsinger yelled at her.

Twenty-nine

Atlantic Ocean east of New Inlet

"Strange, isn't it?" Denning said, after three days at sea during which he hardly uttered a word to his crew outside of the regular orders.

Cogswell was looking through the pilot house window in the last few minutes of light. "What, sir?"

"Our last trip together. We've been through a lot."

"That we have, skipper."

Woodson nodded in agreement, saying nothing. He and Cogswell had observed a change in the skipper and were talking about it before Denning entered the cabin. He was jittery, and his eyes seemed remote and glassy. He was not the Joshua Denning they were used to. And now Balsinger was gone. They wondered how his absence would affect the run to port.

Denning removed his Panama hat. "What are you going to do after this, Homer?"

"Well, sir, I was thinking of catching on with another skipper for a few more runs, then calling it quits. Then take my family to Canada, or maybe Mexico."

"Mexico?"

"Yes, sir. Buy a villa or a farm and stock it with cattle. And I'd buy a sailboat, so I could sail the Gulf."

"Sounds fine." Denning turned to Woodson and said, "You, Ben?"

"Ah, maybe join the Royal Navy, providin' they'll take me," Woodson replied. He had two sons in the Confederate Navy, both officers on the commerce raider, *Baton Rouge*, which was wreaking havoc on Union shipping in the Atlantic. "I'm sure they could use someone with my experience. Since Savannah fell to the Yankees, my wife's been in Atlanta with her parents. But she hates it there. The kids, well, they can look after themselves. They're big boys. What about you, sir?"

Denning gave a quick thought to Marie. "I don't know. I'll have to see what happens." He looked out to the western sky. "For now, let's just get through that," he said, pointing to the cloud forming ahead.

"Some rain coming our way, skipper," Woodson said.

Denning walked out to the rail and eyed the horizon. His lookouts were in place. This was enemy gunboat territory. He pondered his shipment, his biggest military shipment. Probably the biggest ever. Six thousand Spencer repeaters and ten thousand ammunition boxes would cause another roar in Wilmington, much the same way the daylight run did. And what about the medical supplies? The boxes of bandages? The bottles of quinine, chloroform, iodine? And the fifty barrels of gunpowder?

Because it was his last run, he had decided that there would be no high markup domestic items this time. No fancy Paris dresses and hats. No perfumes and other toiletries. No expensive chocolates and dinner mints. The Confederate armies, mainly Lee's Army of Northern Virginia, were his main objective. Giving the shipment away to the army agents wouldn't bother Denning either. To hell with auctions! Get the guns and medical supplies directly to the front! He had made his money on the other runs. This would be his last great effort. The Big Run. The war had opened his eyes to the greed and deceit that was everywhere in the South. The British merchants and rich Southerners were to blame for that. By 1863 every food item was so scarce that trading in luxuries had become a public scandal. No wonder the Davis government was threatening to step in on blockade running.

It was the only decent thing to do.

Three thousand yards away they were waiting.

"Ship ahoy, sir," the *Annapolis* petty officer called down from the mainmast to Captain Carlisle on the bridge. Battling a stiff westerly wind and the sporadic rain, the petty officer brought his telescope to his eye. Visibility was less than two nautical miles.

"What is it?"

"It's the *Silver Sally*. She's turning ninety degrees, sir," the petty officer yelled.

"Smith Island." Carlisle made a face at Farley. "The same as the last time. I'm getting to read him like a book."

"But last time he beat us."

"That was last time," Carlisle snorted. He didn't need to be reminded. "He's planning to hide in the swamps until nightfall, which is," he pulled out his pocket watch, "less than two hours. It's almost high tide now. I like it. I like it! Stay on his tail, Farley."

"Aye, aye, sir."

While the petty officer made the identification for Carlisle, Jimmy Parkens, his eye to his telescope on the *Sally*'s bow rail, did the same for his skipper.

"She's the *Annapolis,* sir."

"How does that bastard Carlisle find me?" Denning asked himself. "We gotta lose him."

South of New Inlet

The sun began to set behind the Cape Fear coast.

"When's high tide?" Denning said to Cogswell and Woodson in the pilot house.

"Eight-ten, sir," Woodson answered.

"An hour ago." Denning heaved a sigh and looked at his pocket watch. "The next high?"

"Seven-fifteen."

Denning pondered the situation. He didn't want to try a daylight run again. They had wasted too much time eluding Carlisle. High tide was subsiding. He didn't want this. They had arrived too late.

Using the *Sally*'s large compass as the only light, Denning held a council with Cogswell and Woodson. Outside, the rain swept against the pilot house. Denning crouched over between his two officers, a chart in his hands. "You'll have to be right on the mark this time, Ben."

"As near as I can figure, Simon's Swamp should be. . . there. Fifteen minutes away." Woodson's voice trailed off. He examined the map of the Atlantic-side of Smith Island's beaches and swamps. "Turn two points to port, Homer."

"Turning two points."

"The rest is up to fate and God, sir."

"And our pilot," Denning added. "We need you now, Homer. More than ever."

"Sir?"

Denning jumped. "What?"

"It's your coffee." Parkens was back with a steamy metal cup.

"Thanks, Jimmy." Denning took it with jittery, eager hands.

Simon's Swamp was a quarter-mile across. It was little known except by a few noted Cape Fear seamen. Simon's Swamp was not for the faint of heart. The narrow opening to it was guarded by three short, narrow shoals too close to the water surface for some to attempt even at high tide. Another advantage for those who used the swamp lay in the fact that it was halfway between New Inlet and Old Inlet, giving a skipper a chance to plot his strategy on which route to take home.

Silently drinking his coffee, Denning moved among his men, watching, nodding, admiring, remembering past runs. These were good men, Southern men, proud like him. And they were hard workers. They hadn't let him down yet. Except Balsinger.

Denning stood on the pilot house in his rain cape, seeking out the Smith Island shoreline. The rain was letting up to the point that gaps in the cloud to the west revealed the occasional star. He saw the surf line. He tapped on the roof to catch Cogswell's attention and Cogswell tapped back. He saw the surf too.

Denning leaped to the deck and waved two sailors over.

"Keep a sharp lookout for gunboats. Pass the word along."

Cogswell guided the *Sally* through the wind, rain, and choppy seas, as the ship furrowed in and out of the eastern shoals off Smith Island. He knew this area well. He and his father used to hunt and fish off the swamp. During the maneuvers every available hand was on deck to provide extra eyes to spot any enemy gunboats. Five Fed warships were picked out in the night, five too many for Denning's liking.

Cogswell took the *Sally* to the gate of Simon's Swamp. "Steady as she goes, Homer," Denning sighed.

Woodson held his breath. "I. . . can. . . feel something."

Denning and Cogswell looked at each other as the ship's bottom grazed the top of a shoal, catching it broadside.

"Don't get hung up now," Denning said to himself, walking out to the rail. The rain had died off. They were at the edge of the swamp.

With a sharp turn of the wheel, Cogswell spun the ship expertly around so her beam was parallel to the beach. The mosquitoes were thick tonight. The harsh smell of weeds and bulrushes surrounded them.

"Drop anchor," Denning whispered to a sailor. "Lower the masts and smokestacks. On the double."

"Aye, aye, sir."

The pounding surf and the ship's gray camouflage were the stealth items in their favor. Denning watched the cloud disappear above him. It would be a clear night, with only a slice of moon. The wind dropped to four or five knots and blew out from the shore. He knew he had to be careful. A patrolling gun ship would catch the slightest sound. The crew were under strict orders to be as silent as possible. From where they were, he saw six gunboats on the horizon.

Within three minutes, Denning held his second council with Cogswell and Woodson in the darkness of the pilot house.

"Which way we going, captain?" Cogswell asked, swinging at a bothersome mosquito.

"I'm open to suggestions. What do you think, Homer?"

"With this mist coming up, I'd try New Inlet for sure."

"Despite the low landmarks?"

"Yes, sir."

"Why? At least the Old Inlet has some trees along the shore to use as bearings."

"Too many ships out there to try Old Inlet, sir. I know we have more space to move around the Frying Pans, but we have to go out too far into the outer line of gunboat defense, and we don't have the surf and shore mist to hide us like we do off Fort Buchanan and Fort Fisher. Out of the swamp, we can hug the coast and slip right in, with the guns on the Mound covering for us."

"What do you say, Ben?"

Woodson nodded. "There's risks, sure. New Inlet is shallow. But there are always risks." He looked over at Cogswell but aimed his words at Denning. "I think it can work. I'm in agreement, sir. New Inlet."

"The only problem we might encounter will be the shoals before the New Inlet's mouth," Cogswell added. "I'll have to steer out over a mile now with the tide ebbing. Whatever we do, let's move before we're too late."

"It's settled then," Denning said. "New Inlet it is." He looked through the glass at the rolling mist.

There was a light tap at the door.

"Captain," Jimmy Parkens whispered. "We might have hit a bit of a snag, sir."

"What is it?"

"I have to show you."

"I'll be right there."

"Stay low, sir."

Parkens and Denning climbed to the top of the pilot house and slipped to their stomachs. The westerly breeze held at four or five knots. Every sound would be magnified now.

"Over thataway, sir." Parkens pointed over the high weeds along the beach, beyond the swamp's inlet. He gave his telescope to Denning. "Keep your eye on that spot in around there. A thousand yards. There's a ship moving back and forth as if she's looking for something. By the outline of its stacks and masts, sir, I'd say it's our old friend, Captain Carlisle. The *Annapolis*. And I bet yuh a horse's ass that he's looking for us."

It took several seconds for Denning to confirm the image of the converted runner in the lens, a trail of low mist surrounding her darkened hull. "There she is. Good eye, Jimmy."

"Thank you, sir."

"Yeah, it looks like she might be Carlisle's ship."

"He might not suspect we're in here and is trying to figure out where we went," Parkens said.

"Maybe." Denning had another idea. "Or he could be decoying, hoping that we move first. He's probably alone, though."

"If he sends up flares, we're dead, sir."

"No. He won't. Leastwise, not yet. He wants me bad enough that he doesn't want help. He'll signal for reinforcements as a last resort only. Jimmy, I'll be counting on you to pass some orders along."

"Aye, sir."

"Put the men on alert and remain here as a lookout until further notice."

"Yes, sir."

Denning slid down to the pilot house to give Woodson and Cogswell the news. "Let's take for granted that Carlisle knows we're here," he said. "But there's nothing he can do about it. He can't fire at us until he's sure. He won't go anywhere near those shoals. He doesn't know these waters like you do, Homer. However, if the mist thickens, we're heading out."

"Still planning on New Inlet?"

"Damn right."

"We're losing the tide, sir."

"I know. I know."

The mist thickened inside of an hour and clung low to the water surface, only a few feet above the hull of the *Sally*. With the masts and smokestacks down, the crew had the advantage of peering over the mist with less fear of being spotted themselves.

"Start up the engines," Denning murmured to a midshipman on deck. "Hold on." The midshipman stopped. To Parkens on the pilot house, he said, "Jimmy?"

"Aye, sir."

"Where's the *Annapolis* now?"

"Can't see her no more. I think she skedaddled."

"Or it's too thick out there for us to see each other. If we can't see them, then they can't see us." He turned back to the midshipman. "Bring the anchor and chains up. Start the engines. Leave the masts and smokestacks down. I want only five knots. And stand by," he said.

"Aye, aye, sir."

The orders speeded to the proper men in seconds. Denning rushed to the pilot house. The engines sparked to life and rumbled at his feet. The *Sally* was moving out to sea. "She's all yours, Homer. You know what to do."

Hands clenched on the wheel, Cogswell steered the ship into the pounding surf of the Atlantic. He crossed himself and swung to port. He felt a sandbar underneath. But the *Sally* slid over it.

Denning climbed the ladder partway to the pilot roof, a good position from which to whisper orders without moving from his perch. "See anything, Jimmy?"

"Nothing, sir. Only the outer ships on the horizon."

"Eight knots."

"Eight knots. Aye, sir," a sailor acknowledged.

The ship speeded up. Cogswell kept the sandy shoreline to his left between one hundred and fifty and two hundred yards.

After three miles, Parkens thought he saw a dark image on the water, through a gap in the mist. "Captain?"

"Yes."

"We're being followed!"

"Where?" Denning asked.

"Off the starboard stern. Eight. . . nine hundred yards. I can see the top of her pilot house. Her masts and stacks are down."

That meant one of two things to Denning. Ordinary Union gunboats didn't have telescope smokestacks, so either she was another Rebel runner making a dash for it, or she was Carlisle's converted runner. "Stop engines!" He waved to a sailor. "Let's see what she does," he said to Parkens.

The ship steamed by abeam to the *Sally* on a parallel course. Now Parkens caught a dim glimpse of whom they were really dealing with. "He's a devil, he is, that one, Carlisle. She's the *Annapolis*."

The eyes of the *Sally*'s crew were on the USS *Annapolis*, now quite vivid against the backdrop of the choppy Atlantic water. She continued on north at a speed of ten knots for several thousand yards and vanished into another fog bank off to their starboard. Denning looked into the telescope. Guarding the approach to New Inlet were three looming Union cruisers. Damn! He was trapped! High tide had long passed and Carlisle was tailing him.

The plan was falling apart.

Carlisle leaned over the port rail of the *Annapolis*, and cursed. He wiped the condensation from his glasses. "We lost him. Denning must know we're after him."

Farley studied the surf and sandy shore as far north as he could see, up to Fort Buchanan and Fort Fisher off the *Annapolis*'s starboard bow. The mist was patchy, but there was no sign of the blockade runner they had been tracking. "Should we circle back, and try and pick her up again?"

"Of course!" Carlisle exclaimed. "We know where they're going. It has to be New Inlet."

"Or maybe it was a feint. She could be heading south for Smith Island right now."

"No! He's trying to trick me, and I won't let him do it."

Parkens stood to see over the mist. "She's turning out to sea, captain."

"Get down. Just what I wanted to hear. Start the engines. Ten knots," Denning ordered a deck sailor.

"Ten knots, aye, sir."

The mist was growing thicker by the minute. Cogswell knew that New Inlet was now about three miles away, well within the range of Fort Fisher's powerful breech-loaders and the powder monkeys who operated them. So were the Union gunboats in range. Could he bypass them in the fog? Then. . . the mist lifted slightly, giving Parkens a view of the land and sea without needing his telescope.

"Captain! Look. Two hundred yards abeam. She's heading into us!"

Denning had only one option available to him. "Hard port, Homer!"

"We got 'er, Farley. We got 'er!" Carlisle couldn't believe his luck. His pilot had made a sharp starboard turn, approaching the runner head-on. "Prepare to fire Big Bear!" he cried from the bow rail. Then a fog bank smothered them.

"Where'd she go?" Farley said.

"Keep going."

"But, sir, the fog. We can't see from one end of the ship to the other. And the shoals. Shouldn't we back off?"

At the last second, Carlisle took his first mate's advice, and ordered a turn out to sea.

Thirty

Near New Inlet

Carlisle's long and tedious search had come up empty. But he was certain the *Sally* had not gotten by him. He had been blocking the entrance. He knew that the *Sally* still had more than two miles until she reached her safety zone of Fort Buchanan's range, the nearest batteries. The cloud cover had lifted. The horizon would start to lighten within the next hour. If he could prevent the *Sally* from reaching New Inlet before sunrise, he'd have Denning right where he wanted him. The rising sun would probably burn off the fog, leaving Denning exposed in the early morning light. Carlisle smiled at his scheme. He was going to bag the pirate this time.

Carlisle ordered the *Annapolis* on a southern course through the dense fog. He then motioned for the engines to be cut. The night was calm, except for the flow of the lapping waves. Any sound should carry well. He watched and waited.

Over the starboard rail, he cupped the megaphone to his mouth and yelled, "Give up, Denning. You're trapped! Denning, can you hear me?"

"Did you hear that?" Denning said, leaning on the pilot house, conferring with Jimmy Parkens.

"Yeah, I did," Parkens replied. "Someone's calling you, skipper."

"It's got to be Carlisle."

* * * *

"Captain, what are you doing?" Commander Farley said. "You'll give our position away."

"Button your lip. This is between me and Denning."

"But, sir. . ."

"Shut up!" Carlisle turned his attention to the area of the beach. "Denning! Can you hear me? You're done for. It's too late for the Old Inlet! The sun will be up soon. The fog won't hide you forever." He took a deep breath and continued yelling into the megaphone. "Your only choice is the New Inlet and there's three ships waiting there for you, if you can get past *us*. You won't get through! Give up now! Save yourself and your crew!"

It was decision time.

Swallowed up by the fog, Denning found it difficult to tell exactly where Carlisle was, but he couldn't be too far away if he could be heard so clearly. "We'll see about that," he said to Cogswell through the pilot house door. "We have an hour till sunup. This is my idea. It's desperate, but what other choice do we have?"

"Let's hear it, sir," Cogswell said.

"Let's go for it all. Straight in. As close to the shore as we can get."

"What if we run afoul of a shoal or the beach?"

Denning pointed out that the mist had started to lift and that the sky to the east was unveiling signs of dawn. The sun would soon burn away the fog. Denning wrestled with the consequences. They had to go in now. "As long as we can get close enough to the mouth of New Inlet, we can beach her and launch the lifeboats, and hope to salvage the ship later."

"If at all. I don't know, captain. We haven't played it this way before."

"Do you have a better idea?"

"Off the top of my head, no, sir," Cogswell said. "I suppose I don't. It's too late for the Old Inlet."

"Well, then. What are we waiting for?"

Cogswell had a sudden sick feeling. As his seafaring daddy used to say, *Something is bad wrong here. Bad wrong.* The captain had waited too long to pull out. "Let's shove off before I lose my nerve."

Denning spun around to Parkens behind him. "I want a full head of steam on the double. Whip the masts and the smokestacks up!"

"Aye, sir. I'm on my way," Parkens said, moving off.

170

* * * *

The *Sally* raced along the surface of the water, Cogswell feeling his way
by the ship's compass and his own calculated guesswork. The mist
was thinning. Cogswell saw the white surf indicating the coastline.
They were too close to shore, much too close. The shoals were dead
ahead—somewhere. It was hit or miss. To the immediate right were
three Union warships, defending the inlet, their smokestacks visible over
the gray of the mist. Were they at anchor? He couldn't tell. On the other
side of the enemy was the rise of Big Hill, a bump on the otherwise flat
coastline, with its lighthouse and the powerful guns of the southern
portion of Fort Fisher. Guns good for four miles. To the left was Fort
Buchanan, the other battery. Four more heavy guns, but not with the
same range as Fort Fisher. Cogswell could see everything. They were
sliding over shoals now, building up speed as they went, faster and faster.

They were almost there. The last run. They were a little more than
a mile off the inlet. The *Sally* was straining to break loose. They were
flying. Then... they hit a shoal broadside. Men lost their footing and
knocked into one another. The top rows of wood crates fell and split,
sending the contents of rifles and medical supplies across the deck, and
knocking down several sailors. Below, one of the stokers in the engine
room wound up in the furnace and came away with burns on his back.

Denning fell from the pilot house ladder. He felt a jolt to the back of
his head and his teeth slammed together. He passed out, then came to,
roused by the noises around him.

Jimmy Parkens ran up, shaking him. "Captain? Captain?"

Denning crawled on all fours to the port rail. He had bit into his lip
and had the taste of blood in his mouth. Other seamen were rising to
their feet. His head whirled as he attempted to consider the situation.
The sky was lighter. Shapes of land and man-made structures were
clearer. The sandy shore off port loomed five hundred yards distant.
The guns at the closer Fort Buchanan and Fort Fisher up the beach to
starboard were in range. Then Denning saw some bright flashes on
shore, seconds apart. Fort Fisher had opened up with their batteries on
the Federal cruisers heading for the runner. Fort Buchanan followed.
The shells were falling around the *Sally* in the path of the warships. The
gunners in the forts were giving him time to escape.

"Man the lifeboats!" Denning cried.

He ran for the pilot house and saw Ben Woodson and Homer Cogswell helping each other to the boats. "Get going, men!" Denning saw his Spencer repeater carbine on the floor. Nobody was going to send him to no Yankee prison.

"Fire Big Bear!" Carlisle screamed to the crew of the Dahlgren smooth-bore, ignoring the inland Rebel shells bursting over his gunboat.

The aimer quickly made his distance and barrel-height adjustment, then pulled the rope of the firing mechanism. A bright red flash and a wall of white smoke followed, sending a heavy shell headed towards what appeared to be a beached *Silver Sally*.

The shell descended with a high-pitched scream and hit the smokestack closest to the *Sally*'s engine room, raining jagged metal and red sparks onto the deck and the water.

When the smoke cleared, Denning could see that the stack had disintegrated, leaving a huge gaping hole in the center of the ship. The shell had missed the gunpowder, but the *Silver Sally* was completely disabled. Denning scrambled to his feet. The lower deck of the ship was filling with water.

Denning reached for his gun, his head still reeling from the force of the explosion. He charged from the pilot house, looked aft of the ship, and saw the *Annapolis*, circling in the morning twilight, at four hundred yards. Denning heard the shouts and the horrifying screams of his sailors, who were making their way to the lifeboats. The stench of burnt flesh stung the air. Men were floundering in the water. The air became saturated with curses. He heard one boat hit the water.

"Get everyone off, including the wounded! I don't want to see anyone left!" Denning yelled.

He saw the danger. A fire caught hold near the engine room. If they didn't get off immediately, they would be killed in a more powerful explosion than the enemy's shell.

"Go, men! Go!" His voice grew more urgent. "Get off the ship before she goes up!"

"Son of a bitch! They're going to ram us!" a sailor shouted.

Denning turned to the open sea. There was the *Annapolis*, a glowing red devil lit by the *Sally*'s fiery glare, heading straight for the *Sally*!

Carlisle had to be a madman. Damn, not with the gunpowder aboard! Denning removed the carbine from the leather case, aimed at the figures on the bow rail, and fired off four quick shots in succession, at different points across the bow.

One of the bullets caught an officer beside Carlisle in the shoulder. He went down in a heap. Another took Carlisle's hat off.

"Go for cover!" Carlisle ordered. "They're shooting at us."

What did you expect? thought Commander Farley, dropping behind the wall of the bulwark and using it as a shield. Shells from Fort Fisher and Fort Buchanan fell into the water around them, forming a cross-fire. Bullets were pinging off the hull. He knew it was too late to stop the *Annapolis* now, too late to stop Carlisle from his headlong insane idea to ram the *Sally*. In the temper he was in, Carlisle was too full of Satan, too intoxicated with hate to reason properly. Farley had learned never to come between a fool and his folly. Carlisle was risking the life of all the good Union seamen aboard just to get even with one man.

The dumb jackass.

Denning watched in alarm as the Union cruiser raced toward him and. . . smashed the hull of the *Sally*.

The forward slam of the *Annapolis* nearly crushed two of the lifeboats in the water and the men in them. The force propelled Denning over the rail, into the water. He lost his Spencer. He touched bottom, and stood up. The sandbar was barely three feet below the water line. He looked around. One of his lifeboats was twenty feet to his right. Cogswell was aboard with two stokers from the engine room. Carlisle's ship ground to a halt on the shoal, alongside the *Silver Sally*. Both vessels were on fire. It was now an all-out scramble for men everywhere, Reb and Fed, to try to save themselves.

"Hurry, captain," Cogswell cried, "before the gunpowder and boilers blow us all to kingdom come!"

"Denning!"

Denning looked up to the hull of his ship. Carlisle was standing against the rail, silhouetted by the fire behind him, a knife in his fist.

"Carlisle!"

"You're not going anywhere!" yelled Carlisle.

Denning removed his knife from its sheath. "Step into my office," he invited him, with a motion of his hand. "Come on. Come on!"

Carlisle jumped feet first into the water, losing his spectacles. He waded toward his long-time enemy. They were eight feet apart. A raging fire burned only a few yards away and they could feel the heat in the water. They stood on the sandbar, knives out in defiance, each waiting for the other to move first.

"Captain! The boilers and powder are going to blow!" Cogswell called out. "Get away!"

"Go! Get the hell out of here!" Denning waved Cogswell off. "Save yourselves!"

Cogswell held back on the oars, looked up at the hull of the ship, then watched the two skippers squaring off. He suddenly realized that the beach guns had ceased their firing.

"So, it's coming down to another knife fight, Denning." Carlisle spat in the water. "This time only one of us will walk away. Too bad Clara won't be around for the winner."

"Leave Clara out of this. She made her choice, wrong though it may have been. This is between you and me, Four Eyes."

Carlisle advanced toward Denning, who met him halfway. It was Carlisle who made the first move, lunging at Denning. Denning caught Carlisle's arm with his left hand and tried to throw him backwards. Carlisle lost his balance, wavered, then recovered, and Denning, with a swift move, swiped at Carlisle, cutting into his uniform and chest. Carlisle returned with a slice of his own, catching the Virginian deep in his neck and shoulder. Denning's knife dropped into the water, leaving him defenseless and staggering. Carlisle had him now. He knifed Denning solidly in the right shoulder, then pulled the blade out.

Denning's gushing blood goaded Carlisle to greater savagery. "How was that, Denning? Want some more?"

Denning staggered. He started to fall, slowly. His vision blurred. Everything began to go dark. Cogswell's yelling was far off, muffled. Denning tried to stay upright but fell to his knees in the water. He could not hold his own. The water was now up to his neck. He wanted to raise himself but couldn't. No strength in his lifeless arms. He was slowly going under and could do nothing about it. Too weak. Carlisle was set to thrust the knife again.

Then a pistol shot rang out.

Nearly delirious, Denning looked up. In the water only a few feet away, a Union officer stood on the underwater sandbar, his hand gun smoking. A Fed had come to his aid. He had to be hallucinating. But he wasn't. Carlisle fell to his knees. He tried to utter a last breath, then dropped head first into the water. And didn't come up.

Denning was dimly aware of Cogswell paddling to him.

"Here, lend me a hand," the pilot ordered the others with him.

They pulled Denning aboard, careful not to swamp the boat, in front of the mesmerized Union officer still holding the gun. Cogswell slowly, cautiously, stripped the officer of the weapon. "Here, give me that."

The officer, Stephen Farley, turned to him, stunned, saying nothing.

Cogswell ignored the fact they were on opposite sides in the war. "Get in the boat, Yank! Move!" Cogswell pushed Farley in. One of the stokers and Cogswell paddled frantically to the shore. "We'd better get the hell outta here before the ammo and gunpowder goes!"

They paddled away like madmen.

Within two minutes, both ships blew up in a ball of fire. A concussion containing three mighty explosions echoed across the sunlit water, bringing with it a wide blanket of eye-stinging sulfur from the ammunition and gunpowder. Pieces of wreckage quickly littered the water. Cogswell could taste the sulfur in the air as he looked down at the unconscious Captain Denning lying face up in the boat. "Thanks, Yank," he said to Farley, spread out in the middle of the boat. "We'll get you to safety somehow. Don't worry. You're not facing any prison. You have my word on that."

"I believe you, Reb. Thanks," Farley said, exhausted, finally emerging from his trance. "I've always known Southerners to be gentlemen."

Cogswell shook hands with him. "I have a name, you know. I'm Homer Cogswell. I'm—I was the *Silver Sally* pilot. You?"

"Commander Stephen Farley, first mate of the USS *Annapolis*. The *Sally* was a good ship," the officer said cautiously. He looked over his shoulder to see more lifeboats in the water, full of gray-uniformed men. He was the only Yankee. He could see a few Union men swimming for shore. It was a queer feeling being in the same lifeboat with Rebs, but comforting at the same time. He trusted the Reb, this Cogswell.

"These are two of the engineers," Cogswell said.

The blackened faces of the stokers gave evidence to their trade in the depths of the runner. They nodded at him. The one at the oars shook his hand. The other, suffering from burns he had received in the engine room during the collision, leaned back, staring doggedly.

"You sure as hell gave us a damn good run for the money, Yank. Now, let's get moving. We're going to have to hide you out a spell." Cogswell looked at Farley curiously. "What you did had to be a first. A man shooting his own commanding officer."

"I had my reasons."

Thirty-one

Smithville, North Carolina

Mrs. Cogswell had been out of bed for more than an hour. As she watched her black maid scurry about in the kitchen, she heard someone stumbling in the front hall.

"Victoria!"

It was a man's voice. A familiar voice. Her husband's.

Mrs. Cogswell hurried to the entrance, and froze at the sight of the five men standing before her. At first she thought they were all drunken beggars. One man, unconscious and bleeding from the chest, was held up by two others. The house suddenly reeked of salt water and sweaty, unwashed bodies.

"It's me, Victoria," one of them said. His face was black from soot and he was cut on his cheek.

"Homer?" She embraced her husband, in spite of his appearance.

"Hello, my dear." Homer hugged his pretty, light-haired, steadfast wife of fourteen years, kissing her on the lips in front of the men.

"Good gosh, Homer. You're soaking wet!" She flicked her hands.

"Victoria. We need a doctor. For one of our men, here," he gestured to the stoker beside him, "and Captain Denning."

She suddenly didn't seem to mind that the men were dripping water on the varnished floor and the carpet. She stared at the stoker and saw his wounds, which didn't appear that serious, then at the unconscious Captain Denning, his arms slung over his comrades' shoulders. His face was a sickly gray with dark circles around his closed eyes. He needed immediate attention. "This man, in the parlor," she said, taking command. "Around the corner. As for the captain, give him the guest room. Up the stairs and second door on the right."

Homer's daughters ran out to greet their father. "Katie! Jessica! How's my girls?" He bent down and put his muscular arms around them.

Victoria called for Silas, the manservant of the house. "Go fetch Dr. Griffith. Right away."

"Yessum." Silas scurried down the hall toward the entrance, then stopped and turned to the master of the house. "Oh, good mornin', Mr. Homer."

"Good morning, Silas."

Then he left.

Victoria realized that the remaining man at the door wore a Union Navy uniform. "My God, a Yankee!"

"He's a friend. Farley, my wife, Victoria."

"Commander Stephen Farley, madam, of the United States Navy. Pleased to meet you." He bowed his head, crossing his hands in front of him.

"What the devil is a Yankee doing in our house?" she said to Homer.

Homer took each daughter by the hand. "Never mind the uniform. He saved the captain's life. It's a long story."

She backed off. "How did you get him here?"

"It wasn't easy. We had to take the back roads. The *Silver Sally* blew up after a collision with a Union gunboat off New Inlet."

"Oh my word." She put her hand to her mouth. She recalled the sounds early in the morning, at dawn. Three distinct booms in the distance had wakened her, the last one the loudest. After twenty minutes she had fallen back to sleep.

"Anyway, I'll explain it all later. I promised to hide Farley till nightfall, then release him to his own side. I gave my word, Victoria. Without his help, the captain would be a dead man, sure."

Victoria looked upon the kind face of the Union officer. "Captain Denning is a good man," she said, changing her tone of voice. "Welcome to our home, Commander Farley."

Farley smiled and said, "Thank you, madam."

She smiled back. "I'm sure you'd like to remove those wet clothes and have something to eat." She looked him over from head to toe.

"Hmm... Homer isn't exactly your size, but we'll find something for you to wear. However, you both could use a little clean-up. Now, get off the floor, you two, before you stain it even worse."

Oak Island

That night, Farley and Cogswell made their way to the beach.

"In you go, commander," Cogswell said to Farley, inviting the Union officer into the *Silver Sally* lifeboat as he held it steady in the choppy water.

Miles away on the horizon floated a row of Union warships. There were more and more these past few months, with no letup. There were so many cruisers now that Cogswell was sure Farley could jump from one ship to another without getting his feet wet. A mile and a half to his left was the lighthouse at Bald Head Point, the western part of Smith Island. To his right were the inner-line cruisers, one of them steaming in closer than the others, less than one mile off shore. Cogswell made it plain to Farley that he should try for that one.

"Now this is what you do, commander. It's low tide for several more hours. Stay to the right. This is the Western Bar Channel right here, the deepest part of Old Inlet. Stick to it and you can't go wrong. The left has all the shoals. Good luck." Cogswell held out his hand across the boat. "And thanks. You realize that if we should ever meet again in this war, I won't show any favoritism."

"Same here."

Farley shook Cogswell's hand and sat down. The Southerner was indeed a man of his word, and his wife had even washed and pressed his Union Navy uniform. He reached for the oars. "Fair enough. I do hope your Captain Denning pulls through. I would have liked to meet him."

"He's in for a rough night with the fever and all."

"Mr. Cogswell, this has truly been an experience I'll have to tell my grandchildren."

"You're not the only one. You never did tell me why you shot your captain."

Farley didn't hesitate. "I had to rid the world of a monster. It was the only way. Justice prevailed."

"I think I understand." Cogswell thought of the order to ram the *Sally*. No skipper in his right mind would resort to such a maneuver.

"And if I get stuck with another skipper the likes of Carlisle, I just might aim to come over to your side."

"We'll take you. You best get moving," Cogswell said to Farley, pushing the boat into the water. "And good luck."

Smithville

Throughout the night, Joshua Denning's temperature soared. The doctor came and dressed the wounds, giving specific instructions to put cold packs on Denning's body to break the fever. If infection set in, he was to be called immediately.

While attended to by Victoria Cogswell and the house servants, Denning's past flashed before him in a series of visions and nightmares over which he had no control. He remembered his father's farm... *then Clara*... he saw Robert Carlisle at Annapolis... his mind recreated the knife fight outside the tavern. He saw the daylight run again... *he saw Clara*... he called out to her and she answered... *he saw Marie*... he remembered the collision... he saw Marie... now Clara was fading away. He called out to Clara, but she didn't return. But Marie was there.

By sunup next morning, Denning still had the fever and was sweating profusely. Blisters started to appear on his body.

At noon, Silas answered a knock at the front door. On the steps was a young, dark-haired woman. "Yes, ma'am."

"I'm Marie Keating. Your master sent for me."

Cogswell stepped forward. "I'll take care of it, Silas."

"Yes, suh."

"I'm Homer Cogswell, Captain Denning's pilot. Please, do come in."

"Thank you, Mr. Cogswell. I heard the news that the *Silver Sally* went down." Marie appeared nervous as she stepped inside. Cogswell closed the door. "How is the captain?"

"Not good, I'm afraid. He's been calling for you for a solid day now. For a while it was another woman, Clara."

She shook her head. "I don't know a Clara."

"At one time, he came to, opened his eyes and asked for you. I thought I should call you. I know your aunt."

Marie smiled. "May I see him?"

"Brace yourself."

Marie took to the stairs, alone. She gasped when she saw Denning in the upstairs room. Not long ago, she was the one lying in bed while Denning looked on and comforted her. Now, the scene had switched. She wondered if she had looked as shocking as Denning appeared now. His reddish-blonde hair was stuck flat to his scalp, and one arm was across his heaving, bare chest. She tip-toed closer. His lips were dry and cracked, and his once-bronze skin was the color of death.

"Joshua."

"Marie," he mumbled, eyes closed. "Marie," he said more loudly, his head moving back and forth.

"I'm here, Joshua," she answered, her voice rising. "Joshua, can you hear me?"

A smile formed on his lips.

The fever finally broke that afternoon, and by the early evening Denning had opened his eyes. He had a strange taste of sulfur in his mouth. Victoria Cogswell brought him a tall glass of water.

Denning drank and returned the glass to her hand. "Where am I?"

"You're in Smithville, Captain Denning."

"Smithville?" He felt his head, barely able to lift himself. "Who are you?"

"Victoria Cogswell, wife of your pilot."

"Homer?" Denning swallowed.

"Yes. Homer is my husband. You're going to make it, Captain Denning. You've been unconscious for nearly two days. You had a bad fever."

"How's Homer?"

"He's fine."

"He's a good man."

"Yes, he surely is."

Denning tried to recall what had happened. His ship was under attack by Carlisle. He remembered the collision. He fell into the water. The knife fight. The pain in his shoulder. It was coming to him in patches only. "Is this your house?"

"Yes, captain."

"Nice wallpaper." Then he looked at her and smiled as if it was difficult. "Now I know why Homer hates being away. You're very pretty."

Victoria laughed softly. "Yes, I think you're going to be just fine. I'll get Homer for you." She withdrew in a flurry of skirts.

Homer bounced up the stairs, two at a time, followed slowly by Marie, who preferred to stay in the shadows of the hall as Homer went in.

"Captain," said Homer, "you're back with the living."

"What happened?"

"The *Sally* exploded, captain," Homer told him, pulling a chair to the bed. "Don't yuh remember?"

"Parkens, did he—?"

"Yes, he made it. And Ben. The others," Cogswell explained with satisfaction. "Everyone, actually."

"Everyone?"

Cogswell nodded. "The whole crew."

Denning was astonished. "They all survived?"

"All accounted for and safely in Smithville. Some a little worse for wear, including you, sir. Four in the hospital. That's a hell of a lot better than the boys of the *Annapolis*. A third or so were killed during the collision and explosions. If you hadn't ordered our men to man the lifeboats, we wouldn't have made it."

"Carlisle? What happened to him?"

"He's dead."

"Good. The bastard."

"His first mate shot him. He saved your life, captain. Do you remember that?"

Denning coughed and closed his eyes. "Yeah. . . I think so. I'm kind of bushed. . . Homer."

Then Denning fell into a deep contented sleep that lasted more than ten hours.

Thirty-two

Smithville

A weary Joshua Denning, despite doctor's orders, got out of bed anyway. He was washed up and stripped to the waist, wearing only trousers, exposing the clean, white bandages on his chest and shoulder. It was warm in the room. He sat in a chair by the open window and looked upon the sparkling Cape Fear River, the waterway he had sailed many times. The outdoor air was beginning to revive him. He squinted in the brightness of the crisp, sunny day. By the position of the sun, he knew it had to be about noon. The ebbing tide was beginning to disclose the shore surrounding the islands in Buzzard's Bay, the weedy and rocky points off Smith Island, and the beaches of Oak Island. He could see the Western Bar Channel and a half dozen Union gunboats on the open water, all in one sweeping glance.

While he sat and recollected, Denning wondered what he would say to Marie when she arrived. Several things loomed clear to him now. The explosion of the *Silver Sally* had propelled him into a new world, as if a line had been drawn between then and now. His new world was free of everything before it—Clara, Carlisle, dirty deals, wicked men, a useless war, too much money to squander, and King Cotton. He was tired, with no reserves on the way. Dead tired. Used up. He had been brought kicking and screaming to his senses.

He was relieved his crew had made it. He would see to it they were all paid what he owed them. Double the normal trip, as he had promised. Denning was out of the blockade-running business for good, although not the way he had wanted. But at least he was through with it, without misgivings. He entered that world for patriotic reasons, for adventure and. . . for money. But times had changed. It was too dangerous, too unfulfilling now that he had something and someone else on his mind. He had been wandering aimlessly for years and hadn't come to grips with it. That would stop shortly, he hoped.

Denning heard footsteps on the stairs and braced himself. Then he saw Marie at the door. For the first time, he saw her not as Clara's double, but as Marie Keating. They were two separate people. One sweet and shy; the other more unpredictable, passionate, and outgoing. The latter was here, now, within reach, a living, breathing individual. She was not a vision. She was his reason to exist, to enjoy life again. Marie wore a cheerful smile. Her new green dress extended down to the floor. It had a low-cut neckline exposing the top part of her creamy-white breasts. Never before had she looked so provocative. She was beautiful. *Oh God, was she beautiful.* He stood for her, slowly, carefully, painfully, using the chair for support. His first thought was to grab her in his arms. No, he couldn't do that. He had to be more tender with a lady of breeding.

"Thanks for coming, Marie." He seemed awkward with his words. His throat and neck muscles were tight. "How's your aunt?" He winced, as she came forward and stopped only a few feet away.

"She's. . . the same. But you, Joshua. What are you doing out of bed? Please, don't stand for me. Sit down." He looked weak to her, and thin, although his shoulders were as square and strong as she remembered.

"I can't. Not yet. Not until I say something."

"What is it?" Marie asked. She looked into his face and detected a peace in him that she had not seen there before. "Go ahead, Joshua."

He took a breath. His mouth curved into a curious smile. "Will you marry me?"

Marie made a muffled noise in her throat. She didn't know if she should reach for his arms or faint or collapse from the shock.

"Will you?"

"We don't know each other. Without proper courting?" Her lips trembled. "It's so—"

"Unexpected." He finished the sentence. He shrugged and winced. It hurt to shrug. "It is, I know. That's the way I work. I'm impulsive. But so are you, and you know it. I think we do know each other. Listen to me. We can forget the Confederacy. Forget the South. King Cotton is one big damn lie. It never existed. It was a figment of some politician's imagination. We can forget war. Forget rotten men like Eli Jacoby and Bobby Carlisle. Let's go to Europe. England or, better yet, France. I'm sure you'd like to see your family. How long's it been?"

It took her several moments to finally reply. "Five years," she said softly.

"We're from the same mold, Marie. The South isn't our country. It won't be anybody's country for too much longer. It'll barely survive another year. Two at most. I for one don't wish to stick around and see its demise."

Marie was overwhelmed. "I thought you weren't the marrying kind."

"Never you mind what I said before. That was in the past."

"But Joshua, I am so. . . flawed."

"As if I'm not. Wait till you see my imperfections."

"We're both so headstrong, so stubborn."

"Go on," he said, smiling slowly.

"What if we should fight?"

"God forbid. But it might be fun making up afterwards."

"*Oui*. It might," she agreed, holding back a smile.

"Is there anything else I must know?"

"I like to get my own way."

"Are you through?" Denning asked.

"I believe I am."

There was a long silence.

"I love you, Marie, like I've loved no other woman. Ever. I've never met a woman quite like you. I love everything about you. Your energy, your drive to be your own person." He moved toward her. Denning forgot about his bandaged shoulder and kissed her with such fervor that Marie thought she was going to pass out. His hands were clumsy on this occasion, lacking some of his previous grace. She didn't care. It would come back to him. She pulled her lips away to gasp for air.

"Of course I'll marry you," she managed to say between breaths, as they held each other.

"You're sure now?"

"*Oui*." As Denning had said, she was impulsive. "Let's leave the South far behind."

"Let's do that. Wilmington can't stop talking about us, anyway."

All of a sudden, she asked, "Who's Clara? You were calling out her name."

"I was?"

"The Cogswells said you were."

"Clara was. . . someone I knew many years ago, Marie," Denning replied, looking deeply into her eyes. "But that was then. This is now. You're here. . . now."

"Was she like me?"

"Yes. . . and no. You're prettier."

She cradled her head between his shoulder and neck, her body pressed to his. "Where is she now?"

"I don't know."

"Tell me about her," she said, without looking at him.

"I'd like to forget her, if you don't mind. Please." Then he thought about it. It was only fair to tell her, someday. "I'll tell you the story. Perhaps, when we're old and gray."

Then their lips met again.

Thirty-three

Captain Clement Sullivan invited Denning and Marie to the crowded deck of the *Hickory Hill*. At twenty-four, Sullivan was the youngest Rebel skipper to command a blockade runner, and he was on his fifth run with the ship credited with eight successful runs so far.

The *Hickory Hill* was in the same class as the *Sally*, one of the new super runners—three stacks, more than two hundred and seventy-five feet long, and built of strong, lightweight steel. Her cargo tonight was six hundred and fifty bales of the all-purpose Georgia Bowed cotton, one hundred and thirty-five barrels of turpentine, and one hundred and ten one-hundred-pound bags of corn seed. While the crew and Denning took for granted the degree to which the ship was loaded, Marie was amazed to find that the deck, the halls, and the cabins fore and aft were tightly stacked with cargo. And piled so high. It was a chore to move or even turn about in her newly purchased gray dress without catching a bale, or a barrel, or a bag in the face.

"Captain Denning." Sullivan nodded to Denning in the darkness. He tipped his officer's cap at Marie. "We just passed Reeve's Point, two miles from New Inlet. I thought you might want to have a look at the proceedings."

"Much obliged," Denning said. "And I'm grateful to you for bringing us aboard on short notice."

"My pleasure. To tell you the truth, I'm honored by your presence."

"Thank you."

"We're fortunate to be let away," Sullivan said.

"Why?"

"I managed to work around the latest Richmond War Department directives. I had to show a complete crew and cargo list. I put you down as Joshua and Andy. You are both listed as cabin boys." Sullivan smiled, his mustache widening. "Therefore you might have to confine yourself to those duties. You have separate cabins for the night."

Denning laughed. "We will comply with your orders, for the first night."

"The other directive, I couldn't avoid. Richmond now has the authority to commandeer half of all inbound and outbound cargo. This shipment is under those rules. Had I not agreed to the new measures, the ship would have been seized."

"Wise move on your part," Denning replied. With the Rebel government poking their nose into blockade running, Denning knew he had got out of the business at the right time.

Sullivan turned into the moderate easterly breeze. "I've decided to take the New Inlet."

"You're the boss."

"I'm sorry I didn't have the opportunity before, so now I want to wish you both all the happiness in the world. Congratulations."

Denning put his arm around his fiancée. "Thank you." In less than twenty-four hours he and Marie would be married at sea.

"Paris will be lovely this time of year. Have you made a decision on whether your fiancée will join you tonight? As long as the rules are obeyed, I won't object."

"I'll ask her."

"Now, if you'll excuse me, I have to attend to a matter. I'll be back shortly."

"Of course."

"What rules?" Marie asked, watching Sullivan withdraw to the pilot house. The couple leaned on the rail, looking down at the black waters of the river.

"Either you can go to your cabin or stay here with me."

"The cabin! I'll go crazy by myself. I want to stay here with you."

Denning smiled in the night. "In that case, when the order is given, I have to caution you to not make a sound. This is serious business. Stay in one spot. Right here is probably one of the best places. We'd be in no one's way. Your dress is the perfect color, the same hue as the ship. It blends in with the surroundings. Nevertheless, keep low behind the rail. Any movement could be detected by the other side. House rules."

"I'm worried, Joshua."

"What about?"

"Getting through."

He put his hand on hers. "No need to worry. Sullivan is young, I know, but he has plenty of experience in blockade running. It's a cloudy night. The wind's light, blowing across from the sea. I've heard tell that since my ship went down the Fed cruisers are keeping their distance from the mouth of the inlet for fear of hitting a shoal. So, you see, everything is in our favor. I just hope they have a good pilot aboard."

Hickory Hill was beginning to make the turn to port. To starboard, Denning saw the Marsh Islands. Dead ahead was Zeke Island, which the pilot scooted around with an easy style. Now they were only a half-mile from the mouth of the shallow New Inlet. Denning's eyes penetrated the night. He knew what to look for. Six deadly gunboats took shape out to sea. The smell in the air was a mixture of the pungent swamp lands off Buzzard's Bay and the salty spray of the ocean to the ship's bow. The waves were choppy. They heard the anchor splash into the water.

Sullivan found his way past the high row of bales to the rail. "Your decision, sir?"

"She's with me, Captain Sullivan."

"Very well. You've explained the rules."

"Yes. I hope you have a good pilot, captain," Denning asked. "The Caroline Shoal can shift."

"I have an excellent man at the helm. While we're waiting for the signal from Fort Buchanan, would you like to meet him? Just to put your mind at ease. He does know the area quite well."

"Yes, I would like to meet him."

Denning and Marie followed the captain to the pilot house. The man behind the helm, a husky individual, was waiting by the table with the navigator, their backs to the visitors. A familiar smell came to Denning's nostrils. Pipe tobacco. *Georgia Navy Gold.*

The pilot turned and said, "Captain Denning. Welcome aboard."

Denning linked the smell and the voice in the darkness. "Homer?"

"That's right, captain."

Denning shook hands with his former pilot. "Captain Sullivan. You not only have an excellent man. You have the best."

"Thank you, captain," said Cogswell, tipping his hat at Marie. "Mrs. Keating. Or should I say soon to be. . . Mrs. Denning."

"It's nice to see you again, Mr. Cogswell."

"My pleasure, ma'am. How are you feeling, sir?" Cogswell asked his former captain.

"Very well, thank you."

The ship's first mate tapped Sullivan. "Sir. Fort Buchanan just gave us the all-clear."

"Thanks." Sullivan stood in the doorway smiling at Cogswell and Denning. "Captain Denning. I'm still an amateur by comparison. Seeing that this will be your final run, would you do me the honor of taking command of the ship during the outbound run?"

"With your qualifications and experience? Captain, you are no rank amateur, I'm sure."

But Sullivan persisted. "I might learn a thing or two from the only skipper to succeed at a day run. Your servant, Captain Denning. I bow to a master." He clicked his heels. "And I insist, sir."

Denning was deeply moved. Marie gripped his hand. "In that case, I'd be more than happy to."

"Very well then," said Sullivan. "I will relay your orders. Would you prefer to stay by the pilot house?"

"Yes, I would."

"I thought so."

The navigator motioned toward the cotton bale against the cabin wall. "Ma'am. Would you care to sit down and observe?"

"Oui, monsieur. Merci."

"Drop the smokestacks and masts," Denning said, giving his first order. The routine was second nature to him. "Lift the anchor and I don't want to hear it. Cover the engine room hatches. Snuff out all lights. And no one is to use the voice tubes. All quiet on the deck. Proceed at five knots."

Sullivan turned to the first mate. They were the standard orders, easy to remember. "You heard the captain."

"Aye, aye, sir."

Sullivan gave Denning a telescope.

"Homer?" Denning looked through the eyepiece. He saw only the outer line of ships.

"Aye, sir?" Cogswell said. Nothing had changed. It was like the *Sally* all over again.

"Stick to the shore up to the Mound Battery. And Homer," he paused.

"I know, sir," Cogswell cut in. He had heard it many times before. "Keep a weather-eye open, and get us through."

"That's right," Denning chuckled. "You remembered."

"How could I forget?"

The engine noise picked up. The *Hickory Hill* slid away slowly through the channel which in another half-mile would narrow down to only two hundred yards across. A pilot had to know what he was doing here. Cogswell did. To either side were the menacing shoals. The ship came abreast of the Mound, the southernmost battery of Fort Fisher, the largest Reb shore fortification on the continent. Denning thought about the South. He was leaving Wilmington far behind. Wicked Wilmington, home to brothels, drunks, greedy speculators who would continue to bilk the Confederacy to its dying day, which wasn't far off now. These shore batteries in Fort Fisher would eventually pay the price too. Denning could see he had no choice but to flee with the woman he loved.

Denning pointed out for Marie where his ship went down weeks before. "Out yonder," he whispered. "You can see a piece of a hull sticking out."

Marie saw a shadow of a ship's outline on the water. She gulped and cleared her throat. The blackened hull served as a reminder to her of the risks of blockade running. *Oh Lord. Don't let that happen to us,* she prayed. She began to wonder if she would be bad luck. She did not belong here. She was an intruder, an alien, a woman. Invited, because of her fiancée's reputation. She remembered how ill she had become on her last Atlantic voyage with her parents. She was sea-sick, irritable and unable to sleep soundly for the entire trip. She did not want that feeling again. Worst yet, she didn't want to be sick for her honeymoon. She prayed again, silently, eyes open, for calm water.

Soft waves rolled up to the ship. Coming around the Mound, Cogswell pointed out a lantern-lit, senior officer's ship two points off the bow, less than one mile away. Cogswell wasn't fooled. He knew that between the *Hickory Hill* and the gunboat lay a shoal that widened out to sea. The officer's ship was trying to lay a trap for the runners leaving port. The runner was a thousand yards out from the safety of the surf but still within gun range of the Mound if his ship needed help. Cogswell steered the ship through the channel like the artist he was. At the same time, he was using the blackened hull pieces of the *Sally* as a marker.

There was no movement by the senior officer's ship.

Denning knew he could stop and take a depth reading here, if he wanted to. The shifting shoal had been a problem before. But no, there was no time. He didn't wish to lose the momentum of the vessel. His main concern was the heavy sound of the engines. "Captain Sullivan, can you tie down the safety valves until we pick up speed?"

"We could. But why?"

"The escaping steam can be too noisy at times."

"Do that and the engineers will fry."

"It'll only be for a short time. Keep an eye on the temperatures."

This strategy was new to Sullivan. "As you wish." He sent the order along.

Denning detected his fiancée's concern for the enemy ship. "He's not moving anywhere," he whispered to her. "He can't. Just pray he doesn't see us and alert the force."

Marie looked through the pilot house glass at the ocean. The darkness of the night, except for the one gunboat, stared back at her. *How can they see anything?* she wondered. Is this what her fiancée had to face on all his runs? She closed her eyes and concentrated on the calmness of Joshua and the coolness of Cogswell, Captain Sullivan, and the navigator, trying to tap strength from these brave men. She wished she could share in their composure. But she couldn't.

She was terrified.

"Enemy gunboat to starboard, sir," the first mate said, receiving word from a lookout on the mast.

"I see him," said Denning. "Steady. Wait and see what he does. Maintain the same speed."

Marie swallowed to keep her stomach butterflies down. She felt a gentle hand touch her shoulder. It was the navigator. "There's no need to fuss, ma'am. We'll get you to Nassau."

She smiled.

The gunship turned away and steamed a course parallel with the shore south of the inlet.

"All ahead two-thirds," Denning ordered. "And release the safety valves before your men burn up."

"Aye, aye, captain," Sullivan answered confidently, as he saw the channel line open up to them.

"Steady as she goes," Denning ordered.

Thirty-four

Atlantic Ocean

The ship's crew waited for Marie to appear. She was late, but it didn't matter. Time had no consequence. Some of the crew were seated in the rows of chairs. The remainder was standing. The smell of hair tonic and cleaned and pressed uniforms predominated. Clad in a white suit, a dark-brown tie, white frilled shirt, and polished boots, Joshua Denning stood with them, his back to the cabin hatchway, the bright sun off to his right side. Standing with him by a makeshift altar made of wood crates were Sullivan and Cogswell.

"How do you feel, captain?" Cogswell asked, his dark eyes on his old boss. He would be Denning's best man today. Standing with a military straightness, the pilot was the proud owner of neatly parted hair, and a clean-shaven face, except for a newly snipped and waxed mustache.

"I'm nervous," Denning said. "This is a first for me."

"You, nervous? I don't believe it. Ah, nothing to it, skipper," Cogswell said. "Take it from me." His dark eyes blinked. He was happy for his captain.

"Do you have the ring?"

"Right here, sir. In my pocket."

"Look lively! Here she comes!" one of the men in the back row said.

Denning turned and gawked.

Never in all his years had he seen a more beautiful woman than Marie in her wedding dress as she slowly came through the hatchway leading to the officers' quarters. She was stunning. Her white dress reflected the sun. He was so lucky to have her. They were of like mind and like spirit. Denning's nervousness quickly vanished during the ceremony, as he stood beside Marie, holding her hand in his. Captain Sullivan took them through the vows. Cogswell produced the ring at the right time and gave it to Denning to place on Marie's finger.

"I now pronounce you man and wife," said Sullivan, his steady voice ringing across the deck. "You may now kiss the bride."

Denning turned and lifted Marie's veil. He kissed her on the mouth. The sailors cheered.

Denning locked the door to what would be the couple's honeymoon quarters in the aft quarterdeck, then lit a gaslight. He watched Marie remove her veil, dropping it on her carrying bag. She smiled at him, tilting her head. He fantasized about what she would look like without a stitch on. That moment was very near. She seemed to read his mind. She stripped to her petticoat, then her underwear and tight-fitting, see-through camisole. He threw his hat and coat to the floor and stopped there, still staring at her, his hands on his hips.

"Is this really happening?" he said.

"You know it is." She removed her undergarments and stood before him. "Now, your turn."

Within seconds, they were naked and under the covers.

Denning reached for her waist with both hands. "I was wondering," he sighed.

"What?"

"What are we going to do for two days at sea?"

"Guess," she said, bending backwards, taking the gaslight and blowing it out. "We're cabin boys," she said in the darkness.

"Right. And we can feast on oysters and champagne."

"I beg to differ," she said.

"Why?"

"I hate oysters."

"Very well, then. Champagne without the oysters."

"Now, where were we," Marie said.

Denning was truly happy for the first time in his life. Yes, there was a God in heaven. There had to be.

That night, mid the calm Atlantic waters, Joshua and Marie were of one mind, one body, one heart, one soul. And Marie was not the least bit seasick.

Nassau, Bahamas

Later that week, under a heavy, hazy sun, Clement Sullivan walked down the ship's gangplank to the wharf, where Denning met him with two sealed envelopes. The *Hickory Hill* skipper looked at the names written on the outside. "I'll see that the proper people get them," he said, stuffing the envelopes inside his coat. "Goodbye and good luck."

They shook hands.

Sullivan turned and made his way up the gangplank. The *Hickory Hill* was shipshape and seaworthy, ready to sail with her military contraband. Destination: *Wilmington*. Denning waved to Cogswell at the rail. Cogswell looked down and waved back, pipe in mouth. They would probably never see each other again. Marie slipped her hand into her husband's. They watched the blockade runner steam out of the harbor. Then they turned their attention to the English freighter on the other side of the wharf. They would be on it inside another two hours.

Denning thought of the contents of the envelopes. They were his idea, approved by Marie. The first envelope bore the name of The Lads of Liberty and the woman now in charge of the organization. Inside was a bank draft in English pounds—a large donation to the cause that Marie worked so hard at. The second envelope, containing two bank drafts, was addressed to Maxwell Toland at the mayor's office. One draft was a donation for a building project along the Wilmington waterfront that the mayor had in mind; the other was for an organization that Maxwell Toland helped found that distributed food and clothing to the poor of Wilmington and surrounding area. Inside both envelopes were notes to say that Denning must remain anonymous.

Denning sighed. He was warmed with an enormous sense of relief. He had now given away more than half the money he had made in the war. The rest, still a sizable amount, he would keep for him and Marie, to start a new life together overseas.

His conscience was clear.

Thirty-five

Liverpool, England—April 1865

Joshua and Marie Denning relaxed in the back seat of the covered carriage and let the driver take them through the wet streets to the docks alongside the Mersey River. It was the kind of spring weather England was noted for, cloudy and rainy.

The driver drew the horses to a halt. The rain diminished, then stopped altogether. The sky remained a somber gray. There loomed a heavy smell of smoke. The Dennings were in the heart of the industrial shipbuilding region of England. Many of the blockade runners had been built here and were still being built for the Confederacy. Joshua took his wife's hand. The two emerged from the carriage and looked upon the dozen or so large runners on the busy dry dock under various stages of construction from the keels up.

"Your friend isn't here yet," Marie said.

Joshua pulled out his gold chain and eyed his pocket watch, puffing on an imported Virginia cigar. "I'm sure he got the message. We got here a little early. We'll wait. There's no hurry."

"I suppose not. There they are, Joshua."

Joshua stared ahead.

The *Silver Sally* had been built in these same dry docks by some of the same skilled craftsmen who were concentrating their efforts on the new ships now. Neither Joshua nor Marie had seen a blockade runner in nearly two years. The sight of the ships beam to beam brought back memories for both of them. Although they were thousands of miles

197

across the ocean, Joshua and Marie Denning were staying informed of the American Civil War by perusing dispatches written by foreign correspondents to French and English newspapers, in particular by young Charles Bishop of *The Times.*

Only two weeks after slipping through the blockade in August, 1863, the Dennings had learned that the Davis government had acted, as promised and as Denning had predicted. The Rebel president took a more major role in the blockade-running business. The War Department bought ships outright, seized majority control of others, and appointed a government official to administer the export supply of cotton. Not only had they commandeered half the outbound cargo space on ships, but they took first option on half the incoming cargo. Captain Denning was not surprised when a Confederate Act of Congress in February 1864 gave the Davis government the power to ban the importation of most non-essential goods. But those in the know saw that it was too late. Fewer and fewer ships had been sneaking through the ever-tightening Union blockade anyway. The beleaguered Rebel armies, including Robert E. Lee's once-mighty Army of Northern Virginia, were being pushed back battle after battle. The Confederacy was starving, dying a slow death due to lack of supplies and equipment to wage war against an enemy that was outnumbering them in every precious category.

Back in January, 1865, the Dennings had opened up a copy of *The Times* of London to read an exciting Bishop dispatch. The Englishman wrote of the daring exploits of skipper Clement Sullivan of the *Hickory Hill.* Clement had evaded capture on an inbound run off Fort Fisher, not knowing that the fort had fallen during a massive and successful Union amphibious operation while he was away in Nassau. The Dennings knew then that with Fort Fisher in the hands of the Union, the last Rebel port of Wilmington was blocked completely to any shipping. The cotton runs were at an end. The news came fast and furious. Since then the Union General William Tecumseh Sherman, after plundering Georgia, had wreaked havoc on the Carolinas. The Rebel capital of Richmond had fallen. Grant had Lee on the run in Virginia. The Davis government had fled South. The once-proud Rebel armies were no longer feared. Although it was a nation only in theory, the Confederacy was still fighting on. But it was as good as dead.

The Dennings looked up.

Another carriage drew up alongside, and a young man in a raincape emerged, a thick newspaper in his left hand. Charles Bishop stood proudly, not the nervous young man Denning remembered. He had grown a thick beard. He had put on some weight, and he was wearing a more conservative suit and tie than the flashy attire he had worn in Nassau. Now he was an experienced and famous overseas correspondent who had returned from the American Civil War.

"Captain Denning."

"Bishop."

"How goes it?" The Englishman asked, sounding like an American.

"Contented."

"It's over, captain. The war's over. Here she is," Bishop said, holding up the afternoon copy of the *Liverpool Express*.

Denning saw the bold headline in front of him. LEE SURRENDERS TO GRANT TO END AMERICAN CIVIL WAR.

"What took so long?" Denning asked, looking at his wife and catching tears of sadness in her eyes.

"There, there, ma'am," Bishop said, gravely. "It's tragic, I know. But the Confederacy was destined to fall. Lee was not invincible. I saw that at Gettysburg."

"This is my wife, Marie," Denning said, a slight smile on his lips.

Bishop politely removed his hat. "Pleased to meet you, Mrs. Denning."

She wiped her tears.

"My husband told me you were aboard the *Silver Sally* during his daylight run."

"Quite right. I was."

"And I was ashore, waving to him."

"Oh, yes, one of the women on the beach. That was you! Remarkable. All three of us were there. Your husband was right about the run."

"How?"

"It made history. He was the only one ever to do it. And *The Times* loved the story. After that I could do no wrong."

"We've been keeping track of you and reading your accounts," Marie said.

"Thank you. I owe it to one man. I'm indebted to your husband, Mrs. Denning."

"Nonsense. You earned it. You obviously had the talent," Denning said. "You just needed a place and time."

"Thank you. That's terribly kind of you. By the way, sir, Captain Sullivan sends you his regards. He joined the Royal Navy. Just spoke to him last week. He hired your old navigator, Ben Woodson."

"They made it. How about that!"

"And I saw Cogswell."

"You saw Homer?"

"Yes. He and his family retired up in Canada—Nova Scotia—before Fort Fisher fell. He bought himself a big sailboat, he did. He took me on it. Fine ship."

"He made it, too! I'm glad." Denning paused. "When did you get back?"

"After Fort Fisher fell."

"What are you doing now?"

"I work for myself. I write stories for a number of British papers and magazines through a news bureau that I helped found. They call it freelancing," Bishop said.

"Is that a fact? Congratulations."

"It's a new, changing world out there. A trans-Atlantic telegraph cable is coming. And just this week I saw a demonstration of a machine that will print stories by pressing letter keys, almost like a portable printing press. It will revolutionize the newspaper industry and corresponding. Yes, sir, this is quite the age we're in."

It was an age the South hadn't been able to keep up with, Denning knew. And it did them in.

"Where are you living, captain?"

"Near Paris. I bought into a country vineyard. A little sideline of mine. Not as profitable as running the blockade, but it's legitimate and less dangerous."

Bishop laughed. "Splendid. We should have dinner somewhere, and catch up on the last two years. I know a wonderful place not far from here. The Palace."

"I saw it," Denning acknowledged. "We'll be along. I . . . I want to look around a while."

Bishop understood. "Of course, captain. I'll run along and reserve a table for us."

"Do that. We'll be along smartly."

"Of course." He tipped his hat to Marie. "Madam."

"Mr. Bishop."

The Dennings watched the carriage leave, splashing through some puddles. As they turned back to the ships, Joshua was the first to speak after a long silence. "They never got into action," he said, his eyes hopping from runner to runner. "It's the end of an era. Funny, you know."

"What?"

"The war. It seems like ancient history. It changed a lot of people. Carlisle. Balsinger. Bishop. Cogswell. You. Me. Some for better, some for worse."

Marie put her arm through his. "Let's forget the war. Let's talk about us."

"Us?"

"I think now's the time to tell you, so that we have something to celebrate at dinner."

"Tell me what?"

"You're going to be a father," Marie said.

The words hit Joshua like a cannon shot. "Are you serious? But. . . I thought. . . you couldn't."

"It must be this English air."

Joshua was so happy he kissed her on the lips. He released her slowly. "Promise me that if it's a boy we won't call him Robert or Bobby. I still don't like that name. I'm not too crazy about Matthew, either."

"I promise, Joshua. No Matthew or Robert." She smiled. "Now we'll be a family of three."

"And maybe more," Denning added. "How about twins?"

"Dear me. One at a time. Please."

Afterword

From the list of *The Cotton Run*'s characters, only Edwin Stanton and Lafayette Baker actually existed. The others are fictional, including the ships and their names.

The Civil War

Three million men fought, six hundred thousand died. Two-thirds of those died from disease and not from bullets. The four years of fighting cost the Confederacy $2 billion, the Union $3 billion. Indirect expenses including property damages, pensions, and such pushed the final combined total to a staggering $15 billion debt. It took years for Washington to sort it all out.

In the midst of a financial boom in the late 1860s, the Northern states could handle the expenses. The Southern economy collapsed.

Gettysburg

Gettysburg was the turning point of the war, as well as the bloodiest battle in the history of the Western Hemisphere. Fifty thousand Americans fell dead or injured over the three-day affair. Robert E. Lee's Army of Northern Virginia was soundly defeated. Some say it was due to Lee's overconfidence. Others say it was his cautious commanders who did not take advantage of opportunities in the first and second days.

After a day of rest, Lee withdrew his battered army to Virginia, never to mount another offensive operation on the enemy's soil. Any inkling of foreign intervention retreated with Lee.

On the same site four months later, Lincoln gave his Gettysburg Address. It lives on to this day as one of the greatest speeches ever made. The following year, Lincoln was re-elected for his second term.

Blockade Running

September 6, 1863 saw Morris Island, at the entrance to Charleston harbor, surrender to the Union, seriously restricting the port to any major blockade-running operations. This left Wilmington the last of the open Rebel ports, until nearby Fort Fisher fell in January 1865 to Union naval forces, in the world's largest amphibious operation until D-Day in World War II.

The Union blockade was instrumental in bringing the Confederacy to extinction. In the first year of war, one in ten ships was caught; by 1862, one in eight; 1863, one in four; 1864, one in three. By the last year of the conflict, blockade running had become a shadow of its 1861-1863 heyday. Only one in two ships was beating the gunboats. All told, sixteen hundred vessels had made eight thousand round trips in the years 1861-1865.

More than a thousand blockade-runners were captured, of which 355 were sunk, burned, beached, or destroyed. The value of the ships and their cargo was estimated at $35 million. In four years, the blockade runners exported 1.25 million bales of cotton and imported $200 million worth of goods, including 600,000 small arms, 600,000 shoes, two million pounds of saltpeter, used in the making of gunpowder, and over a million pounds of lead.

None of the above was enough to win the war.

Lafayette Baker

He was caught spying on Lincoln's predecessor, President Andrew Johnson, at the White House and was fired by Stanton shortly after on February 8, 1866.

Baker published a book, *History of the U.S. Secret Service*, in 1867, much to Stanton's embarrassment. In it, Baker stated that he had given Stanton the diary of John Wilkes Booth (Lincoln's assassin) after Booth had been captured and shot. The statement caused a storm of controversy leading to a House of Representatives commission that eventually found the diary in some forgotten War Department file minus eighteen of its pages.

Baker had escaped several attempts on his life until he died in 1868, a bitter man. Some modern writers have speculated that Baker had been poisoned and that he and Stanton were both involved in a conspiracy to cover up the true details of Lincoln's assassination. It has also been conjectured that the missing eighteen pages contained the names of Booth's clandestine associates, some of them influential Northern businessmen and politicians, people Stanton and Baker knew. There are historians today who believe that John Wilkes Booth was never apprehended and that a look-alike was accidentally shot and buried in his place.

But that's another story.

Edwin Stanton

He saw his dream of a war-time, state-controlled telegraph network under his control come to pass, when he established the Federal Military Telegraph System in late 1863. The service soon employed twelve thousand men and averaged over three thousand messages daily. Stanton saw to it that the military field commanders, including General in Chief of the Union armies, Ulysses S. Grant, had no power over it.

Stanton bitterly opposed Andrew Johnson's soft reconstruction plans and was asked by the president to resign his Secretary of War position in 1867. Stanton refused and was subsequently suspended by Johnson. The Senate restored Stanton's job, only to have Johnson try to remove him again. The Radicals had the evidence they needed and called for impeachment proceedings on Johnson for his actions against Stanton, in addition to his failing to fulfill the Radicals' reconstruction plans and for treating Congress disrespectfully. It didn't work. The Radicals failed by one vote of the Senate two-thirds majority to impeach. Johnson finished his term, only to be defeated by General Ulysses Grant in the presidential election of 1869.

Stanton resigned his post and practiced law until he died in 1869, four days after he was appointed by Grant to the Supreme Court of the United States.

Reconstruction

Five days after Lee surrendered to Grant in April 1865, Abraham Lincoln was assassinated, making it possible for his opponents to rise out of the rubble of political turmoil. With Lincoln and his lenient peace-term ideas out of the way, the Radical Republicans, through a two-thirds majority vote in Congress in the 1866 elections (which could override any presidential veto) were powerful enough to draw up their own reconstruction plans. As a result, the ten Southern states were divided into five military districts, each governed by a major general. New constitutions for each state were drawn up and made to accommodate colored voters. Armed with his own reconstruction plans, Andrew Johnson opposed the Radical Republicans and tried to veto their scheme.

But the Republican majority overruled him.

As a result of the 1869 presidential election, the Radicals had found their man in Grant, who favored the harsh Radical proposals. The reconstruction agenda was passed. For nearly another decade until 1877, the South watched as her land and possessions were seized by Northern carpetbaggers and underhanded businessmen, reminiscent of the era of speculating and blockade running during the war.

Cape Fear

Years after the war, and well into the twentieth century, a new set of speculators came onto the Cape Fear scene in the form of land developers. Smithville was renamed Southport. Smith Island became Bald Head Island. Wilmington grew in size and importance.

Today, the Cape Fear coast is a lively tourist attraction, rich in history, natural beauty, fine sandy beaches, lush-green golf courses, and friendly suburban communities. With pleasant year-round temperatures, Cape Fear is advertised as "a great place to live" and "a great place to visit."

Never again will a daring sea captain round Cape Fear at night, stand on the deck of his sleek runner at high tide and hear his white sails crack in the breeze. Never again will a captain hear the mixture of Southern and British voices, smell the aromas from the galley, and feel the rumble of the giant engines below deck during a dash through the Union blockade. It took a war to do it.

The only war ignited by cotton.

www.ingramcontent.com/pod-product-compliance
Lightning Source LLC
Chambersburg PA
CBHW031232260626
47169CB00007B/2255